THE GODS OF SLEEP

§

A Novel

Robert Mix

To my wife Mimi

For your endless support and encouragement

Everything we call real is made of things
that cannot be regarded as real.

- Neils Bohr

Prologue

The corporate tarmac felt desolate that night. Cloaked in its cinematic shroud of fog, it evoked an image of trench coats, film-noir, and suspense. Moments later, a shrieking turbine engine shattered the still air, the aircraft's disembodied lights blurring through the overcast. Yeung Ki Lam trudged up the stairway of the private jet, his brutal schedule having warped all sense of time and place.

As he settled into the recliner, nothing could have prepared him for what waited ahead.

Thirty minutes later, the sleek Gulfstream soared over the Golden Gate Bridge. The evening sky faded into a deep violet-black, while the city lights dimmed into a distant constellation.

Ki Lam, a fifty-five-year-old banker, was negotiating a casino project on the Malay Peninsula. Finding himself caught between partners that he couldn't fully trust, and the shadowy enemies he'd yet to meet, he no longer remembered the last time he truly felt safe. He exhaled sharply, waving off his concerns as merely fatigue. He glanced back at the two-man security team and took a small measure of comfort in their presence.

Sipping champagne, he fished a copy of the San Francisco Chronicle from his briefcase. The headline posted the latest polling numbers for US presidential candidate Gavin Peakes's bid for office. Ki Lam rubbed his reddened eyes before admitting defeat. By now, reading had become a near Herculean task.

"May I eat a little earlier?" he asked the flight attendant. "I really need to get some sleep." She nodded before returning to the galley. Shortly after his meal, he slipped into the bedding. Ki Lam began to dream—the low hum of the engines slowly transforming into the sound of ocean waves.

***

His dream took him back to boyhood days at a Hong Kong beach called Sai Wan. Ki Lam had always been a powerful swimmer and enjoyed racing his friends to the buoys marking the reef's edge. Today, he started fast and strong, but then it seemed as though the water itself resisted. Something felt off, and he stopped to look around.

The crowded beach was now deserted—friends, family, everyone—all inexplicably gone. Confused, he turned back to shore. Nothing happened. Every stroke, every kick, was met with an invisible resistance—and panic began to set in. His heart pounded with feral force. His breath quickened. *Was this really happening?*

Ki Lam was drowning.

A wave crested over his face and self-control gave way to panic. Snapping his head back, he gasped for air. Through the water's distortion, he stared up at the clear sky, his eyes wide in disbelief. His mind battling for survival. His body continued to fail. And then, for a split second, his willpower faltered. He took an involuntary gasp for air—an instinct beyond his control. Cool seawater flooded into his lungs, burning through his chest. His body convulsed, reduced to a collection of randomly firing nerves.

After a few seconds, the spasms slowed, and then…everything became still. For what seemed like an eternity, Ki Lam's motionless body remained inalterably suspended in the water—as if the universe might be having second thoughts. But then, it began its slow descent into the black void.

High above the Pacific, in the luxurious cabin of the jet, if the flight attendant or his security staff had paid close enough attention, they might have detected a slight twitch in their client's body. But no one noticed.

Near the galley, the lone flight attendant was happy to relax and steal a few moments for herself. In the back, his security team rested in comfort—understandably confident that their employer, ensconced in this metal tube at forty-three thousand feet, was safe and secure from any and all threats.

As the sleek jet cut through the blackness, Yeung Ki Lam lay dead. Murdered in a nightmare. Drowned in his own mind, while submerged in a dream eight miles above the ocean's surface.

Chapter One

New York City.
Six Months Earlier...

Sean Hastings rolled his pen from finger to finger and stopped every third pass to click the mechanism, a quirky habit from college. It was still mid-morning, but he sensed his rising anxiety.

Judging from the hurried glances he'd stolen through the open doors of the executive suites, it was a morning worthy of a postcard. In dull contrast, Sean's cubicle had a more limited view, landlocked, as it were, in the center of the building. The weather at his desk was always a steady seventy-four degrees, and bright—albeit in a cool-white, fluorescent sort of way.

A faint whistling sound escaped his nostrils as he exhaled. He slipped on a pair of noise-canceling headphones and waited for the heavy bass notes of a Dave Matthews song to begin.

This was another typical morning for Sean, slogging through the financial report of a pharmaceutical company rushing its latest drug into production. The lone spark of originality was in the clever use of a butterfly mascot in their advertisements. Fluttering across the TV screen, it implied that patients would experience a metaphorical metamorphosis—and emerge into a pastel-colored world of health and well-being. Sean pursed his lips. Once again, he was fighting a creeping cynicism. His job was to distill all this information into concise recommendations that his firm, Farber Investments, would use to advise their best clients.

He caught the time on the corner of the monitor. Nearly noon. Every Tuesday, he had a standing arrangement to meet his best friend, Keenan, at a nearby Starbucks. He logged out.

***

"You look tired," Keenan said, his tone unvarnished.

"Nice to see you, too," he said, fighting the suggestive yawn. "I'm still not sleeping. Does espresso have more or less caffeine than drip?"

"Less," Keenan said with a grin. "But only comparing shot to cup. It's a concentration thing."

The two had been friends since their freshman year at NYU. Late one night, after flopping onto one of the deeply creased Naugahyde couches in the student lounge, they found a shared interest in film, books, politics, and the arts. Over the next few weeks, they debated everything from race relations and inequality, to a heated discussion on whether Zeppo had significantly contributed to the overall success of the Marx Brothers. Eventually, they rented a small, third floor walkup above a lime-green bodega in the East Village.

"How are things with Karen?" asked Keenan. "Is that why you can't sleep?"

"Straight to the point," Sean said, sounding less than appreciative. It seemed too early to discuss ex-wives. "Not sure. We were working on this new visitation schedule for Abbie, but—"

His voice trailed off as he stared out the café's window, watching the luncheon crowd push their way along State Street. Keenan, ever the patient psychologist, waited for his friend to continue.

"Karen plans to move to Fort Lauderdale," he finally said. "Her cousin has lined up a new job, and the cost of living is cheaper."

Keenan gave Sean a sympathetic look before taking a large bite of lemon pound cake. Sean shook his head. "It's criminal that you can eat like that and still stay in shape. Ever heard of macros? Glycemic index?"

Keenan laughed at the running joke. Sean joined in, although he understood his friend's physique was really the result of an exercise regiment unchanged since his days as an Army Ranger.

"Karen's only part of it," Sean said, after their laugh. "The rest is work. If you fall behind, Wall Street has no problem culling the herd." He leaned in and whispered. "Maybe I should join your PTSD group?"

"Oh, absolutely. My vets would love to hear from someone so tormented with first-world pain."

Sean forced a laugh, but the words cut more deeply than he wanted to admit. He masked his feelings behind a mock grin, and swirled his espresso cup to drag the sugar off the bottom. Then, he pretended to count on his fingers. "Let's see—work burnout, ex-wife problems, insomnia. Yeah, pretty much your average Wall Street stereotype."

"Nah, you're an exceptional Wall Street stereotype." Keenan smirked. "Listen, why don't you come out to the Hudson River courts on Saturday morning? There's a pickup game that starts around ten, it might give you a chance to clear your mind. It's a good group—long on competitiveness, short on talent—your kinda crowd."

Sean glanced at his watch and cursed under his breath. "Sorry, I've got to run," he said, as he stood. "Um, Saturday morning? Yeah, sounds good. With any luck, I'll get some sleep between now and then."

***

Sean's insomnia began a few months back and was only getting worse. He'd tried melatonin, Chinese medicinal mushrooms, tryptophan, even Siberian ginseng. Nothing helped. His preferred remedy was a glass, or several, of single-malt Scotch whisky. Smooth going down, gently euphoric, and it provided near instant sleep. Except for feeling like crap several hours later, it was the perfect solution. At least it tasted better than Chinese mushroom tea.

Keenan wiped a few remaining crumbs off the table with a paper napkin. "I've been seeing this internist at Lenox Hill. Maybe she can recommend something to help you sleep." They pushed their way through the lunchtime crowd. Sean's office was three blocks east, on Pearl Street. Like many of the streets in the lower part of Manhattan, it traced back to the days of the Dutch settlers. Winding, random, and with no discernible pattern. Only Broadway, the precolonial Native American trail, had the moxie to slash diagonally across the city in brazen defiance of uptown's almighty grid system. Manhattan may appear like a set of orderly numbered streets and avenues, but none of that carried into downtown. In the financial district, it was far too easy for unwitting newcomers to become lost and confused.

An allegorical message to be sure.

***

Walking back from lunch, Sean cut through Farber's trading floor. It was a viper pit. A forum for the young and ambitious to battle in a harsh and unforgiving arena. Sean had once planned on making his mark here, but after he and Karen found themselves unexpectedly expecting, his career drifted toward safer waters.

The rest of the week cycled through the same dull loop—work, stress, whisky, and a sizeable sleep deficit. To the few who knew him well, Sean became unrecognizable. He felt it too. He'd always taken pride in being well balanced, considering it one of his better characteristics. Some days sucked, others were great —but it all evened itself out in the end. Lately, that balance seemed to have vanished. And here he was, in the grand funk of funks.

Insomnia was the likely culprit. Its effect gradual—insidious—like making the minimum payment on a credit card. Each day began a little more in arrears than the last. Weekends offered some reprieve, but by Monday, the toll of his deficit had inched a little higher.

To no one's surprise, Sean skipped the Saturday morning basketball game on a feeble excuse, but eventually yielded to Keenan's arm-twisting. He agreed to join him and his new girlfriend at a local club for drinks that night.

***

Keenan was shouting over the music and waving his arms as Sean stepped into the bar. He snaked his way through the crowd at The Inquiry, one of several pubs that recently opened in Keenan's neighborhood. Though it was early, the bar was already buzzing. The cinema-themed decor managed to be charming without trying too hard. Best of all, on the weekends, the DJ spun seventies R&B, and that, above all else, suited Keenan just fine.

"Sean, I'd like you to meet Zahra Segales," said a beaming Keenan.

He smiled warmly and extended his hand. "Pleasure to meet you. Keenan tells me, rather proudly, that you're a doctor."

Zahra responded with a slight giggle. "Yes, at Lenox Hill," she said, glancing at Keenan.

She made an immediate impression—tall, confident, elegant. Sean couldn't be certain whether her remarkable complexion was the result of a blessed inheritance from her mixed-race parents, or a gift from God.

After a bit, Sean stepped away to order another round. Always the traditionalist when it came to libations, he was relieved that no one had requested anything muddled or infused with lychee, pomegranate, or cucumber. While waiting for the drinks, he caught a glimpse of Keenan and Zahra together. They seemed like a good match—comfortable and content with one another—and he was happy for his friend. Still, by the time he returned to the table, his thoughts had turned introspective. His mood dimmed.

Zahra picked up on the change. "Keenan said you're having trouble sleeping. How long has that been going on?"

Sean shrugged. "A few months, maybe more. It's no big deal."

She smiled, with a hint of admonishment. "Utter nonsense. And quite the macho response."

He flinched, caught off guard. Zahra quickly softened her tone.

"It is a big deal, Sean. More than a third of all Americans aren't getting enough sleep, it contributes to things like diabetes and obesity. You might downplay it, but sleep health is now quite fashionable—self-adjusting beds, smart pillows, or sheets that can track sleep cycles. People spend a fortune hoping to get decent rest."

"Okay," Sean grudgingly agreed, "it has affected my life, but I'm lost. I've tried a few over-the-counter meds—they didn't really help. Do you think I need something stronger?"

Zahra's face contorted a bit. "Most of those drugs just flood your brain with a bunch of neurotransmitters. They don't provide the sustained, restful sleep your body needs."

Zahra hesitated, perhaps gauging his openness to new ideas. "Have you tried anything else?"

Sean smirked. "Does whisky count?"

"Actually," Zahra laughed, "I was thinking more in terms of a sleep clinic."

"Sounds like a polite euphemism for a shrink."

"I'm not too surprised you'd say that," she said, "But no, they just help people get some sleep. The number of sleep clinics in the US has tripled over the past fifteen years. So you can—if you'll pardon the pun—rest assured that you're not alone."

Keenan chimed in. "What was the name of that place you had in mind?"

"The Maeda Clinic on the Upper West Side," Zahra said. "It's run by a neurologist, board-certified in sleep medicine. Do yourself a favor and go. I've heard nothing but good things about them."

***

Sean's appointment at the Maeda Clinic was scheduled for eight a.m. on Tuesday morning. He wondered if it was abject cruelty, or a keen sense of irony that prompted the sleep clinic to schedule early-morning appointments for their inherently sleep-starved patients. Why not adjust the office hours to match the schedule of your average insomniac?

"Are you free around…three a.m.?"

"Yes. It dovetails nicely between the waning city nightlife and the start of my workday."

Lately, scattered thoughts and little annoyances like these percolated inside Sean's head. As he headed off to the clinic, he admitted that he wasn't in the best of moods—lacking the open mindset that therapy required. On top of everything else, he was hungry. The clinic instructed Sean not to consume food or drink after midnight for some blood tests. Approaching the 59th Street/Columbus Circle station, the subway screeched to a stop. Sean's stomach rumbled in harmony.

After exiting, he chose to walk the seven blocks north rather than transfer to another train. The morning's air was brisk, made slightly cooler by a light breeze. He followed along Broadway, past Dante Park, and turned left in front of the Juilliard School. On Sixty-Sixth, he continued toward Amsterdam Avenue. The Maeda Sleep Center occupied the ground floor of an elegant residential building— behind a modest brown door with a small polished brass nameplate.

Inside the hushed, absurdly neutral waiting room, Sean passed the time flipping through magazines. One glossy cover promised "18 ways to know if your boyfriend is cheating," while a men's magazine posed, "15 ways to know if your girlfriend is cheating." Sean glanced back and forth, wondering how women had gained a three-method advantage.

A nurse called out his name.

After filling several vials with blood, completing an extensive questionnaire, a brief consultation, and, to his mind, a seemingly inappropriate body-fat analysis, Sean was done. As he headed back to work, a part of him hoped the visit would yield immediate results.

But the next couple of nights were all too familiar: staring at the ceiling, long bouts of restlessness. When the clinic finally called, Sean answered with childlike anticipation. Dr. Maeda reviewed his test results: blurs of numbers followed by units of milliliters, parts per million, milligrams, blah, blah, blah.

"It's all in the email we sent you."

The prescribed regimen included hormones, vitamins, and neurotransmitter supplements: a GABA agonist to calm certain neurotransmitters, 5-hydroxytryptophan to boost serotonin, and assorted supplements to regulate—well—basically everything else. Dr. Maeda even offered a portable biofeedback device to hone Sean's relaxation skills.

I have relaxation skills?

On Thursday night, the shelf above Sean's bathroom sink was filled with ten supplement containers, lined up like toy soldiers in his own personal sleep battalion. With a handful of pills in his left hand and a half glass of water in his right, Sean was ready. After downing the last pill, he carefully settled into a fresh set of sheets, as if any sudden movement might jinx the whole affair. He turned off the lights and, for the next fifteen minutes, actively scanned his mind and body for an indication that something, anything, was happening. When that failed to work, he tried clearing his mind, aiming for thoughts of nothing. But it was like a tornado in there: swirling with thoughts of work, his ex-wife, his daughter, Auntie Em, Toto… the list seemed endless.

Why isn't this working?

The room was cooled to sixty-five degrees, he consumed no caffeine after three p.m., an early dinner, and he even eschewed his usual single malt nightcap. Nothing left to chance, every emailed instruction followed to the letter.

And then—it happened. Sleep came, sooner and deeper than it had in a very long time.

Sean dreamt of sailing aboard a seventeenth-century ship: hearing the snap of the canvas, the creak of the timbers, and the roll of the waves beneath his unsteady legs. The whole thing was crazy, nonsensical, and utterly blissful. When he woke, he was surprised—shocked—to realize that he'd slept undisturbed through the night.

His phone alarm chimed to the Spice Girls' "Wannabe." He stretched, yawned, and then laughed. The song selection was the result of an ongoing prank between Sean and his young daughter, Abbie, who changed his alarm tone whenever she visited. A smile formed at the thought of her, before he canceled the alarm and sat up. Something about this morning was almost weightless, something he hadn't felt in recent memory. He swung his feet out of bed and sang to himself.

"Well, I'll tell you what I want, what I really, really want…some coffee!"

A few nights later, the nocturnal miracle began to fade. While still an improvement, it was slipping away—shallow and sporadic. For a brief period, he'd glimpsed the possible. Why couldn't he do something as natural as sleep? Desperate to put his sleeplessness to bed, he cursed under his breath. He would explain all of this to Dr. Maeda at his follow-up appointment.

***

Friday morning, and Sean arrived early. In the waiting room, someone called out his name. He turned to see a bearded man sitting at the far end.

"Erik Würfel?" said Sean, with a smile.

They shook hands. Erik Würfel was known as a "quant" on Wall Street, though his formal title was head of algorithmic trading. At first glance, or any subsequent one, Erik didn't come across as a Wall Street insider. Dressed in his lumberjack casual attire, with advanced degrees from MIT (none of them in finance), computer programmers like Erik had become the new machine of finance.

"And so," said Erik, grinning, "the sleep-deprived zombies of Wall Street gather at the mad doctor's clinic." He laughed and tilted his head. "I haven't seen you in, what, a year? How've you been?"

Sean offered a half-smile. "I've been good. A few ups and downs—probably a few more downs. You?"

"Oh, still the same. I hate my job, my management, and most of my coworkers, but the pay's great. I'm just building a war chest so I can return to teaching."

"Sounds about right," Sean responded. "I used to think this was the perfect career. Now, not so much. Actually, I've been full of doubts lately."

Sean began openly talking about his divorce, his work pressure, and his general sense of feeling disconnected. He prattled on. This outpouring of emotion was uncharacteristic, but then defining Sean's normal behavior had become more challenging with each passing day.

"I see," Erik said knowingly. "And so naturally all this has manifested into insomnia—and—well, here you are. I came here a few months back and they gave me some supplements. Did they give you anything?"

Sean named the ones he could remember, and Erik nodded as he mentally checked them against his own list.

"The problem," Sean said, "is that at first, they worked fine, but now it's… fading."

"That happened to a friend of mine—great results at first, but then they mysteriously fizzled. Personally, between the biofeedback device and the supplements, it's worked wonders for me." He shrugged in sympathy.

Sean frowned. "What'd your friend do about it?"

Erik hesitated. "It's not for everyone. He's a bit…unconventional." He glanced around the room, before lowering his voice. "Promise not to tell anyone?"

Sean nodded.

"He combined the supplements that Dr. Maeda gave him with a compound from the Amazon."

"He bought them online?" Sean asked, curious.

Erik laughed, a little too loudly for someone trying to be discreet. "No, not that Amazon. The real one, you know, in South America? There's a group compounding this drug using a variety of rain-forest plants: Psychotria vidiris, Manacá, and a few other traditional medicines."

"Never heard of those," he said trying to sound casual. "What's a Psycho-something?"

"Psychotria vidiris? A plant containing DMT."

Sean looked shocked. "Christ, isn't that basically LSD?"

"No, not really," Erik said, motioning for Sean to lower his voice. "These guys have tweaked the dosage and balanced it with stabilizers. It's supposed to give you a deep sense of relaxation—sort of a meditative state, they say. And hey, it's all natural."

"Yeah, but natural doesn't necessarily equate with safe," Sean said. "I think I'll pass." But then after a few beats, he asked, "Did you try it?"

Before he could answer, the nurse called out Erik's name. He stood, but then turned back at Sean. "I did," he said. "It was relaxing. Nothing cosmic or cathartic, but my friend had these vivid dreams for weeks afterward. I guess it hits everyone differently. Got to run. Great seeing you again."

***

Saturday morning began with a strong cup of Sumatra coffee. Sean preferred it to the smoother South American blends. In fact, the older he became, the more he gravitated toward sharper, bolder, and more bitter flavors. He wondered if that reflected some level of personal growth.

During yesterday's follow-up visit, Dr. Maeda told Sean not to worry about his fluctuating sleep. Everything would stabilize after the prescribed neurotransmitters and hormones balanced his body's level of serotonin. Sean accepted the logic, but patience wasn't his strongest suit. He wanted to return to that first night's perfect sleep. How long would this take? He trusted the process, but how was he supposed to manage until then?

What he needed was something to bridge the gap. Something to hold him over until the neurotransmitters had taken full effect. He thought back on Erik's story. Maybe he had overreacted, maybe it wasn't such a bad idea, after all. Besides, this would only be a temporary fix, just until things settled.

And just like that, the quiet process of rationalization had begun.

Chapter Two

Keenan called late Tuesday morning to apologize for canceling their regular lunch. Sean's initial disappointment soon became an opportunity. Two things had been on his mind: a craving for a Reuben sandwich, and an uneasy urge to reach out to Erik about the drug. And he hoped to do so without appearing too eager.

Sean grabbed an Uber to a deli on the Lower East Side, one that he remembered Erik frequented. After placing his order, he hawkishly scanned the crowded room. There, at a small table barely able to accommodate a second tray, sat Erik Würfel. Sean smiled at his good fortune.

Erik looked up from his tray. "A Reuben? They give me heartburn. Which makes no sense because sauerkraut's a probiotic."

Unsure how to respond, Sean waited for an invitation to sit. However, Erik seemed preoccupied with which of his pickle varieties to try first. Finally, he motioned for Sean to sit.

"This is quite the coincidence, don't you think?" Erik said, after biting into the fatter, darker pickle. "Running into each other twice in the same week. Any improvement in your sleep?" He hastily wiped away the pickle juice that had trickled onto his beard.

"A little—maybe." Sean repeated what Dr. Maeda told him. The men sat quietly for a couple of minutes. Sean removed a few pieces of corned beef from his sandwich and pressed down on the bread before taking his first bite. He wanted to ask about the drug without appearing desperate. So, he looked out the window, continued chewing, and waited for Erik to break the silence.

But nothing came. Erik quietly went about his lunch, picking at his potato salad with a plastic fork. Sean's curiosity was palpable and Erik seemed to savor every moment of keeping him in suspense. Finally, he set down his plastic fork.

"If you want to try it," Erik said, "just ask. I'll get you some."

Sean acted like this was something that he hadn't fully considered, and certainly not why he'd chosen to come here today. He wasn't even sure why he was continuing with this ridiculous charade. Still, his insomnia was worsening, and he needed a fast solution. If that solution meant drugs, then drugs it would be. Besides, his industry wasn't exactly intolerant of the use of drugs and alcohol. It was a results-oriented, ends-justify-the-means business—and Sean wanted results.

"I've thought about it," he said, trying to sound indifferent. "I'd need to know more. Like, what's it called?"

"It has a clinical name, but most people just call it Amplius. It's Latin for 'beyond.'"

Erik went on to explain all he knew about the drug's pharmacology. In truth, he knew very little. Any gaps in his understanding were filled by emphasizing that it was "safe and natural."

He boasted that the compound was—or might soon be—approved by a variety of agencies in the European Union. He wasn't sure about which agencies. Had he mentioned that the drug was safe and natural?

Before Erik had finished his dubious endorsement, Sean knew that none of it made any difference. He was ready to throw caution to the sleepless wind. Nevertheless, over the next few minutes, Sean rationalized his thinking to a mostly indifferent and uninterested Erik. He emphasized that taking uncontrolled substances was beneath someone of his stature, and certainly not his normal behavior. Whether Erik cared about any of this or not, it didn't really matter.

Sean wasn't worried about the drug's dangers or its questionable legality. What bothered him were the feelings it stirred: vulnerable, weak, embarrassed that he couldn't control his own thoughts. Erik waited and listened dispassionately to Sean. After sufficiently establishing his precarious foothold on some moral high ground, Sean arranged to pick up the drug later that day.

That night, Sean was too restless and edgy to read or watch television. His stomach was knotted with anticipation. Erik advised him to follow the Maeda Clinic's protocols—then add the Amplius.

He gingerly unwrapped the folded waxed paper packet. Inside, lay a square sheet with small blue-green tablets attached to a sticky white paper backing. The tablets were sublingual, and Erik instructed him to place one under the tongue and wait for it to fully dissolve. Sean held one of the tablets up to the light, trying to imagine the mysterious blend of psychotropic plants and chemicals hidden within. He conjured up images of Amazonian shamans, dense rainforests, topless tribeswomen, trancelike dances, strange piercings, and rhythmic chanting.

After placing a tablet under his tongue, he wrinkled his nose. It was bitter, not chemical, more like plant bitter; a cross between tobacco leaves and days-old black tea.

Sean lay in bed and scanned his brain for the first indications. He assumed that it would begin with a drowsy, tranquil feeling. But there would be no gentle slide into relaxed euphoria. Instead, Sean crashed into sleep at a rate that rivaled the most powerful anesthesia.

Ninety-nine, ninety-eight, ninety-seven, ninety…

***

Inside Sean's dream, he tightened his grip on the reins of his galloping Chestnut brown stallion. His ears filled with the thunderous sound of hooves pounding against the hard, dry ground. Five riders flanked his side.

I'm riding a horse?

High in the cloudless sky, the sun beat down relentlessly. Sean's breath was quick, matching the rhythm of the gallop. Each breath drawing in the dust and heat of the American Southwest. They were riding frighteningly fast, far beyond anything he'd ever experienced on family trail rides. Still, he kept pace—riding through the desert like a cowboy extra in a John Ford film. And then, strangely, for a few seconds, the hooves went silent, the dust hung motionless in the air.

He was jolted by a stark realization.

This was a dream—and he knew it.

Fully conscious within the dream, he knew his name, workplace, address, daughter—in short, everything about his life. A Wall Street analyst galloping through the Old West. Though it made no sense, somehow, in that moment, both lives felt equally real.

"They're called lucid dreams," said Keenan after listening to Sean's story about the previous night's dream. "I remember studying them in school. They were a big deal in psychology journals around thirty or forty years ago."

"It was otherworldly. I could use the dream to work out personal issues. Like it had an intelligence of its own."

Sean failed to mention the psychotropic drug. There was no point in sharing his foray into quasi-legal substances with his good friend, a licensed psychologist. "Do you think it might happen again?"

"Hard to say. There's still no scientific consensus on why they occur. Actually, some psychologists doubt these dreams are even real."

Sean frowned. "Why not?"

"The problem is that people can only describe dreams after they wake up, so the skeptics claim this is a mis-remembrance. Still others are staunch believers. So, the debate continues." He stopped and chuckled. "I read about this female researcher who claimed she was able to control her lucid dreams to such a high degree that she planned, and achieved, an orgasm in her sleep."

Sean laughed. "Really? Then I think I had my first lucid dream at thirteen!"

Chapter Three

Geneva, Switzerland

Morpheus Research occupied a sleek tower near the center of the city, only two blocks north of the Rhône River. Armand C. Locke sauntered into Dr. Adler Daemon's office, settled onto the couch, and helped himself to a bowl of pistachios.

"Jean-Luc called from the bank," he began. "They've confirmed the receipt of the final payment."

Adler looked up from his desk and nodded. "Excellent. I received a call as well. Our Malaysian friends wanted to express their gratitude for our handling of the Yeung Ki Lam situation in Hong Kong. Something about 'removing a great thorn,' I believe. They sent a case of Cristal champagne as thanks."

Adler spent a moment observing Armand, watching the ever-growing pile of shells. It annoyed him, but he kept quiet. He'd become accustomed to a certain level of irritation in dealing with his attorney.

"Well, getting back to business," Adler said at last. "Now that we've locked down Heidemann's travel itinerary—I don't anticipate any further problems."

Armand stood, presumably parched from the salty nuts, and walked to the water pitcher. "I find it rather curious, don't you?" he asked, while filling his glass. "Heidemann will be our second. Why such a sudden animus toward bankers?"

Adler leaned back in his chair and spread his hands. "Probably just a coincidence. Remember what Mark Twain said?"

Armand grunted something that may or may not have been an acknowledgment.

"A banker is a fellow who lends you his umbrella when the sun is shining, but wants it back the minute it begins to rain."

From across the room, a rare chuckle came from Armand C. Locke.

***

New York City

Over the past few days, Sean had grown concerned about the state of his mental health—then worried that thinking about your mental state was, in itself, a sign of instability. The combination of good sleep and the entertaining dreams had brightened his mood. In a strange way, that was the issue. Every drug came with side effects, and the risks with this one were unknown. Sean would keep an eye on his own behavior.

He settled on a little self-evaluation, nothing too elaborate, just a quick mental and physical check he wryly called his "crazy check." So far, the only discernible change was a better attitude. If that was the extent of the side effects, he could certainly live with that.

Each night, he followed the recommendations of the sleep clinic before topping things off with his rainforest-sourced psychotropic nightcap. The resultant sleep was nothing short of miraculous—like cool water to a desert traveler. However, things would not stay the same for long.

Sean had assumed, on the basis of nothing in particular, that the drug generated only lucid dreams, but that was no longer true. Two new dream types began to emerge, each with distinct characteristics.

Sean called the first his "oracle dreams" because they offered thoughtful revelations or life guidance. He dismissed these as merely a collection of subconscious fragments bubbling up from below.

The second kind left Sean stumped. In a literal sense, they were transactional business dreams.

The first of these centered on a midseason baseball player trade, the Yankees trading their best relief pitcher to the Giants. The following night, he observed the acquisition of a small software company with a superior photo-matching application. On the third night; a corporate chairman abruptly resigned amid a scandal. What should he call these dreams?

Bloomberg visions? CNBC dreams?

All they lacked was a ticker tape running across the bottom of the dream. Boring —uneventful—these dreams lacked any symbolism or deeper message. No cataclysmic events. No plane crashes. No tidal waves.

If these dreams represented his vision of the future, then he was in for a tedious future. He wrote them off as a collection of unsorted remnants from work, or the expansion of some chyron he caught out of the corner of his eye on a bar TV.

In his previous dreams, Sean had played a role: a director, a protagonist, or at the least, a witness. But these business dreams were different. He not only lacked a role, but also a physical presence. He was completely invisible to everyone in the dream. Sitting like the proverbial fly on the wall, he seemed completely hidden. All he could do was watch. He tried to discern some moral lesson from these dreams, or find some profundity—but it was just the facts.

The whole thing was perplexing. Still, each night, Sean was grateful to accept whatever dream came his way: lucid, moral, or transactional.

***

On Tuesday afternoon, a well-rested and jubilant Sean sat down for coffee with his friend. Keenan immediately recounted the details of his past weekend with Zahra at a Connecticut bed-and-breakfast. His enthusiasm and animated expressions left Sean with little doubt that Zahra had found a special place in his heart. He listened as Keenan went on about how this or that tasted, smelled, or looked, but Sean knew that he was really describing the smell of her hair, the look in her eyes, and the taste of her lips.

When the conversation shifted, Sean gave him a quick update on his sleep progress and asked him to thank Zahra for the sleep clinic recommendation. Sean leaned forward on the small table, which, being a sugar packet or two shy of level, managed to spill his coffee. Cursing under his breath, he jumped up to get a handful of napkins.

Keenan reached across to the next table, grabbed an abandoned copy of the New York Post, and was busy flipping through the pages when Sean returned.

"Why in the world would they trade Routero to the Giants?" Keenan asked, shaking his head. "It's not like the Yankees have any depth at relief pitching."

Sean rarely paid attention to baseball, but as he wiped the table using the small brown napkins, Keenan's words began to sink in. Sean froze. The room seemed to tilt, suddenly unstable.

It can't be. It has to be a coincidence!

"Let me see that," he said, snatching the sports section out of Keenan's hands. He gave the article a quick scan for details—relief pitcher to the Giants, an undisclosed future pick, $34 million over three years, and the name of Routero's agent. It was all there, exactly as it unfolded in his baseball dream. Sinking back into his chair, he pushed the pile of soggy napkins to the side.

Think. There has to be a rational explanation for this. Maybe it's yesterday's paper, or I heard this from someone at work. Yeah, that's probably what happened. The meeting took place last week and I just heard about it.

He checked the paper's print date and grimaced. It was today's. The article said the official trade was announced last night, at the team's New York headquarters. Sean's mind raced in search of a rational explanation, but everything kept pointing back to the dream he'd had three or four nights ago. He went over the article again, but every detail was identical, right down to the contract dollar amount. It made no sense.

Keenan was watching his friend's strange behavior and cautiously asked if everything was all right. The sound of his voice pulled Sean back into the present. He nodded unconvincingly.

"Everything's…fine. I just remembered something from work."

Over the next few minutes, Sean drifted in and out of the conversation. He needed to get away, to make sense of whatever was happening. He was certain of only one thing; he had absolutely no intention of sharing any of this with Keenan. What could he possibly say? "Hey, I'm taking a black market Amazonian psychotropic drug to help me sleep and I think I can see the future. Do you think this is normal?"

No, it was better to keep this quiet. There was a logical explanation—there had to be. He just needed some time to figure it out.

When he headed out the door, Sean had to acknowledge that today's "crazy check" was not going well.

***

The next day, the confirmation of his baseball dream transformed Sean into a financial news junkie. He kept CNBC running in the background, while pouring over copies of Barron's and the Wall Street Journal. He was desperate to find something—a headline, a blurb, a rumor—anything to corroborate his other two dreams. If one dream had come true, could the others as well?

None of this was the behavior of a stable or rational man, but Sean couldn't help himself. He had tried to explain away the baseball dream as a coincidence— some conflation of news clips, his own imagination, or a divine spark from the vines of the Amazon. Who the hell knew? But no matter how hard he tried, he simply couldn't let go. He was desperate for proof that maybe, just maybe, something extraordinary had really happened in his life.

And he suspected he knew the reason why.

As a boy, Sean had the usual palette of youthful dreams: astronaut, sports star, famous actor. But now he was bound to a desk at Farber Investments, parsing and summarizing mountains of data. Had his dreams been pulled back a little too far? Somewhere along this path, his self worth had taken a hit. He'd come to believe that he was average—perhaps less-than-average—a guy plodding his way through life without ever living it. The thought had cemented itself into his psyche. Of all the shades in his childhood palette, why had he settled on beige? What happened to the reckless confidence that once surged through his veins?

When his alarm went off the next morning, Bruce Springsteen was singing, "Somewhere along the line I slipped off track…."

Sean shut his eyes and sank back into the pillow. It felt like the lyrics were aimed squarely at him.

Restless and dissatisfied at work, could these dreams be his ticket out of a poor career choice? He skipped work and spent the morning searching through headlines for a connection.

After breakfast, he sat at his computer and scrolled through page after page of dreary financial news. Every so often, his thoughts drifted.

> This might be the best thing to ever happen to me. What if this
> led to a spiritual awakening? A breakdown of the barriers
> between consciousness and unconsciousness—maybe unveiling
> the fabric of the universe that binds all of humanity?

Then again, what if it's frying my brain?

He thumbed through a copy of Barron's, and nearly missed a small blurb on the third page of the business section. It was a report on the revised earnings of a major search engine company, but near the end, it mentioned the pending acquisition of a small tech firm called Trace Image. Their photo- and image-recognition software promised to outperform everything else on the market, faster and more accurate than anything currently available.

Facial recognition. A pending merger. A perfect match.

"Yes!" he shouted, startled by the unexpected volume of his voice. He reread the article, as a grin spread across his face.

Perhaps not so crazy after all?

The next day, after a midtown meeting, Sean stopped for lunch at a local diner. The TV behind the counter was tuned to some dreadful afternoon tabloid show dedicated to the exploitation of celebrity misdeeds and their ill-advised tweets. A highly attractive, millennial reporter announced, "Mark Sanders, the newly appointed chairman of Scoresby, the big box retailer, has resigned amid allegations of sexual impropriety."

Three accusers. Harassment. Intimate selfies. It was all there.

Sean's right hand slapped the counter. The startled waitress spun around. Sean smirked and took another sip of club soda.

Three for three. This can't be a fluke.

Too keyed up to return to the office, he stopped to sit on the great lawn of Bryant Park. He needed time to settle down and sort things out, to weigh the pros and cons. As the sun warmed the back of his neck, he stretched his legs and lightly ran his fingers through the cool grass. If this was really happening, he thought, is it a blessing—or a curse?

As he sat in the fragrant, freshly mown grass with his knees bent, he rolled through question after question. How was he to align these enigmatic dreams with his understanding of the physical world? What did he really know about this drug —its origin, its purpose, and its side effects? Nothing. With that sobering realization, Sean stood and wiped away the few loose blades of grass that stuck to his elbows. He needed to call Erik.

***

The adenoidal-voiced receptionist told him, in a polite, somewhat automatic manner, that Erik Würfel had been called away on a business trip to Europe. She was prohibited from releasing any contact information to persons outside the company, but would leave him a message.

Sean hung up. If he couldn't contact Erik until next week, then he'd use the time to document his experiences with the drug. He hunted through several drawers in his home office and managed to pry a brown Moleskine notebook from under some old tax returns. He flattened the book with his palm, planning to journal his future dreams for analysis.

The next morning, while still in bed, Sean sat up and journaled about his latest dreams. The first was an oracle dream, with a rather didactic message about eating healthy and getting exercise. But the second dream held more promise.

The dream started inside the glass-walled boardroom of a midsize semiconductor company. The excitement in the room was palpable. The CEO started the earnings conference call by announcing a new contract with a major cell phone manufacturer for the exclusive use of their low-power DRAM chips in the next-generation of cell phones. The CFO said their revenue would double next year.

Sean leaned against his headboard, scribbling the details. A name, "Sun" something, and a logo with two intersecting triangles. He made a rough sketch in the notebook. Using a Boolean search, he typed, "Sun + technology" into the search bar and up popped DeltaSun Microsystems, a semiconductor company based in Chicago, Illinois. Their logo, prominently displayed on the website, consisted of two intersecting deltas. He saw their earnings conference call was scheduled for tomorrow after the closing bell. Sean leaned back in his chair and rested his folded hands on top of his head. A mischievous smile formed on his face.

Insider trading was a crime under the Securities Exchange Act of 1934. But for many on Wall Street, a discreet amount of insider trading had never held the stigma of a serious crime. More of a minor offense, like peeing in the pool. Rarely talked about, but everyone did it.

Sean bought five call options—a leveraged bet that a stock will increase in price within a set period of time—on DeltaSun's stock ahead of tomorrow's earnings announcement.

Let's see if these dreams have a practical side.

Was it insider trading? Probably. But who can say where our decisions come from? What's the true source of our inspiration? Dreams, hunches, or random encounters? Nah, Sean thought, there was nothing to worry about.

***

When DeltaSun's lucrative mobile chip contract was announced, its stock rocketed. In a wave of glowing comments from analysts and business writers, the stock was the day's big mover. Less than three hours after the bell, Sean closed his position for a $1,500 profit.

For the next several minutes, he barely moved, staring at the trade confirmation. Ecstatic, he was thrilled by the magical turnabout in his life. Of course the money was nice, but for Sean, the stakes were far greater than a few short term profits. This was absolute confirmation that everything he'd experienced in the past two weeks—the dreams, the insights, the timing, all of it—was true and real. His heart raced as he dared to imagine the potential of what was happening. Staring into the monitor, his body threw off a slight chill.

Sean developed a new workflow. As soon as he woke, he carefully journaled the dream, and strategized a trade. Over the next few days, Sean made several thousand dollars, all through small, under-the-radar trades. It was capitalism at its finest. But he had some misgivings.

Receiving an inside scoop through dreams probably met the legal definition of insider trading—it was information not available to the public—but getting caught was another matter. The more he thought about it, the less he worried. There had never been a connection between himself and these companies: they weren't clients of Farber, he never contacted insiders from the firm, and there wasn't a shred of paper for anyone to trail. He was clean. He chuckled when he visualized the prosecutor arguing that Mr. Hastings violated SEC statutes by tapping into proprietary information obtained through his subconscious dreams.

"As co-conspirators, the prosecution also indicts, as yet
unidentified, pixies, fairies, goblins, and spirits."
No, Sean's biggest fear was that they might suddenly stop. The drug came from an unknown source, and there was no guarantee that he'd be able to obtain a continuous supply. Or, the effects might fade, or mutate.

Even the dreams themselves had become a concern. Why these dreams? What if he started dreaming about complete rubbish, like the outcome of corporate bowling league tournaments, or the winner of the MTV Video Music Award? None of these concerns were unreasonable nor unfounded since he had absolutely no control over what he dreamt. What if the dreams turned dark and ominous:

dreaming about natural disasters, terrorist attacks, or plane crashes? Sean saw a few movies about people with those gifts—and things never ended well for them. After spiraling into negativity for a while, he forced himself to breathe. The worries were getting him nowhere. He'd have to wait for Erik's return.

As he got ready for bed, he smiled faintly, anticipating tonight's dream adventure.

***

Erik asked Sean to meet him at Withheld By Request, a wryly named speakeasy located in Greenwich Village. Its mundane entrance—a solid metal door in the middle of a featureless industrial building—might have easily led to a utility room or storage unit. Sean tilted his head until the yellow-orange light from a sodium-vapor street lamp struck the brass nameplate at just the right angle. Pulling the door open, he descended down the narrow staircase.

Reaching the bottom, the dim space opened into a lounge with diamond-tucked burgundy leather couches, olive-green high-back chairs, a generous back bar with bottles stacked twelve feet high, and a sliding library ladder that rode on rails from side to side. Staring disapprovingly at the patrons, and dominating an entire wall, was a large contemporary portrait of Winston Churchill. Sean scanned the room and spotted Erik Würfel at a small table under an oil painting of horses and hounds.

"Thanks for meeting me here," said Erik, wiping the foam of his IPA beer from his beard. "Any trouble finding the place?"

"Kinda thought that was the idea behind a speakeasy. But, no." Sean smirked and then ordered a Manhattan from the waitress.

Erik raised his eyebrows, a faint grin on his face. "So—you want to know more about our little substance?" Sean's expression was answer enough.

"I first heard of the drug from a consultant my firm hired to work on a high-frequency trading algorithm," Erik began. "We were out for drinks one night, and after a few pints, he hints at all the secretive shit his company was doing. They had some technology to access information that no one else could. I figure it's data-mining, or corporate espionage, or whatever. After a few more rounds, he says that this 'technology' was really a drug. A closely guarded secret inside a firm that was already pretty cloak-and-dagger."

Sean leaned in, his Manhattan untouched.

"He said what makes this drug unique," Erik continued. "Its special magic, if you will, was its subjective effect. In other words, it effected every individual differently. You know what I mean?"

Sean's expression clearly indicated that he didn't. Erik raised a hand.

"Trust me, I felt the same. He said that past users reported everything from a good snooze, to the most fantastic spiritual journeys. By the end of the night, he'd agreed to give me a sample."

Sean looked down at his untouched drink and leaned back for the first time since Erik began. He had come looking for answers, but his mind was tangled in questions. What was a financial consulting firm doing with quasi-legal drugs? How did the drug help them get their information? And, most importantly, how did Sean fit into any of this?

He looked up at Erik. "You said you tried it?"

Erik nodded. "We met at his apartment the next day. He looked über stressed, paranoid. He gave me a package containing dozens of sheets of tabs, and asked me to hold on to it for him. Said it wasn't illegal, he just didn't want his company to know he had it. He included a small sample sheet for my personal use."

"And?"

"I slept well. Had a few pretty cool dreams." He stopped and thought. "Yeah, that's about it, nothing special."

Sean plucked the Maraschino cherries from his drink and set them on the napkin. "That's it? There's got to be more. All this secrecy, and you expect me to believe that it's nothing more than some kick-ass form of melatonin. What're you hiding?"

Erik recoiled in defense. "I'm not hiding anything. That was my experience. But the emphasis should be on my experience." He paused to order another beer.

"When I told him what happened," Erik continued. "He said that wasn't unusual, but in some cases, the drug could enable telepathic transmissions, even thought transference. In the rarest cases, when the stars were aligned, the user could step outside themselves—and travel into other people's dreams."

Sean frowned in faint recognition. "Travel into…dreams?"

"They call them incursions—dream incursions. The drug opens a pathway for your consciousness to enter into someone else's dream. They can learn the dreamer's thoughts, see their visions as if they were part of the actual dream. It's like psychic eavesdropping. You could say, 'dream-dropping.'" Erik chuckled. He wet his lips with the cold brew and used a free hand to wipe his beard.

"Until now, I've only heard stories told second or third hand, but judging by the urgency of your call, I'm guessing that you, my friend, might be one of the chosen few. So tell me. Is it true?"

Sean didn't answer. Erik's words rattled around in his mind, colliding with his thoughts and experience. It seemed impossible, too fantastic to be real, but so was everything else he'd been through lately. As implausible as it sounded, Erik's story actually explained a lot. Maybe this wasn't clairvoyance at all. Maybe he wasn't seeing the future, but rather, someone else's present. A glimpse into the future? Or simply an existing deal not yet announced?

Merely? Simply?

Christ! For a brief moment, Sean convinced himself that Erik's explanation made any of this less extraordinary. No, this was something straight out of the pages of fiction. As a young boy, he loved reading Sherlock Holmes. He recalled one of his favorite quotes: "Once you have eliminated the impossible, whatever remains, no matter how improbable, must be the truth."

***

Later that evening, Sean tapped the space bar to wake his computer. To the right of his keyboard, he smoothed out a wrinkled cocktail napkin that Erik had given him. Scrawled on the paper was a largely misspelled list of the plants and chemicals representing the sum of Erik's understanding of the drug.

The absurdity of the situation wasn't lost on Sean. After sixteen days of ingesting the drug, he was finally getting around to doing research. He chuckled, recalling an advertising study that showed most people do their research after purchasing the product. No one wants to be told what to do—but we all need validation.

All of the substances on Erik's list were considered to be entheogens, a class of psychoactive substances that induce some enlightening, spiritual, or developmental outcome. It's what separated them from drugs people used for a recreational high. Over the centuries, entheogens have been used by shamans and tribal healers to access alternate forms of consciousness—to understand a world beyond the material world. Even the name alluded to spirituality: "entheogen," derived from the Greek word "éntheos," meaning, "full of god." It was the root of our word, "enthusiasm."

Sean took a deep breath, typing in the first name from the napkin: "Psychotria vidiris." He read the first few sentences in the description, and rubbed his temples. He was far outside of his element. This was a world of black magic, white magic, trances, rituals, transcendence, and divination. Nothing in his conservative life had prepared him for this.

Psychotria vidiris, or Chacruna, was a plant in the coffee family containing DMT —the "spirit molecule." It was legendary within spiritual circles. Users reported having met entities, communicating with a higher intelligence, the dissolution of their ego, and an awareness of alternate dimensions.

Although often disputed, DMT is thought to be naturally produced by the body's pineal gland. This gland, tiny and pine-cone shaped, was located near the center of the brain, between the two hemispheres. The French philosopher, mathematician, and scientist René Descartes said it was the "principal seat of the soul, and the place in which all of our thoughts are formed."

Other associations between DMT, spirit, and the pineal gland—include the Hindu notion of a third eye, and the crown of pine cones that rest atop the head of a Buddha statue. Considering its powerful, mysterious, and enlightening nature, it probably should come as no surprise that DMT was made illegal by the majority of the world's nations.

He crossed it off the list and moved on to Brunfelsia uniflora, or Manacá. Native to South America, Manacá has been used by shaman's for everything from poison arrows to dream-walking.

Poison Arrows?

Last on the list was Tynnanthus panurensis—clavohuasca—a large, wood-like vine that allows the spirits to present themselves through dreams.

In a manner of speaking, it was a lot to ingest. In his black mesh office chair, Sean felt miles out of his element. He leaned back. Quietly sipping his glass of Macallan whisky, he savored its smooth, mildly burning sensation. Twisting the glass in his hand, he watched the light prism through the golden-brown liquid. Alcohol—one of the world's oldest and most embraced entheogens.

Is it any wonder they're called "spirits?"

Alcohol has played a role in many of the world's great religions. Dionysus, Bacchus, Sucellus, and Osiris were all gods of, or associated, with alcohol. The Greek philosopher Plato even argued for the allowance of alcohol in education, because it provided for the assuagement of otherwise rigid viewpoints. Sean smirked as he pictured the toga-clad scholar. Plato—father of the college beer bash.

Though his knowledge of pharmacology was limited to ibuprofen, he understood the gist of what he had read. Still, nothing explained the way in which he interacted with dreams.

These Amazonian medicines were cultivated to provide visions, to enable transcendent experiences, to unlock new dimensions, or perhaps to touch the face of God. In remarkably drab contrast, Sean was in boardrooms and business lunches, listening to tedious discussions on mergers and acquisitions.

Where was his spark of divinity? His spiritual awakening? Where was enlightenment for poor old Sean?

He let the liquid linger on his tongue, slowly swishing it back and forth. Soon, Sean's thoughts turned to worry. He wasn't sure if he was more concerned about where these dreams might lead, or that they might simply vanish, casting him back to the colorless routine of his former life.

He shook off the negative thoughts. Erik's list was a start, but it was incomplete. The ingredients may have ancient roots, but the synthesis was purely lab-based. Sean began to wonder if, rather than a random side-effect, his experience was, in fact, the exact purpose behind the drug's design. To find that answer, Sean would need to dig deeper. And quirky Erik Würfel might be his only way to the answer. He needed to contact him, though the best he could hope for was a reluctant push in the right direction.

He stared at the screen, the cursor blinking in time with his heartbeat. Everything was beginning to feel untethered and dreamlike.

Chapter Four

On Monday morning, Sean stepped out of the elevator onto the marbled floor of Farber Investments, feeling more confident than he had in weeks. Despite the many vine and chemical names still rattling around in his head, the weekend had left him rested—and red-hot to put his new insights to work.

Late Sunday night, he'd sent an email to his boss. He listed the reasons that Kytel Aerospace, a small-cap aircraft parts manufacturer, was a prime candidate for takeover. Naturally, he made no mention of the dream in which Sean observed Kytel Aerospace being acquired by a large multinational corporation. He recommended that Farber take a position in Kytel.

As expected, his email was flatly ignored. But, by Wednesday morning, Kytel was in the headlines. The stock soared on news of a 55 percent buyout premium. His immediate supervisor was surprised, and maybe a little curious, but wrote it off as a lucky guess.

More "lucky guesses" followed, and with each correct call, lowly Sean Hastings took another small step out of the corporate shadows. Within the offices of Farber Investments, Sean's personal stock was on the rise. Whispers and approving nods, subtle hints of promotion and bonus perks were bandied about. Senior management had begun to notice. For the first time in quite a while, Sean's job was one less thing he had to worry about.

In the weeks that followed, he started to notice subtle changes in the dreams. Tiny details that he'd previously overlooked: people on the periphery, like character actors playing small supporting roles that added balance or color to the story.

An elderly lady sitting in silence at the end of a table, a six-year-old blond girl scattering candy and crayons across a desk, and a Doberman sitting alert in the corner.

After giving these curiosities some thought, Sean concluded that, beyond the main event, these were still just dreams—strange symbolic attempts at sorting through personal matters. Was the young girl the manifestation of the executive's struggle to balance work and family? Was the dog an entrepreneur's only trusted friend? And, was the elderly lady casting judgement on her never-good-enough son, and his unresolved store of mother-son issues? Sean shook his head and grinned.

I need to brush up on my Freud.

***

On Thursday night, Sean dined with Keenan and Zhara at a bustling Mediterranean restaurant. Afterwards, he wished them a goodnight, turned up his collar, and walked the few blocks home. He was in good spirits, buoyed by all the positive trends in his life.

By three a.m., Sean was back in the dream world.

On a crisp winter's morning in July, he was walking up Pitt Street, in the Central Business District of Sydney, Australia. He smiled, appreciating how comfortable he had become to these rapid changes in time and place. Walking behind a group of finely dressed men, Sean tried to pick up the threads of the dream. Twenty paces back, a man in a black turtleneck was following the group.

They entered a symposium on South Pacific mineral rights, and Sean relaxed, sensing the dream's direction. He stood and allowed the narrative to unfold. While waiting, he amused himself by searching for secondary characters.

I bet she's one of them.

A comely blond in a lemon-yellow sundress stood alone. A girlfriend? Ex-girlfriend? Mistress? Maybe the new girl from HR? Sean chuckled. This little game of guessing the story behind fringe characters was becoming the most enjoyable part of dream traveling.

At center stage was an agreement for exclusive mining rights from a tiny Pacific Island nation. Sean found the discussion all too familiar, and frankly, all too boring.

His bosses at Farber were pleased, and his personal investment portfolio was up, but none of that changed the fact that these moments were simply tedious. Who could have imagined that dream traveling would be so boring? The way he looked at it, whether it was done through high tech or high metaphysics, it was still stock research. He wished for something exciting.

Sean sighed, and then looked for another side character for his playful mind game. He spotted the man in the black turtleneck. He had short dark hair, an athletic build, and carried himself in a way that Sean found difficult to pinpoint. Some military training, perhaps? Sean began his little guessing game: a brother, childhood friend, maybe a fallen soldier? He crinkled his brow and paused, there was something different about this man. What was it? Then came a jolt of recognition—a chilled awareness. The man was staring directly at him.

He can see me!

No one had ever noticed him—until now. He snuck another quick glance, but the man had fixed his gaze directly upon him—a solid and unflinching stare. Sean's breath quickened, his heart pounded, his invisibility shattered. A deep visceral fear took hold. Nothing like this had happened before. After all—there were rules.

Actually, I have no idea if there are rules.

Sean's mind was spinning, but only one explanation made sense.

He's the same as me.

How or why the man had traveled here was irrelevant. He was a dream traveler —just like Sean. Until now, he had always believed that the dreamscape was a safe playground. An amusing place to explore, while watching people work through their emotional baggage. Now doubt was creeping in: nothing here was real, right? Parents often comfort their children by saying, "It's okay, it was only a dream."

Were the two worlds as separate as he believed? We've all experienced an emotional or physical manifestation of a dream bleeding into the waking world. Think of an intense nightmare that jolted you awake, with your heart beating rapidly and the sheets soaked with perspiration. Or the warm, flush feeling that left a lingering smile after a vivid erotic dream.

Was Sean safe in this dreamworld? Could he die here? He pushed the thoughts from his mind, mustering the courage to look again. The man was gone. Sean exhaled a huge sigh, and reached around to rub at the tightness in his shoulder. He rejoined the symposium while slowly regaining his composure.

"I am never taking that drug again," he muttered to himself upon waking. It was the kind of statement made while suffering from a raging hangover—hollow and unconvincing. Following the encounter with the man in the black turtleneck, Sean abstained from using the drug—a perfectly reasonable reaction—but deep down, he knew it was only temporary. His life had been a slow parade of failures and disappointments, but the drug had changed everything. Unknown risk or not, he refused to go back to those days. The benefits, both personal and professional, were simply too great. In spite of being rattled by the Sydney dream, he would have to see where this led.

***

A couple of days later, Sean jolted upright before dawn, his sheets drenched in cold sweat. His heart was pounding through his chest, the sweat on his skin glimmering in the faint moonlight. A nightmare, as intense as he'd ever felt, left him trembling in the darkness. He leaned against the cushioned headboard and, like a child, raised his knees to his chest.

Someone had entered his dream. A different face than the man in the turtle neck, but the same menacing presence. The deliberate intrusion of another dream traveler. Sean steadily rubbed his temples with his forefingers. It was a dream incursion, but this time it had been Sean's own dream. His mind reeled with questions.

How did they find him? And, if this was a dream incursion, then why was he aware of it? Dreamers are always unaware—it's the rule.

Why do I keep insisting there are rules?

No one had ever sensed Sean's presence in a dream, so why was this incursion different? There was only one conclusion. He was aware of it because it had been deliberate—because that was their intention. A warning shot, a threat to stay away.

Memories of the dream began to surface: he was trying to flee, doors vanishing into solid walls, escalators abruptly reversing course. A world that could change on a whim. The dream's entire architecture could be manipulated. But why? Sean had certainly never found a reason to alter anything within a dream. Maybe spying on business deals was only scratching the surface of this phenomenon; the true scope of its potential still unknown.

Sean looked at the clock. The hour was absurdly early, but there was no use in trying to go back to sleep. He threw on a T-shirt and headed to the kitchen for some juice. Leaning on the kitchen island, the smothering fear he'd felt earlier was now dissipating, evaporating like the cold sweat from his skin. He wasn't looking for a fight, but in the semidarkness, this upwelling of emotion—this raw anger—caught him off guard. He knew he was unprepared. How could you fight an enemy that appears as an apparition?

He needed answers. He needed to understand what the rest of the world already knew about dreams.

***

In college, he knew her simply as Kate, but today, Dr. Catherine Keelson was a respected historian at Fordham University. Specializing in ontology and metaphysics, she'd recently taken an interest in the spiritual practices of contemporary indigenous civilizations. A bit surprising, considering her life as a devout and practicing Catholic.

Studying the university directory, Sean learned that Kate's office was located in a building on the Rose Hill campus. As he walked up the windowed staircase to the third floor, he stopped to enjoy the view of the New York Botanical Garden.

"Knock-knock," he said, peering into the open doorway.

"Sean! It's great to see you." Kate stood and walked around her desk. She kissed him on the cheek and gestured toward the couch and the two chairs against the window. "Please, have a seat. I've got to tell you, your call really took me by surprise. So—tell me more."

She looked good, he thought, still slim with curly auburn hair, now cut short to shoulder length, and a nice pair of tortoise-framed glasses. She wore gray slacks and a cerulean blouse, unbuttoned at the top, perfectly framing the simple cross that hung from a thin gold chain.

The years have been kind to her.

From the moment he walked through the door, the ease and trust they once shared returned immediately. He decided to take her into his confidence and tell her everything. Well—perhaps not the parts related to insider trading, or the obvious illegality of the drug, or the threatening individuals embroiled in corporate espionage, or the fact that they could manipulate dreams—but, within the confines of whatever was left, Sean was prepared to come clean.

"Remarkable," she said, after he finished. "Sounds like you've experienced something similar to a shamanic passage. I'm not sure what you're looking for, but I assume you want to learn about dreamtime, and things like that?"

"Dreamtime?"

"In Aboriginal culture, dreamtime describes the practice of entering another person's dreams—and helping with healing, guidance, evil spirits, or finding lost souls. Native American tribes, like the Mohawk or Lakota, share similar beliefs. That sounds like what you're experiencing."

"So, this dreamtime is really a thing." Sean looked doubtful. "It's not just my imagination? It's possible for people to travel into someone else's dream? Honestly, none of this jives with anything I've ever learned, I just don't have a better explanation."

She laughed. "It doesn't match 'what' you were taught, because of 'where' you were taught. If you'd been raised in an indigenous tribe, or one of the many developing countries that hold such beliefs, this would seem as natural as the cycle of day and night, or the change of the season. In Western society, these concepts remain entirely alien. We have little interest in things like dreamtime, or any other spiritual concepts or practices."

"Why is that?"

Kate dug a lozenge from her purse and unwrapped it as she leaned back into the couch. She popped it in her mouth before continuing. "There are many reasons, of course, but primarily, for the past two thousand years, it's been the dominance of the Judeo-Christian doctrine that has shaped our thinking. We're taught about the beauty of divinity, told that the divine is all around us, but it can never be within us. The West has created this great chasm between the individual and the divine, one that can never be crossed by man alone. To help navigate this gulf, we have assembled a hierarchical church structure, with stratified layers of priests and other religious leaders that serve as our emissaries."

Sean leaned back in the chair.

Kate continued, "But dreamtime is different, part of a worldview where individuals and the divine coexist. The spiritual separation of the West simply doesn't exist. Shamans are not priests—they only help individuals achieve what they're already capable of achieving."

"Which is?"

"To personally connect with the divine in another consciousness." She smiled.

Sean looked curious. "I hesitate because you sound quite admiring of these indigenous cultures. No offense, but I remember that you were a devout Catholic. I mean," he said, pointing all around, "you still teach at a Catholic university. Have your views changed?"

"No," she said with a warm smile. "My faith hasn't changed, but I've chosen to accept these ideas as an enhancement to my beliefs, rather than a contradiction. Judeo-Christian teachings are young when compared to the spiritual teachings that date back over forty-thousand years. My faith is almost adolescent in comparison—with all the typical growing pains." She giggled and rolled her eyes. Kate leaned back, reflective.

"We've become too infatuated with the individual. The church teaches us to live our life in the service of God, a path to a heavenly afterlife, but it's a life deferred. Society constantly pushes us to divide our lives: work life, social life, religious life, home life. It's arbitrary. Ancient societies integrated all aspects into a single cohesive way of life. To be banished, or cast out, of an ancient society was the greatest of all punishments, the equivalent of a modern day death sentence. But for contemporary Europeans or Americans: leaving your family, moving from city to city, or changing jobs are all routine events and scarcely consequential."

Sean tilted his head, weighing Kate's argument.

"The contrasts are quite telling," she continued. "We seek guidance from external sources—media, doctors, clergy, the internet. Indigenous people seek guidance from dreams, through the embodiment of their deceased elders. We're obsessed with the past and future, but ancient peoples believed in the coexistence of time, referring to it as 'all-at-once' time. Only our youngest children experience that—at least until society can strip away that innocence."

"I suppose I see some of that in my own life," said Sean, in reflection. "Living a day-to-day existence, randomly divided into a series of wins and losses. My marriage—or I should say, former marriage—my work, even my social life… moments I define as either success or failure. In the end, what does it mean—happiness? Success?"

Kate took a sip of her coffee, shaking her head as she swallowed. "It's neither. Success and happiness have become part of the same trap in our society. You're a success when you attain or accomplish a goal, but society will always move the goalpost: if you make a good living—make more money; if you meet your quotas

—they'll raise your quotas. Using this model, success becomes impossible to achieve."

The sunlight glinted off the frame of her glasses. Sean smiled in admiration. She was in her element, teaching and making an impassioned plea for a better world. He wondered if he'd ever believed in anything that strongly.

"To make matters worse," she continued, "people have learned to link their happiness with success, and happiness stays just beyond our reach. If you tell yourself that you'll be happy when you achieve a goal, but then move the goal before you get there, your happiness stays forever over the horizon."

Leaning back into the chair, Sean said, "Well, yeah, that all makes sense, but I'm not sure I know of any other way."

"I think you do. The experience you're having with these dreams is truly special. Most of the West has lost touch with its spiritual roots, and you, for reasons that I can't explain, are rediscovering that missing part of the human experience. The Aborigines have a saying, which roughly translates into, 'Don't try to push a river.' So, my advice is to run with it—don't fight it."

Kate tilted her head and looked at Sean, letting him sit with his thoughts for a minute. Then she added, "The Enlightenment brought us reason and scientific method, but in the process, we've lost the balance between science and spirit. We separate the world into modern societies and primitive societies. Naturally, we consider our technological society superior. But is that true? In Australia, over six hundred Aboriginal tribes live in general accord with one another, in harmony with nature, and in tune with their own spirituality. In contrast, our advanced Western societies are laden with greed and wars, and we exploit nature at every opportunity. I think the early results of our modern philosophy haven't been that promising."

After he left Kate's office, Sean was in disaccord.

I should embrace this as a gift?

He found her uplifting description of spirituality inspiring, but he knew there was another side. What about malevolence? He thought of the man in the black turtleneck and doubted that harmony and accord was the message he was sending. Was there a demon for every angel? He was grateful for Kate's views, but what he was experiencing went beyond her perspective.

What these people were doing felt aggressive, as if technology was forcing itself upon spirituality. This drug was a technological feat, plain and simple. Someone made it for a very specific purpose, and any questions surrounding the true intention of the drug could only be answered by tracing it back to the original designers.

Find them, and you'll find the truth.

Chapter Five

Erik Würfel strolled into the brasserie that afternoon behind Bartholomeu, his Portuguese water dog. The dog's namesake, Bartholomeu Dias, was a fifteenth-century Portuguese explorer—the first European to reach the Indian Ocean by sailing around the Cape of Good Hope. Erik had once considered getting a Spanish water dog, not because of his preference for the breed, but because the Spaniards had a better roster of explorer names.

"I made sure I wasn't followed," whispered Erik, as he sat down and snatched one of the fries from Sean's plate.

"Why would anyone follow you?" Barely ten-seconds in, and Sean was already irritated.

"I don't know. They always say that in the movies."

Sean smiled, playing along. "Then you might consider that dressing like a hipster lumberjack in the middle of downtown Manhattan, with a fifty-pound dog that looks like it slept in curlers, is a poor way to be inconspicuous."

Erik laughed. He was brilliant in mathematics, programming, or anything with numbers, but like many people with very high IQs, he often came across as a little touched to the average Joe. Sean decided to get to the point.

"Look, I need to know where you got the drug—and who made it."

"I told you. It's from a company called Morpheus Research. At least that's who my friend worked for. Not sure if he's still there."

"Never heard of them. What do they research?"

"Financials, mostly. But that's only part of their business. They do a lot of work for governments—sort of a think tank. Not surprised that you haven't heard of them. They like their anonymity."

The dog yawned, and while Sean looked down, Erik used the distraction to steal a few more fries. "A lot of Wall Street firms use them, maybe even yours. Though, it's not something they'll admit."

"How can I find them?" Sean asked, wondering how many influential companies operate on the murky fringes of capitalism.

"What little I know came from my friend. It's not like they have a website or anything. I can tell you this, though: it was founded by two men, but the only name I remember is Dr. Adler Daemon. He studied at the ETH Zurich—the Swiss Federal Institute of Technology. Brilliant. Studied mathematics, then got a PhD in physics. Mind you, this is a school that's produced over twenty Nobel Prize winners, including a fellow named Einstein. Daemon spent a few years at various universities, before breaking out and forming Morpheus Research. It's a private company. No public filings—and no idea about the source of their funding. They're based in Switzerland. Enough?"

Sean thanked him, picked up the tab, and gave Bartholomeu a quick pat on his spiraled and looped head. The dog yawned. Sean headed out.

***

Erik's description of Morpheus as "low profile" was an understatement. His initial search yielded no results. No website, no direct contact information, no financial reports, and no mention in the publication of Who's Who. Not even a single Yelp review.

Most of the results were split between Morpheus, the Greek god of dreams—son of Hypnos, and namesake to the drug Morphine—and Laurence Fishburne's character in the Matrix film series. Aside from a stray reference in an article or two, the company appeared to not exist. In fact, Sean learned more about a Richard Morpheus, a fifty-eight-year-old plumber from Biloxi, Mississippi, who regrettably tweeted something vile during the last election cycle. Sean tried a different tack.

He typed in "Dr. Adler Daemon." This time, there were a few results: a short biography on the Swiss Physical Society's site, a few psychology articles, university affiliations, and an old interview in a magazine called Noosphere: A Cognitive World.

There were a few cryptic references to a project at the Université de Montréal, but from what Sean gathered, it had ended in an undisclosed controversy and was defunded. No articles, postings, or references to Dr. Daemon had been made in the past five years. Sean raised an eyebrow.

What's the good doctor been up to?

He dug deeper and learned that Noosphere magazine was still in circulation. Sean contacted the editor.

****

"Mr. Waxman, thanks for taking my call. I'm Sean Hastings with the Financial Times. I was looking for some background information on a company called Morpheus Research. I understand you might know one of the principals."

A long pause, and then he said, "So, you want to know about Adler? I haven't heard from him in years."

Winston Waxman, the founder and editor of Noosphere magazine, was sixty-four years old, sporting a full head of suspect jet-black hair that turned purple in sunlight. He weighed over 265 pounds, but cheerfully dismissed these as "a few extra pounds."

"How did you meet Adler Daemon?" Sean asked. "Was it through Morpheus Research?"

"Oh no, that came much later. I met him when we did a story on his work at the university, the Human Consciousness and Cognition Project. We were fascinated by its implication for the noosphere. We talked a few more times about the piece, but I'm afraid that was the extent of our relationship."

"Pardon me, you said it had potential for—what was it again? A noosphere? I'm not familiar with the term."

"The noosphere is the sphere of human thought," Waxman said, waiting for the revelation to register in Sean's mind. Finally, with a hint of impatience, he said, "Mr. Hastings. I'm not really sure what you're looking for, or the basis for your inquiry, but it might help if you understood a little about the work that Adler was doing at the Human Consciousness and Cognition Project."

"Yes, please," Sean responded dryly. He rolled his eyes at Waxman's school teacher reprimand.

Waxman cleared his throat. "Around the world, there are a great many scientists and engineers who believe in a unified field of consciousness called the noosphere.

A Russian geochemist named Vladimir Ivanovich Vernadsky coined the term to describe the third stage in the development of our planet. First, we began with the rock itself, planet Earth, and that was called the 'geosphere.' With the introduction of plants and animals, life forms, we moved to the 'biosphere.' Today, we are moving beyond the physical world into one based on cognition. This next stage is the 'noosphere.' The prefix derives from the Greek word for mind. Are you with me so far?"

Sean grunted an acknowledgment over the phone.

"The deeper we move into the noosphere, the more the physical world alters as a result of cognitive activity. Darwin's theory only addresses evolution from a biological standpoint, but as we enter a world of cognitive dominance, evolution occurs through cognition—in essence, bending the physical world through thought."

Sean wondered if this noosphere was more than just a theory, if Dr. Daemon had found a way to gain access through chemical means. "And this was the basis of Dr. Daemon's research?"

"Exactly. Technology has reshaped how we live, how we think. No other generation has experienced anything close to this—it's totally unprecedented. You have to love the irony: Darwin's theory is now the inferior species."

Sean cleared his throat. "Whatever happened to Daemon's Human Consciousness—something—Project?"

"Oh, it's gone, disbanded several years ago. Rumor has it that the university broke with Adler over an 'ethical breach,' whatever that means. A few years later, I heard that Adler founded Morpheus Research."

"Thanks again for your time, Mr. Waxman. Out of curiosity, who are your readers?"

"You'd be surprised." Winston laughed. "We have a small but influential subscriber group: writers, think tanks, scientists, a few US senators, even the Department of Defense—we run the gamut. For what it's worth, I doubt you'll have any luck in getting in touch with Daemon. Instead, you might try to find someone from his team at the Université de Montréal. Have a good day."

***

Montréal, Quebec.
 Four years earlier…

A young Adler Daemon sat across the desk from the dean of psychology at the Université de Montréal. His boss was angry, sputtering and shouting. Adler often had that effect on people. The dean's desk was piled high with papers and loose volumes of books, and Adler moved his head from side to side in a childish take on peekaboo.

"Adler! Damn it." The university dean bellowed at his arrogant young professor. "I have to answer to the Board of Regents. If there's any truth to these rumors, then you've put this university at tremendous risk. What if someone gets seriously injured, or God forbid, dies as a result of your experiments?"

Adler listened with an air of casual dismissal. His blank stare only further deepened the dean's fury, whose pale skin cycled through the red spectrum: baby pink to rose to scarlet. This wasn't their first talk on the subject and it surely wouldn't be the last. He left the dean's office and walked back to his campus laboratory.

Adler Daemon was born in Washington, DC, to parents of European descent working in the diplomatic corps. By virtue of his place of birth, he was a US citizen. Academically gifted, he attended an elite Georgetown school that catered exclusively to the sons and daughters of foreign diplomats. He was well liked, both in and out of school. At the age of fourteen, his parents left the United States on another assignment. By the age of seventeen, Adler had enrolled in ETH Zurich, the Swiss Federal Institute of Technology.

The first light snows of a Montréal winter were falling. Adler shuffled his feet and kicked up the powder dry flurries, mildly annoyed by his dean's reaction. How were they blind to the research's potential? He wondered if bureaucrats ever became frustrated by other bureaucrats—or if they developed some kind of immunity, like clown fish swimming through a sea anemone.

He shook his head in disgust and a few snowflakes fell from his hair. They refused to look beyond the biology, the genomes, and the DNA strands. Human beings were linked together on a deeper level. Adler was convinced that consciousness would be the next step in evolution.

Despite his openness to spiritual ideas, Adler rejected organized religions of all faiths—dismissing them as unconvincing, facile dogma. However, his views softened when it came to polytheistic religions. They were, to his mind, less restrictive, less dogmatic, and more willing to embrace new ideas than monotheistic religions. He'd point to the fact that almost all religious wars had been fought by those worshipping a single god.

Daemon could spend hours reflecting on the big, existential questions of truth and knowledge, though few called him introspective. Most thought of him as cunning, analytical, and relentless. Adler was baffled that no one recognized the contemplative side of his personality. Perhaps, the Human Consciousness Project had been his way of connecting with his inner philosopher.

Crossing the snowy campus courtyard, Adler soon put the confrontation with the dean behind him, and thought about tomorrow's experiment. The psychotropic drug had been modified again. Adler fully understood the risks, not only to the health of the students, but to the survival of the project itself. The dean had been perfectly clear—the university had become suspicious and was watching Daemon's lab. Adler felt the stress.

He pushed on, reasoning that the results were undeniable. Nothing short of stunning. Would that be enough? Adler's subjects could accurately describe places and events for which they had no previous knowledge. He couldn't explain it, but he refused to dismiss it as some cheap parlor trick. They had traveled, if that was the right word, to another dimension and acquired the knowledge firsthand.

One of his student subjects, barely twenty years old, described a Vietnam battle fought more than thirty years before his birth. His account was dead accurate, matching historical records and a recently declassified defense report. Though the student's account was factual, he harbored none of the visceral emotions or trauma one expected to see in a combat soldier. A researcher said it was like they were describing a scene from a movie. Not reliving the moments—but observing them from an emotionally safe distance.

Adler saw this as proof that they had scratched the surface of consciousness. The recollections were like particles from a comet's tail, a collection of debris and remnants that sloughed off along the way. Adler was convinced that universal consciousness was within reach.

Back in his laboratory, Adler tapped his desk in a nervous rhythm. He had defied the university, openly scoffing at their rules. Had he gone too far? Each day felt like he was on borrowed time. Rubbing his eyes, he scanned the laboratory. Stress had turned to slight paranoia. Who could he trust? Who might break? Most regarded him with cult-like devotion, but not all.

He just needed more time. One careless word, one formal complaint, and it would all come tumbling down.

Chapter Six

New York City

Sean made several calls to the Université de Montréal before reaching someone in the Psychology Department. The cheerful voice on the phone sounded almost adolescent to Sean, but insisted that he actually was a professor of psychology.

"Oh yes," he said, when Sean asked about the project. "I was still an undergraduate back then." After Sean pressed him for details, the man confessed that he couldn't recall the scandal, or any of the details.

"Who? Dr. Daemon? Um, yeah, sorry," he mumbled in his French-Canadian accent. The more questions Sean asked, the more blanks the academic drew. The only thing his young, hormone-ravaged mind seemed to vividly recall from those days was a project intern, Olivia Abbott.

Sean rolled his eyes in amusement listening to the young professor describe her in near-photographic detail. He prattled on about how the slightest breeze made her caramel balayage hair dance across her delicate shoulders, the fluid elegance of her walk, and how the sunlight brought out the blue-green color of her eyes.

Caramel balayage hair?

Sean tried to steer the conversation back to the project, but the professor's flames of passion were too close to the point of conflagration. After raising his voice to get his attention, Sean learned that the subject of the professor's lustful desire, Olivia Abbott, had worked on the Human Consciousness team—and still lived in Montreal.

Sean found her office listing in the directory.

"Dr. Abbott, my name is Sean Hastings. I'd like to talk to you about the Human Consciousness Project, and Dr. Adler Daemon."

Several seconds of silence were followed by a long, weary sigh. "I don't know how you got this number, but I can't help you. It was a long time ago—and frankly, a chapter I'd rather put behind me. Goodbye."

The line went dead.

***

"Checking any bags?" asked the ticket agent at JFK later that afternoon.

"No, not today." Sean tucked his passport and boarding pass into his jacket pocket, and headed toward the TSA checkpoint. Montréal was where it all began— and Olivia Abbott was his best chance at unraveling the mystery. Was there a link between the Human Consciousness Project and Morpheus Research? Anything beyond the elusive Dr. Daemon?

Sean walked into the lobby of Montréal's Hotel Place d'Armes around five, and checked in. The luxury hotel, in the oldest part of the city, was extravagant by Sean's standards, but his investment dreams had paid off handsomely—so he splurged. He dropped his bag onto the bed and took an evening stroll around the square and the famed Notre-Dame Basilica. Only a few weeks ago, he would have headed straight for the bar. But things were different now. The annual reports and balance sheets had surrendered to the world of shamans, entheogens, and the strange noosphere.

***

The next morning, Sean showed up at the office of Dr. Olivia Abbott unannounced. It was a shared space with three other researchers and a common receptionist. Judging by the small size of the waiting room, he guessed the researchers rarely welcomed guests. It was an unassuming room decorated with several two-tone travel photographs in plexiglass frames.

"They belong to one of the researchers," the receptionist offered. "He's an amateur photographer." Sean smiled politely and spent the next few minutes admiring the photos.

Thirty minutes later, Olivia strode in, her walk brisk and full of purpose. In person she was even more striking than he'd imagined from the professor's description. It wasn't just her physical attributes, Olivia projected an aura of confidence and strength. For a moment, he felt awkward, almost like a gawky schoolboy. He felt off-balance. In the midst of this juvenile fog, he heard the receptionist announce his name.

"Hastings?" Olivia queried with knitted brows. He'd hoped for a warmer tone.

"I told you on the phone that I wasn't interested in discussing either Dr. Daemon or the project," she said bluntly.

"Yes, you did," he said, as he tried to collect himself. "But I thought if you heard me…as a person."

God, I sound like a moron.

"I'm sorry, but no. I have another appointment" With a deft pivot she turned to walk down the hall.

"I've had dreams!" Sean blurted out. "I've traveled into other people's dreams!"

This was not how he'd rehearsed the moment.

Olivia stopped abruptly and turned. "What do you mean by traveled?"

"Visitations, incursions, dreamtime—whatever you want to call it. It started after I took this drug, and…look…I know this sounds pretty crazy."

Olivia stood motionless in the hallway and tilted her head. She stared at Sean for a long minute, perhaps deciding what to make of the stranger. Sean regained his composure and, for the first time, noticed the intensely blue-green color of her eyes. His thoughts briefly returned to the young professor.

"Susan," she turned to the receptionist. "Would you be kind enough to bring us two coffees? Mr. Hastings and I will be in my office."

Her office was remarkably neat for a researcher. Sean could still recall the paper-strewn chaos that many of his former professors seemed to prefer. A single green glass vase with three pure white calla lilies sat on the desk. Books on psychology, biology, and philosophy lined the shelves behind her. A small marble bust of the Greek philosopher Parmenides watched from the credenza in the corner.

Sean felt an impulse to fire away with dozens of questions, but he stopped himself. Olivia's face indicated that this was going to be a case of "you go first." Fair enough. Over the next twenty minutes, he took her on his journey from sleeplessness, to ingesting Amazonian drugs, to the dream incursions, to the financial dealings, everything all the way up to, and including, the threatening stranger that recently crashed his personal dreamscape. It felt like a confession.

Olivia listened without interruption. Her expression conveying neither skepticism or doubt. After he finished, they sat quietly for a minute. Now it was Olivia's turn.

"I was in my doctoral program when the Human Consciousness and Cognition Project recruited me. I thought they were interested in my biophoton research, but that wasn't the case. I almost left because of it, but the project was so intoxicating, brimming with brilliant people. And so I stayed."

"What was the project's goal?"

"We were searching for empirical evidence of global consciousness—the inner world that runs parallel to the outer world we experience everyday. We can't see it, so most people doubt its existence. We call this inner world 'universal consciousness.'"

Olivia sipped at her coffee and watched Sean's reaction.

"We wanted to explore the idea of a multi-dimensional universe," she continued. "Emphasizing consciousness and the noetic sciences. Are you familiar with these?"

"Something to do with knowing?" Sean asked tentatively.

"Was that a guess?" She laughed. "You're right though. Intuition, guesses, hunches, gut feelings—all the subjective things we know but have difficulty explaining. We understand concepts like love and fairness, or abstract ideas like freedom or patriotism. But how? How do you teach the meaning of love?"

"I think I understand. These concepts are instinctive, natural to all humans."

"Exactly. We started with parapsychology experiments, but we soon focused on dream research. Are dreams a jumbled mess of the day's thoughts and feelings, or a pathway to understanding consciousness?" She cupped her coffee in both hands.

"What about Dr. Daemon?" Sean asked, too intrigued to be cautious.

"Adler? Brilliant, also relentless, obsessive, and highly demanding. The trouble began when Adler prescribed sleep medicine to a few of the student-subjects in our dream research. Nothing outrageous at first, just the usual stuff physicians prescribe to half of America. But after some promising results, Adler persuaded two of the students to experiment with psychedelics."

Olivia gently shook her head as she recalled the moment.

"Most of us objected, drug therapy was well outside the scope of our research grant. But Adler pushed, and eventually the team caved to his will. He introduced peyote, psilocybin, 5-MEO, and other drugs to the student subjects—and we suspected that he began using the drugs himself. An obvious breach of ethics, but the results were stunning. Subjects could recall, in amazing detail, places they'd never been. One student woke up knowing every last detail of a small town in southern France—we had to use maps to verify the information. The student had never been to France."

Sean was completely riveted and his coffee cup, still full, had gone cold.

I still need to know about Morpheus.

"Adler began to change," she went on. "He withdrew from the group. Traveling, on several occasions to the Amazon to look for more native compounds. Somewhere between the dubious travel invoices and Adler's surly attitude toward the university administrators, enough flags were raised to put the project under scrutiny. When a student filed a complaint, the walls began to crumble. When the university learned of Adler's personal drug use, the walls finally collapsed. Funding and facilities were immediately frozen, all the research seized."

Sean shifted in his seat and looked at Olivia. It was a fascinating story, but several questions still burned in his mind. "When I first mentioned dream traveling," he paused with a squint, "it looked like I hit a nerve. And, when I told you my story, which almost any sane person would think was completely nuts, you barely raised an eyebrow. I can't accept that everything was just packed away and forgotten. I know that what I'm going through is linked to a company called Morpheus Research—and to Adler Daemon. How are the Human Consciousness Project and Morpheus connected?"

"The university," she said, with a resigned sigh, "confiscated the work, but we always knew there were hidden copies. Adler left Canada shortly after the fallout and returned to Europe. The rest of the team scattered to the wind. I went on to complete my PhD in biopsychology, then moved into teaching."

Sean frowned. "I've looked into Morpheus Research, but they're a ghost."

"People talk, of course." Olivia said, her shoulders shrugging slightly. "The rumor was that Daemon returned to Switzerland and, with a business partner, founded Morpheus Research. I'm ashamed to admit it, but at the time, I believed he only wanted to continue the research we had started."

Olivia studied him for a long while. "Are you sure you wish to pursue this? Morpheus is highly influential. They move in powerful circles."

Sean shrugged it off—an ego-driven reaction. Beneath the surface, he was less confident about facing off against a foe that had already demonstrated its superior abilities.

"Okay then," she said, taking his response as a yes. "I'll be in New York next week. There's someone there I'd like you to meet."

Sean thanked her for her time, the coffee, and the background information. As he walked out the door, Olivia appended her previous thought.

"Mr. Hastings—Sean—I was quite serious when I said you should give it some thought. In the meantime, keep a low profile and refrain from any inquiries into Morpheus."

"Well," Sean said with a smirk, "considering that they've already done a dream incursion on me, a low profile is no longer an option. Thanks again."

***

Geneva, Switzerland

It was an idyllic autumn day in Geneva. A crisp, invigorating breeze flowed from the snowcapped mountains, and Dr. Adler Daemon strolled leisurely, taking pleasure in every second of the short walk. He crossed the river at the Pont des Bergues, in no hurry to meet with his associate.

At the Riverside Café, Adler chose a quaint outdoor table by the water. He glanced down through the wrought-iron railing and smiled. A mother duck and her ducklings glided along the waters of the famous Rhône River. He took in a deep, relaxing breath. It was a perfect day to enjoy the sights of Geneva: the calm of the lake, the white peaks of the Alps, and the spray plume of the Jet d'Eau, a 140-meter fountain that defined the cityscape. In as much as any place was home, Daemon could claim Geneva as his.

He had attended university in Zurich and preferred the German influence of northern Switzerland over the French south. Still, this move had been for business, and logistics demanded a base of operations in Geneva. The city's blend of alpine beauty and cosmopolitan energy matched his interests and mood. In short, he felt comfortable here.

The warmth of the late afternoon sun played against the cool lake breeze in a most delightful way. The temperature was quite agreeable for wearing anything from a light polo to a three-piece suit. Naturally, Dr. Adler Daemon opted for the latter.

A blond waitress brought him a glass of Châteauneuf-du-Pape, his favorite wine from one of the regional vineyards of the Rhône Valley. He ordered a platter of assorted cheeses and cold cuts to complement the fragrant red. As the sunlight warmed his cheeks, he closed his eyes, and savored his first sip of wine.

A shadow crossed over his face. He opened his eyes in time to see a silver-suited man in his mid-sixties sitting down at his table. The man brusquely grabbed the menu from the table, pointed at the wine, and asked, "Any good?"

"Very," replied Adler, with a certain weariness.

"Okay, let's grab a bottle." He motioned for the waitress.

Armand C. Locke was Adler's personal attorney. He'd monogrammed his initials on everything—briefcase, shirtsleeves, pocket squares, robes, and more. His business card read, "Armand C. Locke, Lovewell, and Jones, LLC, A Law Firm."

Why he had insisted on the unorthodox use of his full name in the title of a law firm was anyone's guess. Why his partners, Lovewell and Jones, had put up with it was yet another mystery. Armand was licensed to practice law in New York and Virginia, but he'd spent the last few years abroad, working exclusively with Adler and Morpheus. Back in the United States, Lovewell and Jones were happy to forge on without their namesake partner. It was strictly a marriage of convenience. As far as Lovewell and Jones were concerned, every day spent away from that horse's ass was a good day.

"Have they agreed to the terms?" asked Daemon.

"Yes, all the necessary papers are signed and digitally encrypted. I'm waiting for Jean-Luc, at the Banque du Genevois, to confirm the first of the payments has been processed."

Armand possessed a remarkable gift for the nuances of international law. Since Morpheus's services were usually of a legally questionable nature, Armand's creativity and legal mastery proved invaluable in safely navigating the treacherous reefs of international trade, commerce, and security laws.

A waitress arrived at the table, opened the wine, and poured two glasses. Adler quickly downed the remaining sip of his first glass and looked at Armand. "Tell me what you think—a little bolder than most."

"Yeah, not bad," assessed Armand after a quick swig.

Armand Locke was a difficult man to read—even harder to like. Adler once called him a "longshoreman wrapped in an Armani suit."

To the best of Adler's knowledge, the man only cared about fast cars and fast women. A ridiculously worn cliché, especially for someone in his sixties. Still, over the years, Adler had learned to tolerate his many contradictions. If it hadn't been for Armand's keen legal mind, he wouldn't have bothered to try.

Armand wore Savile Row suits and Italian shoes, drove finely engineered automobiles, and bought acclaimed examples of contemporary art, but he eschewed the other traditional symbols of upper-class society like opera, ballet, fine food, and wine. He tried to project an air of sophistication, but in his heart, he was a crude man. In their personal lives, the two men had absolutely nothing in common, but in business, they formed the perfect couple.

"Are you sure this will work?" asked Armand, reaching across the table and picking a slice of mortadella from Adler's platter.

"We wouldn't have taken it this far if there was any doubt. We've settled on the time and place that provides the most impact for our client."

"They specified Jackson Hole, right? During the financial symposium?"

"Yes, but we still need to confirm his travel itinerary," replied Adler, as he sliced a section of gooey Brie. "We know he prefers short afternoon naps, so the timing of his nap is our narrow window of opportunity. The greatest challenge is to avoid killing him in the process. Three or four minutes without oxygen and his brain will be damaged. Stretch that out to, say, five or six minutes, and well—he'll be dead. I'm confident that we can stop the inhibition of his breathing in time, but unfortunately, there's no guarantee he'll start respirating on his own. Which is why we need to know the details of his security team's protocols. They'll need to be alerted at precisely the right moment so they can administer CPR. If all goes as planned, our friend will be alive—but permanent brain damage will have occurred."

"Like boiling the perfect egg," said Armand flatly.

Adler drew a heavy sigh. "A crude…but remarkably accurate analogy."

Armand's cell phone buzzed. He looked at the caller ID and said, "It's Jean-Luc calling to confirm the first installment."

Chapter Seven

New York City

Sean walked past the famous LOVE sculpture in Midtown Manhattan and followed Olivia's text directions to the Center for Change Potential. In front of the steel-and-glass clad office building, he double-checked the address before stepping through the revolving door. The CCP was a respected consulting group and think tank that specialized in helping once-successful companies overcome stagnation.

Olivia Abbott was waiting in the reception area when Sean arrived. Before they finished their hellos, a receptionist politely interrupted. "Good morning. Please follow me. Mr. Maxwell is waiting."

"This is your last chance to get out," Olivia said with a grin as they followed the receptionist. Sean smiled, mostly out of politeness, but wondered why she persisted with the spooky rhetoric.

At the end of the corridor, Morgan Maxwell was waiting. He exuded a subdued elegance. His office interior—decorated in a burnt-orange palette, calfskin leather chairs, and a tigerwood inlaid desk—was refined and stylish. He struck Sean as a man whose composure would never falter, or be out of place. A man that would never show an outward sign of doubt.

"Your experience is not that uncommon," Morgan said, in a reflective tone. "Dream traveling doesn't fit into Western beliefs, but in primitive cultures, these practices are an essential tool for helping one another. Of course, we aren't living in a primitive culture."

Morgan moved toward the window, leaning on the wide sill. With his back still turned, he said, "Our instincts are rarely so altruistic. Look at your own behavior Mr. Hastings—using this knowledge for financial gain and career advancement."

Sean shot a fiery glance at Olivia.

I said that in confidence! What the hell's going on?

"There's nothing to be ashamed of," Maxwell said, his tone almost reassuring. "It's who we are as a culture. We believe that an individual's pursuit of gain benefits society as a whole—a rising tide, and all that. It's the basic tenet of capitalism. But, in indigenous societies, when they encounter something like dream traveling, their first instinct is to use it to better the lives of the group. Ours is to profit—to consolidate power." Morgan poured himself more coffee, and lifted the pot as an offer to refill. They shook their heads.

"A client first told me about Morpheus Research," Morgan said. "They were being whispered about in corporate circles and at cocktail parties. They were offering a unique and highly effective form of corporate espionage. The person telling the story usually finished by expressing their indignation. But at the same time, you knew that every executive in the room was already imagining how to contact them."

He threw his hands open and shrugged.

"Later, at a colleague's beach house, I met his son, Ryan, who wrote his graduate thesis on the behavioral patterns of type A individuals. His father joked that he could've saved time and money by simply staying home and observing his own family. Soon, we were all sharing stories about the insanely driven people we've known, but Ryan said it was nothing compared to his old boss, Dr. Adler Daemon. Ryan had been a research assistant on the Human Consciousness and Cognition Project. As you've guessed by now, he introduced me to Olivia."

Sean frowned. "Okay, so Morpheus offended your sense of fair play, or clouded your true-blue vision of capitalism. Why does any of that matter?"

Morgan carefully selected a sour candy from a bowl and offered some to Sean and Olivia. They declined. Crumpling the plastic wrapper, he looked up.

"You're right," Morgan said. "This goes beyond stealing corporate secrets. Olivia told me about your dream incursion. Were they able to alter parts of the dream? Change the surroundings?"

Sean nodded, stunned. He hadn't mentioned that to Olivia.

Morgan smiled and flashed his brow. "That was merely a demonstration. Once Morpheus learned how to enter dreams, they moved on to manipulating the dream's constructs. Now, they're focused on controlling the dreamer—which leads to the endgame."

Sean furrowed his brow, curious about where Morgan was headed.

"Morpheus plans to weaponize dreams."

Sean nearly laughed. It sounded like a B-grade sci-fi movie plot. He looked over, but no one else was smiling.

Olivia picked up where Morgan left off. "We've been told that dreams are dreams, and reality is reality. But what if that isn't entirely true? What if Morpheus was able to hurt someone in a dream—and it resulted in actual physical harm? Imagine a cardiac arrest or a respiratory failure induced in a dream—and triggering an actual biological failure."

"An actual failure?" asked Sean incredulously. "But that would be…" He stopped and looked at Olivia to make sure he heard her correctly. "You're talking about killing someone—inside a dream?"

"Assassinations," added Morgan while nodding. "Exactly. Since we all have to sleep, everyone is at risk. Armed security teams, corporate jets, secure military facilities—it doesn't matter—everyone, everywhere, is vulnerable. Think about it. No bullet holes. No stab wounds. No poison. Just an autopsy confirming death by natural causes."

Sean wondered if he detected a slight hint of admiration in Morgan's voice.

Tapping him on the arm, Olivia said, "We think it works like this. Are you familiar with the parasympathetic nervous system?"

Sean gestured a degree of understanding.

"It controls autonomic functions of the body—breathing, heart rate, temperature. We believe Morpheus has found a way to hack into this system during dream incursions. Suppressing the autonomous system without the use of drugs or invasive tools."

Sean looked confused. Something wasn't adding up.

"But those functions are automatic," he said. "If I was choking in a dream, my body would react. Even in a dream, I would still breathe—I can't simply choose to suppress it."

Olivia leaned against the edge of Morgan's desk and crossed her legs.

"We think the answer lies in anesthesia," she said. "Under general anesthesia, those same autonomic functions are inhibited. It's what makes anesthesia so useful —and dangerous. Modern medicine has learned to control the variables—like patient size, drug interaction, existing conditions, etc.—but no one fully understands how it works. In the proper dose, a patient can be adequately sedated, and safely and painlessly undergo surgery. If it is improperly administered, a patient can overdose, causing a severe pathological depression in the part of the brain known as the brainstem, or medulla—stopping respiration or heart functions. In other words—it's lethal."

Morgan's secretary came in to exchange coffeepots. After she left, Olivia stood from the desk, and resumed.

"We think that Morpheus can simulate the effect of anesthesia—tricking the brain into reacting as it would to a physical sedative. A virtual, drug-free—potentially deadly overdose."

"Is that really possible?" asked Sean, astonished that anyone conceived of something so outlandish.

"We believe so," Morgan responded.

"When Daemon left the Université de Montréal," Olivia continued, "he disappeared for a while. When he resurfaced in Switzerland, he was flush with cash: recruiting staff, purchasing equipment, advancing his research. Three years after he left the university, Daemon founded Morpheus Research. Whatever the source of his funding, it far exceeds anything obtainable through academic grants."

Sean fell back into his chair, his mind racing. Did they actually believe this? He was tempted to walk out the door, but then something struck him. "You said our understanding—are there others?"

"After the Human Consciousness Project ended, the team fractured," Morgan explained. "Daemon had his loyalists, all devoted more to the man than to any research, but most went their separate ways. However, a few understood how dangerous this knowledge could be in the wrong hands."

Olivia moved closer to Sean. "When we heard that Adler was recruiting people from the original project, we decided to keep tabs on his activities. Sort of a watchdog group. Now we have almost a dozen members."

Morgan stepped in. "Everyone brings something unique. I handle business and connections. Olivia's our biochemist. We have a forensic accountant, an expert in electromagnetic radiation, a neurologist, a psychic—and now—you."

Their interest in him should have been obvious, but Sean was genuinely surprised. "Me? What can I do?"

Olivia softly touched Sean's left arm. With a smile she said, "You're too modest.

When most people have a flash of intuition, they dismiss it as a hunch. They never consider it might be a long-dormant sense. Animals can sense earthquakes before they happen, or navigate enormous distances to return home. We marvel at their instincts—but we tend to be brutal skeptics about our own intuition. This drug has unlocked an abeyant skill in you, Sean. And what's so remarkable, is how far you've come entirely on your own."

"Morpheus is gaining ground," Morgan said gravely. "You can help turn the tide."

"Remember, they already know about you," Olivia added. "I doubt they know what to make of you, but you're causing them concern.

Sean sat up and took a heavy breath. It all sounded insane—but also strangely magical. The dreams had transformed his once tedious life into something extraordinary. Was this a second chance? An escape from the sad routine that had led to his sleeplessness and depression?

"If I was interested," he said cautiously. "How would this work? Everything sounds theoretical."

"You'll understand more after you meet the rest of the team," Morgan said. He took off his wire-framed glasses, and rubbed the bridge of his nose. "Sean, the stakes couldn't be higher. Governments, corporations, terrorists—all willing to pay an obscene amount of money for an untraceable method of assassination."

He stepped in front of Sean.

"So, Mr. Hastings…are you in?"

Sean turned toward Olivia and stared into her deep-blue-green eyes. She returned his gaze. He was looking for guidance, wisdom, perhaps a lifeline? This was not an easy decision. Time slowed.

Finally he said, "Sorry, but no."

***

It's one of the curious quirks of human nature: once we become aware of something, we see it everywhere. A car, a watch, an idea—suddenly, we see dozens of examples everyday. Carl Jung called it synchronicity.

After his meeting with Olivia and Morgan, Sean felt besieged by talk of spirituality. Articles, interviews, podcasts: all in some way discussing spirituality and human consciousness. It was everywhere. Had he always been unconscious about consciousness?

Killing time before an appointment, Sean scrolled through Instagram. A meme of a wild, fuzzy-mustached physicist stared back at him:

> *Everything is energy and that's all there is to it. Match the frequency of the reality you want and you cannot help but get that reality. It can be no other way. This is not philosophy. This is physics. — Albert Einstein.*

Sean huffed and rubbed the back of his neck. Someone, or something, was definitely trying to get his attention. How long could he ignore it? The dreams had pulled him from his humdrum existence, but there was still so much he didn't understand. Perhaps, it couldn't hurt to wade a little deeper into these spiritual waters. He called Morgan's office.

"Mr. Maxwell is out of town," said the secretary. "But he left you a message, dinner at eight p.m., Friday. Samir's restaurant in Tribeca."

Sean found the invitation presumptuous, but sighed in resignation. Of course he would go.

***

Samir was working the reception desk when Sean arrived. The fifty-year-old restauranteur was a picture of trendy elegance in a white Ralph Lauren shirt, dark jeans and leather sandals. His carefully coiffed jet-black hair pulled tightly back, seamlessly transitioning into a full beard. All of this hair was visually separated by a pair of mirrored sunglasses.

"Welcome. Mr. Maxwell and his party are already seated."

Sean followed Samir. He observed the restaurant's penchant for unorthodox lighting: mismatched chandeliers, pendulum lights, Tiffany pieces, the occasional icicle strand. The disparate style included high ceilings, creaking dark wooden floors, and arched doorways of the beaded and non-beaded curtain variety—all reflecting the eclectic charm of its Lebanese owner. After navigating the maze of narrow hallways and rooms, they rounded the last corner. Sean's pulse quickened. Olivia was seated at Morgan's table.

Morgan rose. "Sean, glad you made it. You already know Olivia," he said, as he turned, "and this is Dr. Landon Maeda."

Sean reached out to shake hands, but froze. It was the doctor from the sleep clinic.

Morgan noticed his reaction. "I'll explain in a moment, but first, I'd like you to meet Noble Gareth, our psychic."

He was a trim and handsome man in his early forties. Sean was immediately charmed by Noble's Scottish brogue.

The seat next to Olivia was vacant and Sean hoped that was by arrangement rather than blind luck. He sat and looked around the table.

"We're waiting for one more," Morgan said to Samir, as he took the drink orders.

Addressing the awkward moment earlier, Morgan said, "I see that you recognize Dr. Maeda from the clinic. It was Landon who brought you to our attention."

Sean nodded slowly. Wondering what it was about Morgan that made him feel uneasy.

Maeda turned to Sean. "Morgan and I go way back. When he teamed with Olivia, we developed a dual mission for the clinic. We looked for someone who was —I want to say susceptible, but that isn't the right word—let's say, receptive to the drug. As a neurologist, I identified certain suitable genetic traits, ones compatible with the drug. When we did your blood work, it showed you were a good candidate for dream incursions."

A voice from behind Sean said, "Good evening."

He turned around and immediately recognized the man in a Stumptown plaid shirt, blue jeans, beard and glasses—Erik Würfel.

Morgan smiled and continued. "When Landon identified you as a candidate, we asked Erik to approach you at the clinic. The fact that you knew each other was purely chance. We assumed that if the drug worked as planned, you'd reach out to Erik. When he was called away to Europe, we decided to put things on hold. But then Olivia called to say she'd just met a man named Sean Hastings. Well, you can imagine our surprise."

Sean felt manipulated. "So it was all a setup? The consultant story, the drug? All of it?"

Erik shook his head. "No, that was true."

"When you went to Montreal," Morgan said, "either out of curiosity or sheer determination, we knew we'd found our man. Destiny, you might say."

Sean wanted to be angry. But beneath his outrage he felt something that was closer to gratitude. There was no denying that, in these past weeks, he had felt more alive than ever before. His old life had become a rather sad cocktail of insomnia, boredom, and loneliness. Now, he was feeling exhilarated, euphoric, ebullient…and many other words that mean basically the same thing. Sean glanced around the table. These people were clever, and he enjoyed their company. Now he faced a choice: redirect his life and embark on a righteous crusade against evil—or sit, pout, and pretend to be upset.

I want this…no…I need this.

Finally, Sean smiled and nodded. Everyone took it as an acceptance.

***

After dinner, Samir insisted they cap off the evening with a round of eau de vie, a digestive drink first introduced to Lebanon during the postwar French occupation. Though it translated to "water of life," after one sip of its high alcohol content, one would be tempted to call it the "firewater of life." Morgan raised his glass.

"Now," he said, turning to Sean, "let's talk about how you and Noble will work together. The memory of dreams fade the moment we wake up. Until they invent a cerebral DVR, we appear to be out of luck. Unless…" Morgan held a lengthy, dramatic pause and Sean was again amused by his attempts at gravitas. "I'll let Noble explain."

With a stoic expression, the Scot said, "Alright, let's start by reading your palms."

Sean frowned, but extended his hands, palms up. Olivia giggled.

"Sorry," Noble laughed. "I haven't got a clue what I'm supposed to see." Sean felt annoyed, a little embarrassed at being the butt of a joke in front of Olivia.

"Everyone's always teasing me," Noble went on. "Asking me to read their palms, 'roll the bones,' or contact Marilyn Monroe."

Still chuckling, he said, "It brings up an interesting point, though. Parapsychology is quite specialized. Clairvoyants perceive people, objects, or events using extrasensory perception. Mediums communicate with the deceased. Prescience is the ability to see future events, and telesthesia is the ability to see distant objects without the use of normal senses. While there's some overlap, we generally stay within our skill set."

Sean grinned, seeing an opportunity for payback. "Aw, just when I hoped to see some spoon-bending or a floating table."

"That's telekinesis and levitation, respectively," Noble replied, without missing a beat. The amiable Scot had an accommodating spirit. He sipped his drink, grinned, and then continued.

"Want to hear about some of the more obscure skills? There's psychic surgery, the ability to make surgical incisions using concentrated mind energy, or thoughtography, the ability to print physical photos on paper using only mental images and thoughts."

Sean laughed. "Okay, now you're just making this shit up."

"Nope, they're on the official list of recognized psychic abilities." Noble raised a glass in a silent toast to the arcane. He slammed his shot, with its contrasting blend of gentle peach and fuel-grade alcohol.

"So, down to business. Whenever we focus on a problem, or recall a memory, our brains emit a faint energy wave. And each energy wave possesses a unique frequency. Our goal is to capture a Morpheus agent's frequency during a dream incursion, so that we can identify and find them later."

Sean stared blankly at Noble. Even after a few drinks, it sounded loopy.

"How can any sane person be expected to buy into this?" he asked.

Noble listened politely and smiled. "It may sound far-fetched, but look at what you've experienced recently. The impossible has transformed into the possible. Our minds are like tight muscles or tendons—it's painful to stretch and grow beyond the paradigms we've become comfortable with. Consciousness—shared thought— is destined to be the next great advancement of humanity."

Olivia reached over to gently touch Sean's arm. Her hand was soft and warm, and the sensation of her touch distracted him.

"Schopenhauer," she began, "is credited with saying, 'All truth passes through three stages. First, it is ridiculed. Second, it is violently opposed. Third, it is accepted as being self-evident.' Throughout history, every major scientific breakthrough was called 'revolutionary.' I think it's because that word reflects the conflict between those who embrace change, and those who fervently cling to the past. We've had the cognitive, agricultural, industrial, and informational revolutions. But none of these has prepared us for the revolution of consciousness. Its potential is too great to be corrupted by the likes of Adler Daemon."

Sean stared at the edge of the table, considering all he'd heard. He felt something shift inside. The fortressed walls of Sean's mind were showing its first cracks. Was it Noble's deep conviction, the buzz from the eau-de-vie, or the sensual warmth of Olivia's touch? Either way, Sean's skepticism was slipping away. He felt untethered—and uncertain—like he was learning to swim, finding the courage to let go of the dock for the first time.

He looked around the table. They were joking, laughing, and enjoying each other's company. He liked these people. He liked their cause.

"So," he said with a soft smile, "where do we go from here?"

Morgan leaned forward. "In a few days you'll meet another member, Reinhold Haas. He's flying in from Munich to explain the technical side of the process."

"And," Olivia said with a laugh. "You won't understand a single word of it… none of us do."

Chapter Eight

The instructions seemed simple enough. Reinhold was tasked with renting a discreet office in Manhattan—something inconspicuous for their equipment and operations. But now, standing outside the building, Morgan, Olivia, and Sean were trading looks of bewilderment. They double-checked the address. It was correct.

"Pardon me," said a young man with a partially completed neck tattoo as he brushed past them. Above the entrance of this ragged two-story brick building was a large red and black sign: SQUID: Ink and Body Scarification Salon.

The trio stood there, speechless. Finally, between their consternation and amusement, they smirked and went inside. On the immediate right was the entrance to the tattoo parlor, the muffled sounds of needles buzzing and a little soft chatter. Further down the hallway was a creaking, wood-planked staircase that led to the second floor. When they reached the top, they were met by Reinhold Haas—enthusiastic, beaming, oblivious to their dismay.

"Welcome, welcome," he exclaimed. "Well, what do you think?"

Morgan scratched his head. "It's…not exactly what we discussed."

"I know! So much better, ja?" He gestured all around. "This whole building used to be a machine shop—fifty amp circuits, reinforced floors. But the best part…the thing that really sold me, was the name on the building."

Olivia stifled a slight giggle. "You mean Squid?"

"Yes, but in all-caps," said Reinhold, with a wink. "It's an acronym for Superconducting Quantum Interference Detectors. Part of our equipment. The sign is perfect. It's like we're hiding in plain sight."

Sean exchanged a knowing look with Olivia. Her earlier comments about the German were starting to make perfect sense.

Reinhold showed them around the room and, despite a shaky first impression, they had to admit that it wasn't bad. White walls, epoxy floors, and fluorescent lighting—all lending the room the look and feel of a laboratory. Nothing like they'd expected from the gothic leanings of the first-floor neighbors.

Reinhold had partitioned the room into two spaces. On the left, a break area with a secondhand sofa in a light-brown corded fabric, an oak and glass coffee table, and an area rug with a faux-Persian pattern. A vintage refrigerator, the type with rounded corners and a large metal lever, gently hummed next to the sofa. After taking a look at Reinhold, Sean assumed it held more beer than food.

The entire right side of the room was dedicated to the laboratory. Dozens of pieces of electronic equipment filled the space: a sea of blinking diodes, low hums, and faint clicks and whirls. Sean glanced over at Morgan and Olivia. They seemed impressed. So he followed along, nodding his head, and pretending to understand.

In the center of the room was a six-inch-high platform, carpeted in Berber and supporting a comfortable-looking recliner. Reinhold jumped on the platform like he was hosting a sales event.

"So, this is our Sean," he said cheerfully. "I've heard much about you."

"All good, I hope."

"Natürlich."

At thirty-one, the German national had a slender frame, a close-cropped beard, and spiky, gelled hair. He had two passions in life: electronics and soccer. Though often called a savant in electronics, sadly, no one had ever been tempted to use that term to describe his soccer skills.

Reinhold Haas turned to the whiteboard and began scribbling in a flurry of IP addresses, frequencies, and some kind of math. Sean couldn't be sure if it was trigonometry or calculus—as if it made any difference to him. When Reinhold finished, Sean tried to absorb the gist of what he heard.

"So, if I got this right," he said tentatively. "We all emit electromagnetic waves that correspond to a unique frequency. And you want me to help you find the one that belongs to a Morpheus agent?"

Reinhold nodded. "Ja."

"Will this actually work?"

Morgan leaned back and crossed his legs. "Back in the sixties, fingerprints were the principle forensic tool for solving crimes, they can be recorded, cataloged, and cross-referenced. But now police rely on a different method of identification."

"You're referring to DNA."

"Exactly. Not that long ago, with the exception of a few genetic scientists, almost no one had heard of DNA. In a similar way, frequency is not currently accepted as a form of identification, but like its DNA predecessor, it's destined to be recognized as a valuable resource."

Olivia asked, "Have you ever wondered why your dream incursions are so random?"

Sean chuckled. "Almost every night. I could fill a notebook with questions about how the drug works, why the incursions happen, or what's with these business dreams."

"I'm not sure we can explain the business dreams," Olivia said, "but we might be able to help you control where the dreams take you."

Morgan nodded. "Morpheus spies on companies that are about to break out, to make a significant change. Erik has given us an algorithm to narrow the potential candidates. Noble will telepathically target some top individuals working for those firms. And then its up to you."

Olivia smirked and said, "Are you ready for the technical part?"

"I thought that was the technical part."

They approached a strange device—a cross between a tilted front-loading washing machine and a sheet-metal lathe. Reinhold rested an arm on the machine and proudly said, "Meet MEG, our specially modified magnetoencephalograph. It uses a sensor-equipped headband to scan and process Noble's brain activity and convert it into binaural tones. Each tone represents a target's frequency. Sean, when you hear them in your headphones, your subconscious will translate the sounds into the agent's frequency."

Sean said, "Let's pretend I understood that—the whole brain thingy with the tones. How do I avoid being detected? Getting caught?"

Olivia stretched her slim frame. Her tone confident. "Dreamers can't detect an incursion. The same goes for their agents. They won't know you're there."

Sean frowned. "Well, the Morpheus agent in Sydney obviously knew I was there. And at that point, neither of us knew anyone else was doing dream incursions."

Morgan shuffled in his seat. Olivia chewed on her lower lip. "Actually," she confessed, "we're not sure about that. An anomaly, perhaps?"

"I was hoping for a better answer."

***

A few days later, Morgan laid three dossiers on the table. "Erik's algorithm has identified these companies as Morpheus targets."

Noble glanced over without interest. Olivia casually thumbed through a couple, before tossing them back onto the table in frustration. Morpheus was moving quickly—and the group was always two steps behind.

Naturally, all this led to a collective anxiousness—often expressed through an odd sigh or a prolonged, distant look. The pressure was most apparent on Morgan. His once warm smile and compassionate eyes were now hidden behind a near-permanent look of exhaustion.

It hadn't always been this way. The catalyst for this change came on a clear September morning.

Of the many images etched into people's memories on the day the twin towers collapsed, for Morgan Maxwell, it would forever be the sight of paper. From his nearby office window, he watched as hundreds of thousands of sheets of paper descended from the buildings, falling like autumn leaves.

The contrast of the day was chilling: the tranquility of gently swirling papers, and the chaos that overwhelmed the city. He watched the papers fall. Documents that, minutes earlier, had seemed so important. Work that came at the cost of lost sleep, missing children's recitals, or the sacrifice of what would be their last precious hours with friends and family.

Through the horror, Morgan saw the absurdity of chasing money, chasing power. He had an epiphany that day, though his corporate colleagues would coldly characterize it as "losing it."

He called it clarity.

He quit his job in finance and established The Center for Change Potential. His many detractors were soon silenced by his rapidly growing client list. In his personal life, he began reading books on spirituality and attending lectures.

Years later, at a talk by Bruce Lipton, he met some former members of the Human Consciousness and Cognition Project. They told him about Morpheus Research, and how Daemon was perverting the science. Their message aligned with Morgan's new mindset, and he agreed to find the funding.

***

Noble slumped onto the laboratory's couch. He looked tired.

Sean asked, "Rough night?"

"Aye." He crossed his arms and sighed. "Having a hard time isolating the frequencies from Erik's algorithm. Too much damned noise—cell towers, radios, microwaves—it's like trying to pick out a single violin in an orchestra."

Sean nodded. "You're not the only one. Reinhold has been a bit snippy, rewriting code and tweaking the headband."

It wasn't all bad news. Sean proved to be remarkably receptive to hypnosis. Noble joked that Sean could go under "like a cruise ship anchor."

As Reinhold finished translating Noble's psychic data into a series of binaural tones, Sean leaned back into the recliner. He slipped on a pair of headphones, while Noble adjusted his mic.

"Relax," said Reinhold, "Think of it as music."

This isn't music, Sean thought. It sounded like a cat walking on a piano, not unpleasant, but hardly musical. The notes sounded nonsensical, but under the hypnosis, Sean's brain heard more than a collection of random sounds. It was a secret code that only his subconscious could decipher.

The human brain operates in five modes of activity called brain-wave patterns: alpha, beta, theta, gamma, and delta. One state is normally elevated above the others, making it the dominant pattern. Sleep was the most common way humans shifted from one brainwave pattern to another. Meditation, hypnosis, or the use of drugs and alcohol were the other common methods.

Of the five, theta waves were the most interesting because of their association with creativity, inspiration, and spirituality. In this twilight state, just before deep sleep, our minds are filled with dreamy imagery, and we're left in an euphoric, oh-so-relaxed feeling. Noble's job was to keep Sean hovering in the theta state—half asleep, half awake—while the tones did their thing.

***

That night, in the laboratory, Sean settled in for a night's sleep. The binaural tones had implanted the executive's frequency information in his subconscious and, if everything went as planned, he would enter the dream of one of the three potential targets for a Morpheus incursion.

It did not go as planned.

Sean ended up in an unrelated dream. "What happened?"

Noble and Reinhold exchanged glances.

"I…I really don't know," Noble said frowning. "We'll try again."

The next night, the same result. On the third night, Sean woke looking visibly disturbed.

"You found the Morpheus agent?" asked Reinhold, with hope.

"No. Worse. I wound up in the dream of a fourteen-year-old girl." Sean shook his head and chuckled. "Guess I'll have to keep a close eye on Abbie when she becomes a teen."

Noble and Reinhold had begun arguing, an angry exchange in German and Scottish accents.

Sean ignored them. His thoughts drifted back to what had brought him here in the first place. What seemingly inconsequential decision had changed his life's trajectory? Was this a new chapter—or a whole new life? Whatever the answer, this version of himself felt completely foreign. Unknown to his ex-wife, colleagues, friends, even to himself.

Until his mind was freed, Sean realized that he had never felt trapped. Had a radical life change been the answer all along?

***

The next night, Sean wriggled in the recliner and pulled himself upright into a more comfortable position. Reinhold announced that he'd corrected the programming error.

Things were good, and Sean's life was on a better track. Change was never easy, but he liked the man he was becoming, he liked the people around him, and most of all, he liked the prospect of a new beginning.

Noble dimmed the lights in the lab. "Ready, Sean?"

Sean smiled, reflecting on his new part-time job—reconnoiter of hidden Morpheus agents in the curious world of dreams. The binaural tones soon began, and Sean wondered what waited for him on the other side.

Chapter Nine

S ean's arrival into the night's dream began with the brisk sting of spray across his face. He could taste the ocean on his lips—a salty reminder of the enigmatic line between dreams and reality.

The boat's crew moved with deft precision, keeping the A2 spinnaker in its groove. The racing sloop heeled hard to port. Off the starboard side, Jeff Carl's nemesis was sailing a forty-five-foot Swan. The two boats sprinting with less than a thousand yards to go. Carl's boat had hoisted its big-shouldered sail a fraction of a minute earlier than the Swan. Now, the spinnaker's advantage was beginning to pay off. Carl's boat surged across the line ahead of the Swan.

Sean recalled the file Erik had prepared on Jeff Carl. He'd built his technology company around batteries, optimizing the performance of lithium-ion batteries. Wall Street rumors said the company had made a major breakthrough in the time it took to recharge. If true, Jeff's company was ripe for a takeover—making it a prime candidate for a dream incursion. This would be the group's fourth attempt at finding a Morpheus agent. So far, they'd yet to encounter a single one.

With the sun beating down on his face, Sean sat on a large winch and watched Jeff Carl's dream unfold. He smiled, grateful that his tendency toward sea sickness hadn't translated into the dream world. He looked at the man steering the yacht, recalling the interview where Jeff said he felt more at ease at the helm of a boat, than the helm of a corporation.

After the race, the dream shifted to the clubhouse. Sean sat at the yacht club's teak bar—highly polished under an ungodly amount of varnish. Jeff moved in celebration from guest to guest, laughing and drinking. Club members, some in navy blazers, mingled with Jeff's loud and rowdy racing crew.

Standing well apart from everyone else, both physically and in appearance, were a few men that Sean assumed were business associates. Their attempt at blending in was almost comical. Dressed in their "what do I have in my closet that looks nautical" outfits: white chinos, pastel polos, and reddish-brown leather deck shoes. The celebration began to wind down, and Jeff Carl slipped off to a small conference room. The gaggle of pastel polos followed.

Framed by a wall of pendant flags, trophies, and a clock made from a ship's wheel, Jeff Carl thanked the men for agreeing to meet "in such an unorthodox surrounding." The auto executives were painfully late in entering the electric vehicle market—something they hoped to rectify by acquiring Jeff's company.

Sean watched with tepid interest, and his mind wandered.

Had they bought their deck shoes from the same catalog?

When he looked up, the light at the far end of the room had begun to bend and shimmer in a most peculiar way. Was this part of Jeff's dream? The light pulsed and flickered for a few more seconds—then disappeared. In its place stood an athletically built man in a dark-gray sweater.

Morpheus!

Sean's heart began to pound and his mouth went dry. The same fear from the Sydney dream returned, and he tried to hide behind an absurdly thin flagpole. He struggled to remind himself that this was the moment they'd worked for, but now what? Sean knew he was a neophyte dream traveler, with barely a clue about how all this worked.

Across the room, the agent casually walked around the table. No one noticed him. No one except Sean, who was shuffling around the table trying to maintain some distance from the man in the sweater.

The agent took a few steps toward Jeff Carl. Sean slid to the opposite side—a game of cat and mouse. When Jeff Carl reviewed some documents, the Morpheus agent stood directly behind him, peering over his shoulder. Sean was so fascinated watching the action that he almost forgot about his fear. It was like a scene from some Cold War spy drama—mini camera in hand, snapping images for later analysis.

Sean inched closer. The man turned suddenly. Sean froze, bracing for his discovery, but the agent passed him without so much as a glance. Sean let out the breath he'd been holding.

I'm okay with being the mouse, as long as the cat doesn't know I'm here.

Then he remembered Noble's instruction: focus on the agent.

What did that mean? How close do I have to be? Did focus mean touching?

He wasn't sure which earthly actions or sensations translated into the dream world? He was here, but no one could see him. He could shout, but would anyone hear him?

Back in the lab, Noble stirred when he sensed Sean's body twitch. The movement jarred him and he sat upright. He leaned forward, palms hovering over Sean's forehead, searching for a faint signal revealing the agent's frequency.

In the dream, the pastel garbed associates began to fade from view—quite literally—first blurring, then vanishing altogether. Jeff's subconscious had tacked to a new course, and he was swapping sailing stories with an elderly gentleman sporting an impeccable beard.

Just like that, the moment was gone. The Morpheus agent had also vanished.

Sean sighed. He knew what came next—the waiting—the worst part of the incursions. Morpheus agents came and went as they pleased, but Sean was stuck here until his body woke up. Bored and disinterested, he watched the yachts rock in their moorings. Then, a strange shimmer near the dock caught his attention. He sat up. But it was simply the late afternoon sun reflecting off the water. Sean blew out a breath and felt a twinge in his stomach. Was he ready for what the dreams demanded?

***

The smell of coffee was the first sensation to break through Sean's foggy return to consciousness. That, and something else—smoky, earthy, faintly familiar. Noble handed Sean two cups; one with coffee, at Reinhold's suggestion, and one with whisky, at Noble's. All in the spirit of camaraderie, Sean supposed.

"How'd it go?"

"Everything we hoped for. And you?"

"Well, the agent couldn't see me, so that's good news." Sean shook his head as he remembered. "Remarkable, really. He moved and gathered information at an impossible pace."

Sean downed the espresso in a single gulp, and then slowly sipped at the whisky. "So, did we get the agent's frequency?"

Noble grinned broadly. "Reinhold's preparing the headband as we speak. Don't worry, you did well."

Cradling the Styrofoam cup, Sean watched Reinhold work—his hands a blur of keystrokes and mouse clicks. Noble went off to slip into some form of meditation. Sean shrugged and leaned back in the lounge chair. His part was done. Tomorrow, the hunt for Morpheus would begin.

***

The next afternoon, Reinhold texted Sean: We've completed the translation of the agent's frequency data. Ready to introduce the tones into your subconscious.

Walking into the building, Sean passed one of SQUID's clients. His neck tattoo read, That which does not kill us makes us stronger.

Sean wondered about the sudden interest in Nietzsche.

Halfway up the steps, his mind turned to what lay ahead. How safe was it, really —having something inserted into his subconscious? What were the long-term effects? Hell, what were the short-term effects? By the time he reached the top of the stairs, Sean forced the doubts from his mind.

I suppose if it hasn't killed me yet…

In the lab, Reinhold and Noble were fine-tuning the equipment, while Morgan and Olivia chatted in the corner. Morgan looked up and gave Sean an awkward thumbs-up; he returned the gesture with an uncomfortable smile.

Olivia was smiling too—but in a more measured, subtle, La Gioconda sort of way. She looked radiant in a white blouse and a green skirt that flowed like liquid with her every movement. Distracted, Sean barely noticed when a distinctly German voice called from across the room. "We are ready."

He settled into the recliner, the faux leather creaking beneath him. Noble came over with an incredibly soft, fuzzy brown blanket. "A gift from Olivia," he said. Sean smiled, hoping her thoughtfulness represented more than just practicality.

He donned the headphones, adjusted the fit, and heard Noble's Scottish baritone voice. It was reassuring. Pulling Olivia's blanket up to his chin, he felt a peculiar kind of serenity. After all, he was about to surrender his mind to something unseen and unknown. His breathing began to slow under the hypnosis, and his left arm slid to the side. Noble's voice soon trailed off, and Reinhold began playing the tones that matched the Morpheus agent's frequency.

Two minutes later, it was done.

Noble counted up from five, snapping his finger after each number. On the final snap, Sean awoke. He removed the headphones and looked at Noble.

"Now what?"

"A fair question," said Morgan, stepping forward. "If we got the tones right, we'll find this agent. But to find them, they'll need to be dreaming—or controlling a dream incursion."

Sean nodded as he folded the fuzzy blanket across his lap.

"We'll try tonight," Morgan added. "In the meantime, anyone up for dinner?"

***

At the restaurant, Olivia set her wine glass down and looked at Sean.

"Tell me a little about your daughter."

Sean was distracted by the maroon imprint of her lipstick on the rim of her glass. He smiled wistfully, then turned to answer.

"Abbie? She's nine." He scrolled through his phone and found a recent picture. "She's a bit of a prankster—nothing serious. Little things, like changing my ringtone to one of her favorite pop songs."

"She sounds adorable," Olivia said, looking at the photo. "And she's quite pretty. Nine's a nice age. Any signs of the looming teenage angst?"

Sean laughed. "Not yet, but I'm bracing for it. A coworker of mine has three daughters. He said it's like a lunar mission—at some point, they go around the dark side of the moon, and you lose all communications. You don't recognize the person they left in their place, or know where the real one went. You just wait—and you hope. Then one day—they're back—acting like they never left."

Olivia's laugh was warm and genuine. Her eyes sparkled in the soft light, and something stirred inside Sean.

"It feels so natural to love and protect Abbie," he said quietly. "I'm not sure why I said that, or found it surprising."

Olivia smiled. "So, before she launches into orbit, are you able to spend much time with her?"

"For now," Sean replied. "Karen and I have kept things amicable since the divorce. I'm lucky and grateful for that."

"What made you say, 'for now?'"

"She got a job offer in Florida. I'll still see Abbie, but obviously the distance makes it harder."

The waiter stepped in to refill their glasses, and a comfortable pause settled between them. They picked and nibbled at the charcuterie plate, neither rushing the moment. After a minute, Sean asked, "So how about you? Any children?"

"No, not yet. Though I've thought about it. Haven't met the right man, I guess."

"I can imagine a lesser man might be intimidated by dating a bio...what was it again?"

"Biopsychologist," she said, with an amused crinkle of her brow. "It's the study of how behavior and emotions are influenced by the biological functions of the brain."

Sean leaned over in a playful, sparring mood. "But Aristotle argued that all our thoughts and feelings originate from the heart."

"An unfortunate error—one that's still perpetuated in the movies. Thankfully, Hippocrates and Plato had the heart to correct it, giving the brain its due."

"Yes," Sean countered, "but doesn't this biological approach of yours—these chemicals, electrons, and physical structures—simply reduce us to nothing more than a bio-machine. How do you explain love?"

"Dopamine, norepinephrine, serotonin, oxytocin, and vasopressin," she teased, before laughing. "And, in your case, a healthy dose of testosterone."

"Ouch," Sean said, pretending to wince. "Just when I thought we'd chipped away at that scholarly, erudite veneer."

The main course arrived and the conversation took them late into the evening. Time passed quickly. Morgan thanked everyone for a lovely night, but said, that for some, the workday was far from over.

***

Back in the lab, the air felt uncomfortably cool. Sean was grateful for Olivia's blanket. He smirked and took some personal satisfaction in that she hadn't offered one to Noble.

Sean settled into the recliner. With the frequency information from the Morpheus agent embedded into his subconscious, now was the moment of truth— finding the agent in a dream incursion.

Noble was leaning against the equipment rack and Reinhold retreated beneath his personal headphones. The fluorescent lights were turned off and a floor lamp next to the recliner was dimmed. Everyone and everything in its place. If it went well, this would be the first step to unravel the mystery of Morpheus Research.

When Sean awoke, he kicked off the blanket and pulled himself upright.

"Did you find him?" asked Noble.

"No. Nothing at all. I'm not even sure what I dreamt about."

Not what they'd hoped for.

The frustrating pattern repeated itself for three more nights—each ending in failure.

No agent. No incursion. No progress. Things were definitely not in their proper place.

The mood in the lab grew tense. Sharp words exchanged, casual conversations turning brusque. Finally, they all agreed on taking a night off, though no one could really rest.

As Sean left the lab, he knew Morpheus was out there—waiting for him on the edge of his dreams.

Chapter Ten

Jackson Hole, Wyoming

Franz Heidemann stepped gracefully from the rear seat of the black SUV, buttoned his jacket, and looked up at the grandeur of the Teton Range. It was his first visit to Wyoming. The summer sun had melted the last of the snow, but as an avid skier, Franz couldn't resist imagining some of Jackson Hole's amazing runs. Come December, this verdant mountainside would be blanketed in white—dressed in the colors of green, blue, black, and double black. He silently vowed to return, but next time for pleasure.

This was no holiday. The annual Economic Policy Symposium gathered the world's financial elite—central bankers, economists, and industry leaders—to discuss global economic trends and strategize future global policy. For Franz Heidemann, the former head of the Deutsche Bundesbank, this was a crucial event. As the odds-on favorite to lead the European Central Bank, a good showing here would go a long way toward securing the position.

Heidemann was known for his sharp intellect and aggressive views regarding the future of the EU, but his divisiveness had left few people indifferent to what he meant for Europe.

After the long flight from Frankfurt, he still had a few hours before the opening cocktail reception. Accompanied by his two-man security detail, Franz made his way to his suite in the five-star resort. He instructed his staff to wake him at four, and then closed the sliding doors between the salon and the bedroom. Within minutes, the weight of the fatigue set in. His breath slowed, and a soft snore drifted through the louvered doors.

Franz began to dream.

In his dream, his wife was annoying him. He had made it perfectly clear that they had to leave for the opera gala no later than seven, but now that wasn't going to happen. She'd gone shopping for a new gown and, between the traffic and her indecision, she'd returned far too late. Now they were in a rush. Franz hated being late—after all, he was German. When she was finally ready, he practically pushed her out of the door.

As the elevator arrived, she gasped. She'd forgotten her evening clutch in the room.

"Hold the elevator, I'll be right back," he bellowed, already sprinting down the hallway. Swiping the key card and opening the door in one fluid motion, he grabbed the clutch and ran back toward the elevator. His face flushed with exertion and exasperation.

"Go, go!" he exclaimed, leaping through the elevator door. His wife perfectly timed the release of the hold open button. Franz landed and spun around just as the elevator doors shut, but it clamped down on his loose tie above his shiny Bundesbank pin. Franz cursed, but the elevator had already started moving. The sudden pull lifted him off his feet, smashing Franz's face against the top doorjamb. He attempted to cry out, but he was choking. His frightened wife frantically pushed every elevator button like an unsupervised five-year-old. Dangling helplessly, suspended only by the fine silk threads of his tie, Franz's vision narrowed from the lack of blood. He passed out. The elevator abruptly stopped at the next floor and the doors opened, releasing him from bondage.

In the banker's suite, outside of the bedroom where Franz was sleeping and dreaming, a staff member answered the phone. A calm voice reported that a threat had been made against Mr. Heidemann, and asked if he was all right. A staff girl, in her early twenties, immediately became flustered and alerted his security team. Bursting through the bedroom doors, the guards found him sprawled on the bed—alive, but not breathing. One began CPR, while the other called for help.

By the time the ambulance took Franz to the hospital, the crisis appeared to be under control—a tragedy averted. His rattled staff regained their composure and turned to mitigating the incident's impact on the symposium. More to the point, the effect it would have on Franz's ambitions. They just needed to plan the next move carefully.

What no one knew—not his staff, not the doctors—was that Franz had been deprived of oxygen for precisely four minutes. A brain starved of oxygen for four minutes suffers permanent damage. How impaired still remained to be seen. For now, it was a safe bet that Franz Heidemann would never be president of the European Central Bank.

In some corners of the financial world, that was considered very good news, indeed.

***

New York City

Sean spent his night off at home, a decanter of single malt fueling another round of self-analysis. Why couldn't they find this agent? The frequency information had come directly from Jeff Carl's dream, yet somehow the man remained elusive.

There were a number of possibilities.

First, a matter of bad timing. The agent may have been in another time zone, or in a different sleep cycle. Second, an error in the frequency information itself—in short, they were dialing the wrong number. But the third possibility was the one that disturbed Sean the most. Morpheus had become aware of their plan and was shielding their agents from detection.

He poured another drink, his fourth—maybe fifth? The taste of earthy peat lingered on his palate. Then another thought crept into his mind. What if Morpheus no longer needed the drug? Sean's throat tightened. If that was true, then the team wasn't merely behind, they were now obsolete. His mind continued to spiral into ever deeper what-ifs, until the questions evanesced like match smoke —and Sean passed out where he sat.

He woke in the morning to savage clarity—and a headache to match. After slugging down a couple of ibuprofen with some black coffee, he picked up where he left off.

In the Jeff Carl dream, the Morpheus agent had vanished the instant the business meeting ended. In torturous contrast, Sean was left in limbo—stuck in that damn yacht club long after Jeff's dream ran aground. If Morpheus could exit at will, could they enter at will?

Sean's dream incursions only worked while he was asleep, deep in a delta brain wave state. Did that state have some physiological or metaphysical limitations? What if the Morpheus agents were using a different brain wave altogether—something like—theta? If Morpheus was operating in theta—then Sean's group had been tuned to the wrong signal from the start.

***

"Ja, it's a pretty easy fix," said Reinhold, after Sean asked if the theta frequencies could be programmed into the binaural tones.

"Really?" Sean had assumed the task was more problematic.

With an indulging smile, Reinhold pushed his office chair back from the desk. "Each brain wave operates in a defined frequency range," he began to explain. "They're expressed in Hertz. Delta waves are at the lowest, and above them are the theta waves. If your theory's correct, the agents will be on the lowest band of theta, just above delta. We just have to shift the Hertz—no big deal." Reinhold scooted his chair back toward the keyboard. Then he stopped and turned back to Sean.

"You know, it's quite interesting that you chose this particular range. Thomas Edison experimented with this same boundary—between theta and delta. And he used meditation to do it."

Sean looked curious. "Meditation?"

"Edison believed that theta waves unlocked creativity, visualization, intuition, recalling blocked memories…things like that. He thought meditation was the best way to get into that state—the deeper you go, the greater the benefit. The problem was, every time he got close enough, he fell asleep—slipping over the edge into delta. So, he began meditating while holding a small rock over a metal pail. The moment he dozed off, the rock fell from his hand, jarring him awake. After some practice, he was able to hover on the very edge of deep sleep."

Olivia came from across the room, drawn by curiosity, and unable to resist joining the conversation.

"Since we're into trivia—children spend their first seven years predominantly in theta—watching, learning, mimicking—literally absorbing the world around them. It's a cliché that children are like sponges, but it's because they're in a dominant state of theta. They learn new languages by simply playing with other children. Theta is one of the two principal ways in which humans learn."

"And the other?" Sean asked, brows raised.

"Repetition," she said. "Old fashioned repetition or practice—whatever you prefer. As adults, we can no longer simply absorb information—we have to grind our way forward."

Sean thought about it for a moment, and nodded. "Then it sounds like theta is the key. So far, it feels like we've broken into the bank, but can't crack the safe."

"I'll handle the recoding tonight," said Reinhold. "Start a new run tomorrow?"

Facing another free night, Sean remembered that Abbie wanted to see the new exhibit at the Children's Museum. He decided to swing by and pick her up.

***

Sean woke to a gorgeous autumn morning and he mumbled something to that effect. Until recently, this was unimaginable, such an outpouring of positivity before his first cup of morning coffee. No hangover. No restless edge. He'd slept well, and did so without his usual triad of drugs, alcohol, and flat-out exhaustion.

After spending a couple of hours with Abbie at the Children's Museum, he met Keenan and Zahra for dinner. Afterwards, he took a quiet walk in the night's air, an agreeable ten-block walk home. He climbed into bed at an early hour and fell asleep. That night, the only dreams were his own dreams.

He woke up all sunshiny and perky. An ordinary night for most, but for Sean, it bordered on the aberrant.

This wasn't the only change he noticed. At work, he had breached the imaginary cubicle barrier—chatting with coworkers, and even agreed to meet a few for drinks at some ubiquitous Irish pub.

The hunt for Morpheus had put a spotlight on what his life was missing—a sense of purpose, belonging, and energy. His thoughts were focused. His awareness heightened. It was like falling in love—suddenly hearing a rhythm in the city's din, finding meaning in wispy clouds, or the poetry in a song lyric that had long ago become tiresome.

He called Karen to say that he supported whatever she chose to do about the move. She sounded surprised—or wary—or a little of both. He told her that quality time spent with Abbie mattered more than the quantity.

What was happening to Sean?

He was as confused as anyone. Was this his higher purpose? The answer to the insomnia that started him down this path? Either that—or Sean was falling in love.

***

The following night, one floor up from the house of tattoos and scarring, Sean settled into the recliner. He wrapped the fuzzy brown blanket around his shoulders. Reinhold had finished reprogramming the tones, and earlier that day, Noble implanted the theta-delta, dual-frequency information into Sean's subconscious under hypnosis.

"Let's see if this works," Sean murmured, to no one in particular. Olivia's words still echoed in his mind: Children learn in theta waves.

Well, until he learned to use theta to enter dreams, the old method would have to do. He settled in for a night's sleep.

When he woke, Noble was gently snoring next to him, halfway out of his chair. Sean chuckled and then nudged him in the ribs.

"Anything?" Noble asked.

"Nope. You?"

He shook his head.

"I have no idea what's wrong." Sean groused. "We're missing something."

"Maybe it's a drink?" Noble rose from his chair and walked to the lounge, stretching and twisting with each step.

"I'm convinced theta waves are the key," Sean said.

Noble handed him the glass. "What'd you have in mind?"

"I have to learn how to do this in theta," he said, taking his first sip. "I'll call Morgan tomorrow morning. He's well connected. Maybe he can find someone reputable to teach me how to stay in theta. If Morpheus is using it—then we should too."

The two men clinked their glasses in a toast to the unknown.

Chapter Eleven

Sean stared at Morgan, incredulous. "A shaman? That's your brilliant idea?"
Morgan folded his hands on the desk, and offered a warm, if somewhat amused, smile. Sean had asked to learn how to reach and sustain the theta brain-wave state—and Morgan simply provided a solution. The rant continued.

"Let me guess," Sean said, now pacing the room. "Ram's skull headdress, bear fur wrap, facial makeup in a general, white skull theme—maybe a claw necklace draped across his bare chest."

Morgan started to interrupt. "I think you'll find—"

"Oh wait," Sean cut in. "And various skulls of who knows what hanging from his belt." Clearly not what Sean had in mind when he asked for help.

He sighed in frustration. "I was thinking more along the lines of clinical psychologist, or neuroscientist. Maybe even a well-respected hypnotherapist—not some raving voodoo priest rolling the bones."

"As I was saying," Morgan responded, as if he were explaining this to a child, "your preconceptions, although delightfully amusing, aren't accurate. Shamanism is the oldest spiritual practice known to man, dating back at least forty thousand years. Before dismissing it, you might consider that it has endured for a reason."

Morgan paused as Sean calmed down. Then he continued, "You came to me for help—wanting to learn a new skill. The fastest way to do that won't be through the front door of traditional Western science. Think about the changes you've already experienced, and what brought you here. Everything so far has been a blend of two distinct worlds: scientific and spiritual. The rational and the mystical. You want progress? It won't come from some geeks in lab coats, armed with traditional diplomas."

"It just isn't what I had in mind." he said, his tone turning deferential.

Morgan leaned forward. "Sean, you're mind has never been in control of this journey. Fate, destiny, chance: they've been guiding you all along."

Morgan clapped his hands together in a prayer and said, "Do me a favor. Meet with this shaman. I think he can bring together the parts of you that are lost or disconnected."

He looked up at Morgan with a pouty expression. "So, what's he anyway? Native American or something?"

"His name is Ulgen Khan. He was born in Bürenhayrhan, in the Altay Mountains of Mongolia."

***

The next afternoon, when Sean arrived at the Center for Change Potential, he was shown into a private conference room: leather seating, Balinese tables, Persian carpets, and lots of expensive-looking original art. It could have easily passed for an upscale private lounge.

Sean's pulse quickened. Why was he feeling nervous? Maybe because this whole thing was just plain weird. Hadn't he already made allowances, adjusting to the group's eccentric requests? Wasn't that enough?

Shifting uncomfortably on the sofa, he flopped his head back. He closed his eyes —and listened for the telltale sounds of rattling bones from somewhere down the hallway.

A few minutes later, the door opened. Morgan entered, followed by a tall man in his early sixties. His round face was sun-weathered, his cheekbones pronounced. The deep creases in his face and his crow's-feet lent character and expression to his sharp and alert eyes. The heritage was undeniably Asian. Fit and formidable, he stood six foot tall.

"Sean," said Morgan, "I'd like you to meet Ulgen Khan."

The two shook hands. Sean snuck a sheepish glance toward Morgan, who was stifling a laugh. He seemed to utterly enjoy Sean's shattered expectations.

Ulgen Khan had chosen to forgo the ram's horn helmet and the belt of small animal skulls for something a little more subdued. He was wearing a cadet-blue Armani sport coat, a tight-fitting black T-shirt, and wool slacks. The very picture of fashion perfection, all the way down to his British Northampton Oxford shoes.

"Not what you expected?" asked Ulgen, grinning.

Sean was taken aback. "No…not at all," he sputtered.

So much for hiding my thoughts.

Ulgen laughed with a deep ease. "You'd be surprised how many people think I'll show up wearing bearskins and tribal makeup, and bleached bones dangling all about."

Sean offered a weak chuckle.

"You might say I'm more of an executive shaman." He appeared quite amused by his own phrase. "I suppose that's what happens after fifteen years of living and working in Manhattan."

He picked a spot on the leather sofa. "So, Morgan told me a little about your situation. I'd like to hear it in your own words."

A secretary appeared with a few refreshments and then stepped back out. Sean began. For the next forty-five minutes, he retraced the sleepless steps that had led to the clinic, the encounter with Amazonian drugs, the dream incursions, meeting the group, and the confrontation with Morpheus.

When he was done, Sean slumped back into his chair and exhaled. Hearing it out loud made it sound even more astonishing.

Ulgen Khan had listened without interruption—his expression stoic and unfazed.

"You still find this hard to believe?" Ulgen asked.

"Of course, don't you?" Sean responded with raised brows.

"Not at all," he said calmly. "Where I come from, this is all quite natural. We've come to accept spirituality as an integral part of our world." He paused. "Though I have to admit, this Morpheus element is an interesting twist."

He leaned in. "So, do you have any questions?"

"Oh, I definitely have questions."

Ulgen leaned back, gesturing for Sean to go ahead.

"Let's start with how you can help me."

"For that answer, you must first understand Shamanism. At the simplest level, we're teachers—or what your corporate world would call facilitators. Through meditation, my spirit will leave my body, traveling into the unseen world to find your helpers. To assist you in retrieving what you've lost."

"And what is it that I've lost?"

Sean felt silly—like he was playing the spiritual edition of a Socratic dialogue. It sounded ridiculous, as if these questions were better asked on a mountaintop while in a lotus position.

"Yourself, Sean. You have lost and forgotten your true self. Our western civilization may be advanced, but most of us have forgotten who we truly are."

Ulgen paused to selectively pick at the refreshments.

"This ability you're seeking—to move freely in the theta brain pattern—this is only the beginning. You've asked to learn a specific task, but there is so much more to gain. I'll help you reconnect with the parts of you that already understand."

Sean gave him a blank stare. "Understand what?"

Ulgen Khan smiled with bright eyes. "That this material world is not material at all."

Sean blinked. "I'm sorry?"

"This world," Ulgen said, gesturing around the room, "these chairs, the building, your body—they are only perceptions, an illusion. Part of the accepted and pragmatic world we call reality. When you've accepted this truth—that there's much more to this world than what we see—it will forever change your life. At that point, you'll have the skills you're looking for. And much, much more."

"No offense," Sean retorted, "but this sounds like a bunch of mystical double-talk—some sort of shaman-speak."

"A little, perhaps" Ulgen said, unfazed. "But it's also the language of quantum mechanics."

Sean froze. Quantum mechanics? That's certainly not what he expected to hear from a shaman. Ulgen had upended yet another preconception.

"Newton explained the world we see around us: gravity, planetary movements, changing states of matter. We feel comfortable with these ideas because they fit within our human senses and perceptions: visible, tangible, visceral. However, this naturalistic approach falls apart at the atomic and sub-atomic level. What I'm telling you is something that many people have already realized—from the perspective of both spirituality and science—nothing is real until it is observed."

Sean glanced over at Morgan. He wanted to dismiss it as complete nonsense, but there was something about what Ulgen said that seemed almost familiar—like a distant recollection.

"You don't look satisfied," Ulgen observed.

"Yes. No. That's not it," he replied slowly. "I'm still not sure how I fit into all of this."

"A scientist named Hoffman once said that evolution has given us the perceptions that we need for survival, but part of the deal, is that the rest is hidden from us. And the rest? Well that's nearly all of reality."

Ulgen took a sip of tea and paused to savor it for a moment. He nodded his approval and put the cup and saucer back on the coffee table before continuing.

"You want to know how this applies to what you're trying to do," He leaned forward, his eyes piercing. "What you call reality is, in truth, only energy in its observable form. It's everywhere—and everything around us is derived from this vibrational energy."

Sean sat on the edge of his seat, doing his best to keep up. Although he sensed that his skepticism was beginning to yield to curiosity.

"Sean, open yourself to the possibility that there's more to this world than we can see, even if it's something you can't fully grasp or accept for now. I'm sure your recent experiences have already strained your ideas about what's possible. Now, it's time to take it further."

Sean looked like a man trying to solve a magic trick.

Ulgen broke the silence. He asked Sean to close his eyes and breathe. It was time to meditate—to give Ulgen an opportunity to understand the parts of Sean that were left unspoken. When they were done, Ulgen rested his hand on Sean's shoulder.

"I'm going to ask for a small favor. Just a little research before our next meeting."

He handed Sean a slip of paper. "String theory. Superposition. Entanglement. The double-slit experiment."

Sean furrowed his brow as he read the list.

"Not exactly light reading," Ulgen said, "but it is enlightening."

Then he grinned at Sean. "You know, Einstein spent his life searching for a unified source of the universe. Now we've reached a point where the ancients, through spirituality, and the moderns, through science, are forming an unlikely partnership to fulfill Einstein's dream."

He rose and said, "Morgan, Sean, it has been a great pleasure."

As Ulgen was leaving, Sean couldn't resist a little parting jab. "Any relation to the other Khan?"

"Who?" Ulgen paused, feigning misunderstanding. "Chaka Khan?" He laughed heartily. "Ah yes, Genghis. Maybe. Probably. Did you know that Genghis Khan has one of the greatest lineages in human history? Around sixteen million men in Mongolia share his Y-chromosome—that's one out of every two hundred men on earth."

As he walked out the door, he recited, "Our father, who art in Mongolia…"

Sean left soon after.

Once alone, Morgan reached down and unlocked a desk drawer. He pulled out a second phone.

"Triple Yankee, six, eight, four," Morgan said, after the voice prompt.

"Go ahead," said the voice on the other end.

"He's getting close."

Morgan ended the call, replaced the phone in the drawer, and sat motionless—staring at the door that Sean had just exited. Then he softly sighed, biting his cheek.

***

After hitting enter, Sean's computer unleashed a torrent of search results—each more intimidating than the last. Hyperlinks, footnotes, and jargon seemed to mock his every mouse click—quietly intimating that he was far out of his depth.

With a sharp exhale, he began to slog through the scientific labyrinth: making a sincere effort to read, or at least skim, through dozens of articles and research papers on quantum mechanics.

What the hell is a Copenhagen interpretation?

Faced with more bone-dry academic papers, he looked for an easier way. If nature always chose the path of least resistance, then who was he to argue? He opened YouTube, and was warmly greeted by hundreds of short videos about the subject. Relieved, he let out the breath he'd held.

The titles were far less intimidating than the lengthy academic research papers—though credibility was an issue. It ran the gamut from Noble prize winning physicists, to someone named CosmicGuy24.

By now, the hour had grown late and Sean had watched a few dozen videos. A theme had emerged.

Everything is connected to everything else.

The world is more than a random collection of plants and animals.

Everything is connected.

From the perspective of a New York stockbroker, all this sounded like New Age fluff. But the conclusions were backed by science. Sean liked the idea of an intelligent design without all the trappings of formal religion. Like many, he'd spent much of his childhood attending church. Now, he couldn't recall the last time he'd gone. What did that say about him? About faith?

He closed the laptop, his head still buzzing with theories, colorful graphics, even the echo of the narrator's voice. He had so many questions—perhaps more than when he began.

Sean scratched his chin. He'd need help separating the science from the mystical. Kate might know of someone to help make sense of it all. He decided to call Dr. Catherine Keelson at Fordham University in the morning.

***

She was waiting for him in the university's main cafeteria. Weaving his way through the collapsible tables and benches, the surroundings were all too familiar. Did the smell of damp plastic food trays, stale coffee, and college pizza stay with you for life?

Catherine was looking down at her mobile phone when he approached.

"Two calls in ten years, and this one more cryptic than the first. Is this going to be a pattern?"

"I don't think so," he replied, "but then my crystal ball's been a little off lately."

"How's the shamanic journey coming along?"

"I met one!" He exclaimed, far more enthusiastically than he intended.

Kate giggled. "A shaman? And?"

"He was wearing Armani."

She laughed, probably wondering at what point her friend had gone off the rails.

He quickly clarified. "What I meant to say was that, while he did dress quite nicely, he wasn't what I expected. Very unorthodox for a shaman—or at least how I pictured a shaman."

He swung his leg over the plastic bench and sat opposite Kate. "We had the most amazing conversation. He talked about spirituality, but also philosophy, physics, and the sciences. He said they're all related—all tied together. Before he left, he asked me to look into some of the theories in quantum mechanics."

Sean raised his brow, and shook his head. "Kate, I tried my best, but I need some help. I thought that, if we met with someone in the physics department—maybe the two of you could be my guides."

Kate studied him for a moment, fascinated by his strange transformation. She smiled, grabbed her coffee, and stood.

"Well then, my inquisitive stockbroker friend, follow me. Since you've already traveled in dreamtime, and communed with Armani-clad shamans, let's take the next logical step and see Carl Yong."

"The psychologist?" Sean asked, somewhat confused.

Kate laughed. "Wouldn't that be a trick? No, the Chinese spelling, Y-O-N-G. He's a professor in our Physics Department—and as an added benefit, this one's very much alive."

***

The physics professor appeared much younger than his age of thirty-five: shoulder-length black hair, rounded Lennon glasses, and a well-worn Yankees baseball cap. Dr. Yong was one of the department's more enthusiastic proponents of the unified field theory. Despite the equivocal nature of his message, Kate had assumed that Sean was looking for someone with more progressive views.

"So we're looking for a crash course in quantum physics?" asked Carl. "Would that be with—or without?"

Sean and Kate exchanged puzzled glances.

"Equations," the professor quickly added.

"Oh God. Without, please," Sean said. "I just want to understand what quantum mechanics has to say about the nature of reality."

"My friend's on a bit of a vision quest," Kate teased. She grinned and patted his knee like a big sister.

"Okay," Carl said with a chuckle. "Do you want to start with the apple? You know, the one that fell on Sir Isaac's head?"

Sean shrugged.

"Newton's physics revolved around the physical world, the things we can see, feel, touch. It worked well for centuries—until we started studying the strange world of atoms and subatomic particles. They weren't just smaller, they also behaved radically different from objects in the physical world. To explain this behavior, physicists built a new framework, and called it quantum mechanics."

Dr. Yong spent the next half hour explaining the key points behind the unified field theory: zero point energy, super-strings, particles, waves, and the influence of observation, etc.

"I'm not sure that answers my question," Sean said after reflection. "I'm hearing one theory replaced by another—then another. How does this explain reality?"

Carl Yong smiled. "It's simple. Quantum mechanics says it's the observer that shapes the world they see."

Sean had been sitting on the edge of his chair, leaning forward. He lifted his elbows from his thighs, and rubbed his eyes.

…the observer shapes the world they see?

He looked at Carl Yong and furrowed his brow. "So if I understand you—what you're saying is—"

Sean hesitated. "Reality is subjective. You're saying we create our own reality?"

Carl swiveled in his chair, placed his hands on his head, and smiled broadly, "Yeah, that's right," he said. "You got it."

Chapter Twelve

In the days following his meeting with Carl Yong, Sean wrestled with the professor's explanation. Like boxers in a ring, the questions and answers circled each other, with no decisive verdict. Before long, Sean found himself standing at the door of Ulgen Khan's surprisingly warm and welcoming Manhattan apartment.

Ulgen greeted him, ushering him inside. The tasteful decor blended Western and Eastern art, with Indonesian furnishings. As he passed through the foyer, Sean detected the pleasant, earthy aroma of incense: cedar or sandalwood, or some kind of wood—he couldn't be sure.

"You have a lovely home."

"Thanks," Ulgen replied with a smirk. "I usually keep the animal skins and skulls in the solarium. We'll save that for another time." He held a perfectly deadpan expression, but then winked and laughed heartily. Sean followed him into the bright living room and provided a quick update on the research he'd done into quantum mechanics, as well as his meeting with a college physicist.

Ulgen reclined into a plush sofa, an expansive view of Brooklyn and the East River filling the large windows behind him. He motioned for Sean to sit.

"So," he began, "do you know why I asked about quantum mechanics?"

Sean was glad that he anticipated the question and had prepared a response.

"I think it was meant as a bridge. My tendency is to think in analytical terms, but if I can accept what quantum mechanics teaches us about reality—how observation changes what's being observed—then I can accept the same type of uncertainty in spirituality. I'll come to understand both sides."

"Excellent!" Ulgen smiled, his eyes almost crinkling shut in his expression. He placed a hot cup of particularly fragrant tea in front of Sean and leaned back.

"Science is always evolving—new theories, new discoveries, new technology. That's what gives the discipline its strength. But the spiritual world is very different. It's ancient. Unchanged."

Sean considered this for a moment. "Are you saying the spiritual world is superior?"

"No, it's not a competition," he said, shaking his head. "I merely wish to point out that we live in a time when these once separate worlds have begun to converge. Like rivals that are now coming together as old friends."

Sean tapped his upper lip as he listened. Ulgen continued.

"There is what we know, what we don't know, and then there are all the things we don't know that we don't know. These are the known unknowns, as your Donald Rumsfeld once put it."

Ulgen grinned at the eclectic reference.

"Quantum mechanics has pulled these two worlds closer than ever before. A convergence. Morgan says you've been given an incredible gift, but he fears that your assumptions and beliefs will hold you back. We need to question those beliefs, soften them up a bit, so that your mind will open to new possibilities."

Question those beliefs?

Are there any beliefs left unquestioned?

Maybe Sean's old world wasn't exactly perfect, but at least it made sense.

He gave Ulgen a long look and studied the man's face. Deep lines radiated from the corners of Ulgen's eyes, like a map revealing a thousand years of wisdom. Had he been too quick to judge this man? Somewhere in the weighty discussion, Sean decided that he could confide in him.

"I've lost my faith," he said softly, as if God might be listening. "One day, it was just gone. A close friend of mine has kept the faith his entire life. In many ways, I'm envious. How comforting it would be to have that kind of certainty. Instead, I'm left with neither a god, nor a suitable replacement—only a void."

It was rare for Sean to share his private thoughts. "And a void is a pretty depressing place to be."

Ulgen tilted his head and looked at him sympathetically. "You're not alone, Sean. Fewer people are following traditional religions. People aren't sure where to turn next. Some are like you, earnestly searching for answers. Others choose to play semantical games, saying things like, I'm not religious, I'm spiritual. But these are vague and empty statements. What they really mean is, I want to believe in something greater, but I can't put a name or face to it."

"So what do I do?"

Ulgen shrugged. "Now you're confusing me for a psychiatrist. I'm only a shaman."

Sean's face dropped and Ulgen smiled, watching his childlike expression with amusement. The corners of Ulgen's eyes softened and he sighed.

"Anyone can be spiritual, Sean—but it won't be the same for everyone. It's not the how that really matters, only that you find comfort and strength in searching for something greater than yourself. That's the starting point for all faith. It's something you can do—a choice you can make today."

Ulgen looked compassionate. Sean looked lost.

After a minute, Ulgen said, "In our last meeting, I started to explain what shamans do, but perhaps I should elaborate."

Sean nodded with a short shrug.

"We're concerned with the souls of the living. And the souls of the dead. When a soul becomes lost or disconnected, we guide them back to where they belong."

Sean smiled half-heartedly. "Is that what I am to you—a lost soul?"

In a reassuring voice, Ulgen asked, "Isn't that what you've been saying all along? That you feel adrift? But maybe you're not lost at all—maybe you're actually drifting toward something. I believe you're much closer than you realize. It's been said, 'There's nowhere you can be that isn't where you're meant to be.'"

Sean reflected on the quote. "Buddha?"

"John Lennon," Ulgen said with a grin. "Shall we begin?"

They talked for hours. Ulgen spoke to Sean differently now—more like a peer than a pupil—or, at the least, a respected apprentice. Gone were the academic references to physics and psychology. In their place, he told stories of his childhood, his first experiences with the unseen, and the moment that changed his life forever.

He described a time when a group of foreigners arrived in his village with a young girl who'd fallen quite ill. The visitors were frantic, rapidly speaking in a language that no one understood. After listening for a moment, young Ulgen realized something extraordinary. He could comprehend their language, and began translating for the village doctor.

Ulgen believed that moment was a sign—an illustration of his life's course—of his calling. Sean sensed that Ulgen was drawing a parallel to what was happening in his own life.

Khan spoke about life and death, and reincarnation. He explained how shamans could deliberately enter dreams, walking freely through another dimension. He taught Sean how to attain deeper forms of meditation, the type involving visions and quests that move beyond conscious thought.

By the time their meeting drew to a close, the sun was setting on the day. The first city lights flickered on in the neighboring buildings. Ulgen Khan leaned forward, his voice assured.

"You'll see the changes soon," he said.

Not only would Sean learn to enter dreams in the theta state, but it would only be the beginning—the first step in a long and unpredictable journey.

"Stay open," Ulgen urged. "The limits you've placed on yourself aren't real—just illusions created by the ego. Keep your mind free, and you'll find your potential is more than you've ever imagined."

As Sean stared out at the East River, he sensed a subtle shift taking hold. In the rhythm of his breath, he felt the first stirrings of possibility—of hope.

Chapter Thirteen

After his meeting with Ulgen Khan, Sean took every spare moment to practice his new meditation techniques, eager to put his mastery to the test.

But when he returned to the laboratory, things didn't go as planned. Entering the theta state was fairly easy, but staying there was another matter. The line between theta and delta was finer than he'd expected. Time and time again, Sean pushed a little too far, and fell asleep, only to have the frustrated Scot nudge him awake.

Annoyed looks were exchanged, and then the whole process started over. He began to feel like a political prisoner, subjected to a form of sleep-deprivation torture. By now, the hour had grown late and resisting sleep, either in or out of meditation, was nearly impossible.

"Let's just go back to what we were doing before," pleaded Noble, his patience worn thin.

"No, no," Sean insisted. "Theta is the key."

They pressed on a little longer, but exhaustion was winning out. They traded weary looks and decided to quit for the night.

When they returned the next day, they were rested, hopeful, and ready to try again. But after Sean nodded off for the third time, Noble's frustration surfaced. He kicked Sean's chair in anger.

"Seriously?"

They tried again—and failed three more times.

Neither was sure who was getting the worst of this deal. They were getting nowhere, so they raided Reinhold's refrigerator and his beer collection. Popping open their selections, the two sat on the couch.

"So," Sean said, after swallowing, "How'd you get into this whole psychic racket?"

Noble laughed. "You make it sound like a trade," he said. Juggling his hands as if weighing the options. "Let's see, carpenter, electrician, maybe psychic?" He shrugged and smiled. "I'm not sure, it's just something I was aware of at an early age."

Sean nodded and assumed that Noble wasn't interested in elaborating. But then the Scot sat up. "Actually, there was one moment in particular. When I was six years old."

He shared with Sean the story of his fourth-grade assignment: to draw a picture of what his town would look like at Christmas. The rest of his class drew sleighs, fir trees, and icicles—but Noble drew an odd semi-circle with a blue stripe running down its side.

A month later, on December 21, 1988, terrorists detonated a bomb aboard Pan American 103 as it flew over Lockerbie, Scotland. Large sections of the aircraft rained down on his neighborhood, killing eleven people on the ground and all two hundred and fifty-nine people aboard the 747. A widely published photograph showed the nose of the aircraft, split in half vertically and lying on its side in the dirt. An iconic and everlasting symbol of terrorism.

"When my drawing and the photo were placed side by side," Noble said, "it was a near-perfect match."

Sean stared at him for a long time. Neither spoke. An occasional swish of beer was the only sound to disturb the silence. Sean gave thought to Noble's story— tragic—but inspiring. It was also confirmation of everything that Ulgen Khan had told him. If there was more to this world than we see, perhaps there was more to Sean than he believed.

"Would you mind if we took another shot at it?" he asked.

They tried again. This time, Sean maintained the theta brain state for an extended period. He began to trust in the process, to gain confidence in his ability to find that comfortable hollow between theta and delta.

They practiced some more, and then Noble announced, "Okay, let's call it a night. We'll take the next step tomorrow."

Sean knew the next step was to add Amplius to the meditation. If all went as planned, he would soon move through dreams while in theta—just like a Morpheus agent.

The next afternoon, he began meditating as soon as the first sensations of the drug kicked in. Sean felt himself descending, slipping through various layers of consciousness. This time it felt different, as if entering a series of trap doors. He felt himself going deeper, almost as if he was being pulled down by some invisible force. His heart beat faster—and he felt scared. What was Amplius doing? Was he losing control? Sean's mind resisted, like pulling his hand away from a flame. He knew he needed to let go. He imagined Ulgen's words echoing in the blackness, "Stay open."

But where was it taking him? What was waiting for him?

Then, just ahead, something familiar—it was theta. Now it felt almost tangible, like an actual place. He began to breathe again and readied himself for the usual dream incursion.

But—it started moving again—his mind dragged deeper into the unknown. Sean tensed, fighting the instinct to escape—to make it all go away.

A distorted voice drifted through the fog. "Are you all right?" Noble sounded very far off, like a long-distance transmission through a worn and crackly speaker.

"I'm good," said Sean in a whisper, reassured by Noble's voice, his touchstone to the world.

How much further?

Sean felt as though his mind had separated from his body, leaving him drifting freely in space.

No gravity. No time. No reference.

And then, Sean arrived at the bottom.

I am here.

Exactly where here was, he wasn't sure. A world of nothingness, absolute and pure.

No self. No identity. Just a complete sense of being.

And just like that, he understood what Ulgen had been trying to tell him. This was his true self, his higher self. Everything stripped down to its most fundamental form. The fear began to fall away. The experience calming. He smiled inwardly, embracing the feeling and wrapping it around him like a warm blanket.

And then, in an instant, everything changed.

It came to him as a bright flash, as intense as a lightning bolt. His fear sensed its opportunity to rise, but he resisted. Then he imagined a hole had begun to open at the top of his skull. A rush of knowledge started flooding in—a deluge of information—astonishing, reassuring.

When he surfaced, Sean was overwhelmed with emotion: harmony, indivisibility, and oneness. He drew a shuddering breath, and rocked his head from side to side. He turned and saw Noble staring at him.

He grinned and said, "Nigel's opened a gallery."

"Nigel who?"

"Your childhood friend from Lockerbie. He's an abstract painter with a studio in London."

The look on Noble's face was priceless. The same perplexed expression that Noble's psychic feats had elicited from people over the years.

"This will work," Sean muttered. As he spoke, he wondered about the fear that he'd felt during the descent. Was that his ego trying to exert its will? Or, had Sean clung to his beliefs too firmly?

The next morning, he arrived early, collapsed onto the lab's aging couch, and propped his feet on the armrest. He felt sharp, almost cocky. However, his moment of triumph was cut short by Reinhold's voice announcing that it was "time to begin."

Sean began the meditation and slipped into theta waves. Reinhold had already uploaded the agent's frequency information from the Jeff Carl dream. All Sean had to do was relax—and allow his subconscious to guide him.

***

He slipped into the agent's dream effortlessly. Until now, the transition had been a clunky, inelegant affair, more like tumbling down a laundry chute. This time, it felt sublime.

As the dream opened, Sean found himself in the Swiss Alps. Outdoor seating encircled the mid-mountain chalet: picnic benches, clusters of crossed skis and poles dotting the snowy banks, and expensively dressed skiers enjoying their lunch in the alpine sun. The aroma of sausage, red cabbage, and potato pancakes hung heavy in the crisp air. Sean strolled around, scanning the faces to find the agent. He spotted him, thirty feet away, sitting at a bench and removing his gloves.

So far, so good. Now, he just needed to get the man to talk, maybe disclose a little information about himself or Morpheus. But how? Sean hoped for some brilliant idea to well up from below, but nothing came. He had to hurry, this man wouldn't stay put for long. Was he overthinking the process?

Then he remembered the fear he'd felt yesterday, the uncertainty, the doubt.

Relax. Trust.

If his subconscious had found the agent, then he should allow his subconscious to finish the job. It was time for a gamble. He walked over and sat at the bench, opposite the agent.

"Have you heard from Adler?" Sean asked, moving on instinct. Hoping his many weekends of playing poker were about to pay off.

The agent looked up, startled. "I beg your pardon?"

"Adler Daemon. I haven't heard from him lately."

No reaction. The man finished the last of his beer in a single gulp, like he was planning a hasty exit. "You've mistaken me for someone else," he said. "Sorry, my friends are waiting."

He untangled his legs from the picnic bench and began to stand.

"Weren't you the agent assigned to the Jeff Carl dream?"

"I have no idea what you're talking about," he said, with a dismissive wave of his hand. Half-standing, he paused for a moment, and then dropped his gloves back onto the table. "I didn't catch your name," he said sitting.

"Simmons, Gerard Simmons. I'm surprised you didn't hear I'd joined."

The agent gave Sean a long, intensive stare, like he was scanning a detailed image. The seconds ticked away. Finally, he gathered his gloves and stood. His expression cold and detached.

"As I said, you've got me confused with someone else. A pity, really—it all sounds rather mysterious." He calmly zipped up his jacket and said, "Tschüss."

Sean felt the moment slipping away, but then the agent accidentally dropped one of his gloves onto the table. They both reached for it. Sean grabbed it first.

"Perhaps the altitude added to my confusion. No hard feelings?"

"None at all," said the agent, pointing to the glove in Sean's hand.

"Whoops, sorry." Sean handed over the glove with a sheepish smile, and the men shook hands.

The agent walked toward the ski rack and unlocked his skis. Knocking the snow from the bottom of his boots, he pressed down on the bindings and listened for a sharp click. After adjusting his goggles, he put in two strong skater kicks, and disappeared down the mountain.

Sean leaned back against the table and muttered, "Well that was a bust." He sighed, tilted his head back, and closed his eyes. He felt the sun pressing against his face, when a bright light flashed across his eyes. He bolted upright.

What was that?

Okay, he thought, looking around. I'm okay—still in the dream, still on the mountain, and still in theta.

Random images began forming in his mind's eye. He saw himself shaking hands with the agent, but arcs of electricity were now flowing between them. Other images followed: a building, a middle-aged man with a salt-and-pepper beard, a city, a lake, a fountain, and a flood of names, one after another.

What is this?

Then it hit him—it was Morpheus Research—names, locations, assignments—the works.

Ulgen Khan's words echoed in his mind. Stay open to new possibilities. It would unlock a potential beyond anything he could imagine.

Was this what he meant? Was this the beginning of something greater?

He found sleep was impossible that night, though not for the usual reasons. The moment he closed his eyes, the flash returned—waiting and buzzing. Had he found a greater truth? He couldn't wait to tell the others.

***

His text was succinct.

"Meet me at Morgan's office tomorrow morning at 10 a.m. It's important."

Sean arrived brimming with energy. "Something remarkable happened last night," he began. "Truly remarkable."

Morgan frowned. "We've gathered that. So what happened?"

"When the agent left the dream, I thought we failed. Another disappointment in a long series. Then, these images began forming in my mind—names, places, and dates. At first, none of it made sense, but then I realized these were the details about Morpheus Research—organization, history, the works."

Noble, Morgan, and Olivia exchanged stunned looks.

"Morpheus Research," he continued, "was founded by Adler Daemon and a man named Ian Bishop. After leaving Montréal, Adler's career cratered, ostracized by the academic community. He continued his research, even publishing a few papers.

Although none of the mainstream journals would publish his work, he cobbled together a few small grants from antiestablishment groups."

Sean leaned forward and picked up his coffee cup. He leaned back before continuing.

"One of his papers, in particular, stood out. It posited that the body's autonomic functions could be controlled through noninvasive means, no anesthesia or any physical contact. He proposed that this could be done through telepathy—or, by entering a person's dreams. No one, aside from the conspiracy theorists, paid any attention. The one exception was Ian Bishop."

Sean glanced back and forth. He'd piqued their interest.

"Bishop was an arms dealer from South Africa. After the fall of apartheid, he took his business global—staying ahead of Interpol, and creating ties with corrupt political and business leaders around the world. When he found Daemon's paper, he immediately saw its potential. Bishop understood two things very well—weapons and the black market. He quashed all existing copies of the paper and then made Adler an offer."

"An offer?" Noble asked.

"He'd fund Daemon's research in exchange for the exclusive rights to the technology. Adler was broke—the choice was easy. Morpheus Research was formed with Daemon as the public face of the company, and Bishop as the man behind the curtain."

Morgan exhaled sharply. "And you learned this…in how long?"

"In an instant."

Olivia crossed her arms and frowned. Her tone clinical and detached. "You really expect us to believe that?" she asked. "I'm not saying Sean is lying, but…let's be real. This story was probably planted in your head by Morpheus."

Sean was shaking his head. Olivia appeared unswayed and went on. "It sounds like Morpheus was the one doing the manipulating. It's like one of those NDEs, near-death experiences. People swear that they've seen God, or a divine light, or traveled to distant planets."

"I actually believe in those," interjected Noble quietly.

Olivia shot him a dark look suggesting that his input was not welcome.

"Look," she said. "I know what chemicals can do to a brain's function. I'm not sure what Sean actually experienced—a hallucination, some kind of Amplius delusion? Either way, it's wise to be skeptical."

Morgan placed his palms on the table, his voice steady as he cut her off. "Is it really that hard to believe? Daemon's research, and our whole purpose in opposing him, is based on an unseen, and largely unknown, force in the universe."

He turned to Olivia. "You know, better than us, what Adler's capable of. The wiser choice is to admit that we don't really know what we're up against."

Stung by Olivia's strong reaction, Sean met her gaze. "What I saw was real. As real as anything I've ever experienced. I can't explain it, but that doesn't mean it isn't true. I don't need to understand microwave technology to use a microwave."

"We need an edge," Morgan interjected. "Morpheus will commit crimes that don't appear to be crimes at all. It's like the old adage about the devil's greatest trick." He shook his head. "Imagine the pure, intoxicating appeal of killing or maiming—without any impediments, without any personal risk?"

Sean nodded in agreement. "I think we finally have an edge. Morpheus has never experienced what I experienced last night—something bigger than all their grubby little espionage and murder schemes."

Over the next hour, the group pieced together the structure of Morpheus Research—a small company with an oversized global reach.

Time was running out.

Morpheus was evolving from espionage to assassination.

For the first time, though, it felt like the group wasn't just catching up, but closing in.

Chapter Fourteen

With an evening to himself, Reinhold decided to find a proper gasthaus, but then corrected himself. No, in America they're called bars, or pubs. For all his technical brilliance, Reinhold had only recently discovered the bizarre joy—or curse—of social media. Now, he had Instagram, Tiktok, and Facebook accounts. Most recently, he uploaded his profile to something they call Tinder.

He smiled. He liked this country.

Opening Yelp, he found one of the oldest pubs in the nation was located close by, near NYU. The reviewers said it was raw and rowdy—peanut shells and sawdust strewn across the floor, and a five-star rating for its beer selection.

Reinhold threw on his favorite nylon bomber jacket, the one with a green exterior and orange lining, and headed out. His step had a natural bounce to it, pushing up and forward with his calves conditioned by years of playing soccer. Walking south, his mind trained on the frosty pints and good music ahead. He never noticed the stocky, balding man that followed a half block behind.

He cut through Washington Square, circling the central fountain. Up ahead, the bright neon signs marking the clubs near the university came into view. Glitzy reds and oranges shimmered against the deep violet sky. Behind him, the balding man kept watch.

The bar was on a cobblestone side-street, located in a Colonial-era building. Reinhold stepped over the high sill. Right away, he felt at home. Low ceilings. Wooden beams. Walls strewn with memorabilia.

Peanut shells and wood shavings stuck to the bottom of his army-style boots as he made his way to the bar. At the far end, he found an empty stool and ordered a beer. Reinhold looked up and saw the sign above the bar:

We were here before you were born!

He grinned, and chugged half the beer before wiping his mouth with the sleeve of his jacket.

A girl sat down next to him—a brunette with shoulder-length hair and straight bangs that came down past her eyebrows. She wore a black beaded choker under a silver chain and cross, a Led Zeppelin T-shirt, a short denim skirt over black knee-high socks, and a pair of worn Doc Martin boots. Laces untied, of course.

Sneaking furtive glances, Reinhold tried not to be obvious. His pulse quickened. She ordered a beer, and when it arrived, she asked him to pass her a coaster. The conversation was underway.

"Oh my God, you're from Germany?"

Reinhold laughed, surprised by her candor. And so it went. Her name was Lyzabeth. When she mentioned she was studying computer science at NYU, Reinhold's evening turned into his best night in America. His life had always been organized, orderly—but Lyzabeth seemed liberated. Like a free spirit, loving every moment of life.

They talked about her studies, they drank. They talked about his work, they drank. When they thought they drank too much, they ate something greasy.

They agreed to meet again the next night. Reinhold offered to show her the lab. Lyzabeth agreed—on the condition that he'd tell her all about his mysterious computer program. He crossed his heart with his forefinger and smiled. In the raucous and crowded bar, surrounded by students and sawdust, he kissed her.

Later, he walked her back to her dormitory. They held hands, playfully bumping into each other while slowly weaving their way through the streets of New York. A fair night in the city, with just the suggestion of a breeze. At the dorm's entrance, Reinhold kissed her again. Slurring in his German accent, he mumbled, "Du bist perfekt."

After another kiss, she bounded up the short flight of steps. Standing in front of the wood and glass double doors, she threw him an air-kiss, a quick wave, and disappeared inside. Reinhold stood there: dazed, happy, tipsy.

When he left, although it hardly seemed possible, there was a little more bounce to his step.

In the shadows of a brownstone stoop across the street, the balding man watched Reinhold Haas walk away. He flicked his cigarette butt, pulled out a cell phone, and made a short call. Moments later, a dark sedan pulled up to the curb. The man climbed in, and the car slowly pulled into the night.

***

Sean downed the last of his morning coffee, grabbed his jacket from the kitchen barstool, and headed off to work. The city was already awake and bustling. He stepped from the building and joined the flow of pedestrian traffic. As a native New Yorker, Sean's commute was ingrained—a small role in the city's choreography. Oblivious to the noise and hustle, the briefcases and the backpacks, Sean descended down the stairs to the subway station.

The A train was the first to arrive and he slipped into an empty seat, still warm from a departing construction worker.

Sean dreaded what lay ahead, another anguishing day at Farber Investments. A fruitless search for meaning in the endless parade of market upticks and downturns.

The coffee had left a bitter aftertaste. As he exited the train, he reached for a small packet of gum in his coat pocket. Stuck to the pack was a crumpled scrap of paper with the name and number of Winston Waxman, editor of Noosphere magazine. He huffed and shoved the scrap back into his pocket. He'd almost forgotten about him.

As he climbed the crowded stairway to the street, the name tugged at him. Waxman had mentioned something about universal consciousness. At the time, Sean dismissed it as sheer nonsense, but now he wasn't so sure. Could that explain the strange sensations he was experiencing while in theta? Before he reached the street level, he'd decided to call.

Sitting on a lengthy granite bench in his building's enormous lobby, he dialed the number.

"Mr. Waxman? This is Sean Hastings. We spoke awhile back about Adler Daemon."

A pause. "Oh, I remember. You're the journalist. But I think I told you everything I know about Adler."

"Actually, I'm not calling about him. It was something else you said at the time—something about a universal field of consciousness. The noosphere, I believe?"

"Yes, that's right." Winston paused for a bit longer. "But aren't you a financial reporter?"

"This is more of a personal inquiry. I hoped you wouldn't mind explaining the concept again. Preferably in layman's terms."

Waxman sighed. He often complained that talking to a mainstream reporter was a complete waste of time. No matter how many solid references he made to the physics—or any of the psychological or biological evidence that supported his theories—in the end, they arbitrarily dismissed his ideas. When the article finally came out, poor Winston was once again tossed into the bin with the Sasquatch and Loch Ness loonies.

Sean waited.

"Okay, Mr. Hastings," he said, after a few seconds.

"The noosphere is a world centered on thought—the cognitive. Our magazine explores using thought as a creative force. Everything begins with a thought."

Winston paused briefly, perhaps a little surprised that Sean hadn't interrupted him so far.

"So," he continued, "we ask, what is consciousness? Traditional science says that it's in our mind, a function confined to the brain. But there's considerable evidence to suggest that consciousness isn't just in our heads, but part of a much larger external system."

Sean listened, his mind flashing through recent memory. "So, you're saying that consciousness can exist outside of us?"

"Exactly. I think the potential to connect to this power is the greatest of all human strengths."

Sean murmured, almost to himself. "There's nowhere you can be, that isn't where you're meant to be."

Waxman cleared his throat. "I'm sorry?"

"Nothing, just something a friend once shared with me. So how does one connect to this consciousness?"

"Well," Waxman sounded a little surprised, as these questions usually came slathered in sarcasm.

"For now, meditation seems to be the best path. Functional MRIs have shown that during deep meditation, the entire brain lights up—revealing total coherence. Normally, parts of our brain are idle—activating only when they're needed. Then, they go dormant again—like an office building, where some lights come on and others go off. But the functional MRI shows a different picture during meditation. It shows increased blood flow to the entire brain—the whole thing—all at once. Clear evidence of an increase in coherence."

"And you say meditation is the best path to achieving this?"

"Oh yes. With advanced practitioners of meditation, the deeper they go, the more activity their brain's register."

Waxman paused, and chuckled. "It's quite interesting. You'd think that the deeper they went, the more internal the experience. But it's just the opposite. Instead of going deeper into their own mind, they expand outward. For those of us who believe in the noosphere, this is proof that everyone, and everything is connected. It's only a matter of time before everyone will be able to access universal consciousness."

***

It was early evening, and Sean turned onto Greenwich Avenue. The surrounding buildings bathed in the last sienna light. The city streets felt warm. Sean was meeting Olivia at a cozy Italian restaurant near Christopher Street. He was replaying their earlier conversation in his mind. Somehow, between the light-hearted banter, his invitation and her acceptance, they never established if this was, in fact, a date.

Since the divorce, Sean had been on plenty of dates, but never felt a connection. The women he'd met through work struck him as shallow. Obsessed with more of everything: better titles, greater wealth, more elegant parties. He recognized the hypocrisy—he'd used the same criteria to gauge his own success. Still, seeing it in their eyes made it seem more blatant and superficial.

On West Tenth Street, he waited for the light. Busy anticipating the evening, he was unaware of the man in a black suede bomber jacket who was had followed him since he left his office. The light turned green. Sean crossed. The man waited by the curb.

In the restaurant, the tiny bar was packed with the after-work crowd. Olivia had snagged two seats at the far end, where it narrowed, hemmed in by the glass shield that blocked patrons from the fiery stone pizza oven. She looked up as he approached and handed him a glass of red wine.

"Italian?" he asked.

"A Malbec. From Argentina. Recommended by a bartender from Montenegro." She giggled. Sean smiled. He felt a warmth, one that hadn't come from the pizza oven.

They talked about work, and all the idle topics people use to acquaint one another through their expressions, intonation, and body language. The hostess interrupted to say that their table was ready. Tucked away from the world, in their little nook, they grew comfortable with one another.

Across the street, on the pedestrian triangle, the man in the black suede jacket flicked a cigarette onto the sidewalk. Through the window, he watched Olivia react to something Sean had said. He stamped out the butt with his right foot and exhaled a billow of smoke into the night's air. His eye twitched as he fumbled for another cigarette.

***

By the end of the evening, Sean had agreed to meet Olivia in the morning, to accompany her to JFK. She had to fly to Montréal for meetings.

Sean gave her a quick kiss on the lips, and watched as she passed through security for the short flight to Montréal.

He had his own meeting that morning. Joining the taxi queue outside, he waited, his phone in hand. When he glanced up, every head in front of him was bent at the same angle, thumbs swiping tiny screens.

We are truly sheep.

In an act of minor rebellion, he shoved his phone back into his jacket pocket. He observed a group of Caribbean travelers dressed in bright golds, reds, and greens pass by—a vivid contrast to the dark blues and grays of the business shuttle crowd. The taxi line inched forward.

Sean's eyes wandered. A young man in his mid-twenties stood by the curb. He had an unusual beard, it had been trimmed into the shape of an anchor.

No baggage. No movement. Was he waiting for someone?

Sean watched for another minute, but then he reached the front of the queue. Seated in the yellow cab, he was ready to dismiss the whole thing. But as they drove off, he looked out the back window. The man was on his phone—and his eyes were fixed directly on Sean.

"Good morning," Olivia said the next day. "Did I wake you?"

"Not at all. I've got a late start today."

They talked for a while. She asked about Sean's evening.

"I watched a horror movie," he responded.

"Any good?"

"I can't really say. I didn't make it to the end. I can't handle scary movies—the victim of an overactive imagination, I guess."

She laughed. "I think I can relate. Yesterday, I kept seeing the same man everywhere: the security line, on my flight, and again, at the store on the way home. Probably nothing, but it sure felt weird."

Sean froze. The man with the anchor beard flashed in his mind.

"I'm sure it's nothing," he said, trying to sound reassuring, but his gut was telling a different story. He knew there had been something off about the man at the airport, but Olivia confirmed his suspicion.

They were being followed.

"Well, call the police if you see him again." He paused. "When are you back?"

"Not for a few days, at least."

They talked a little longer, but Sean couldn't shake the uneasy feeling that somewhere out there, someone was watching. And he suspected he knew who it was.

Chapter Fifteen

When the third call went straight to voicemail, Sean felt the irritation in his chest. With one hand on a pole, he braced himself as the downtown train swayed and rattled along the track. He was starting to think that Reinhold had forgotten their meeting. His frustration mounted, his grip tightened.

He's a tech guy. Just answer the damn phone.

He checked his messages again, as if he'd missed a response earlier. Nothing. He was still shaking his head when a large man in a Burberry raincoat bumped into him. Sean kept his balance by pinching a subway pole, his phone tenuously gripped in the bottom three fingers of his hand.

If Reinhold forgot our meeting…

A seat opened at the 23rd Street stop, but was gone before Sean could react. There were only two stops left, but it wasn't helping his souring mood. As the train lurched from the station, Sean was again knocked off balance by the human bumper car.

When he arrived at the lab's building, Sean peeked inside the SQUID salon. A girl was having a color fill done on a shoulder tattoo. With a shrug, he moved on, climbing the warped and creaking risers of the wooden stairs. He muttered to himself with each step, convinced that Reinhold had skipped their meeting. When he reached the landing, a narrow beam of light was spilling from the laboratory's door.

Expecting to find Reinhold hunched over his terminal, Sean pushed the door open. With his first step inside, his arm started to prickle with goosebumps—

something wasn't right.

In a faltering voice, he called out, "Reinhold?"

Silence.

Sean's eyes darted around the room. Everything appeared normal, but the strong feeling persisted. He scanned the room: instruments, braided cables, coils—and then—an empty space. The large MEG machine was missing.

Confused and curious—a little worried—he pressed further into the room. His field of view widening with each step. Finally, just behind the computer desk, he spotted Reinhold.

What's he doing on the floor?

He stepped closer. His confusion quickly turned to alarm when he saw the tiny trickle of blood at the base of his friend's skull.

"Reinhold?" His voice quivered.

Maybe he fell and hit his head.

But Sean's gut was telling a different story. Reinhold was slumped over, awkward and unnatural, almost like he was folding in on himself.

Sean leaned in for a closer look, but then staggered backward. He'd never seen a bullet wound before—or a dead body—but none of that mattered. The truth was undeniable. Savage and raw.

When he moved in front of Reinhold, he felt his leg's weaken. Sean's jaw went slack as he slowly sank down against the equipment rack. Sitting opposite Reinhold, he looked at his friend's eyes, open with a calm, if incongruous look on his face.

No scream. No panic. Just an empty, hollow feeling.

It was as if all of Sean's emotions and thoughts had crashed—waiting for a reboot. Minutes passed. He could do no more than sit on the floor, staring at his friend's body. Eventually, the fog began to lift, and with it came an upwelling of emotion. Sean forced himself to draw steady breaths. To focus.

He'd never given any thought about what to do if he stumbled upon a murder. The obvious choice was to call the police, but he quickly realized how badly that would go. They would ask a lot of questions and it was highly unlikely that any of his answers would satisfy your average beat cop.

"What kind of work was Mr. Haas doing?"

"Is there anything missing?"

"Can you think of anyone who might wish to harm him?"

Sean cringed at the thought of his response. Any truthful answer—dream incursions, frequency identification, magnetoencephalographs, an evil Swiss group —would not go over well. He pushed the thought aside.

Sean edged toward the computer station, careful to avoid Reinhold's body.

He tapped the keyboard to wake the computer, but nothing happened. He turned the desktop around and noticed the hard drives had been removed. Just the empty slots and a few short retaining screws that remained scattered on the desk. Then he remembered that Reinhold kept some flash drives locked in a cabinet on the right.

He found the lock broken, the drawer empty. He cursed in anger, covering his mouth with his fingers.

The more he thought about it, the more resigned he was to the idea that no one would ever find any evidence: no fingerprints, CCTV footage, or anything else. No trace of the people who committed this dreadful crime. "Professionals," he muttered with some disgust.

Now, he needed to plan his next move. The police could wait—there was too much at stake here. Sean phoned the closest thing he had to a fixer. His hands trembled as he pressed the contact number for Morgan.

***

Geneva, Switzerland

Dr. Adler Daemon sat at the far end of a long conference table on the second floor of Morpheus's headquarters in Geneva. The table's mahogany surface was inlaid with a blue-green polymer resin that ran the full length, creating the illusion of water flowing from one end to the other. Adler designed it himself, inspired by an Italian river he once saw from the window of a private jet. It snaked through deep and narrow valleys, and widened as it neared the open bay. The image of its effortless beauty stayed with him.

Daemon had an affinity for merging nature with technology. An amalgamation of God's vision and man's vision, he often said. Nature held everything necessary for the next evolution of mankind.

Even in his earliest experiments, Adler shunned the use of synthetic drugs in his research, arguing that truth could only be found using entheogen substances: DMT, psilocybin, or peyote. These plants would not only bring humanity closer to God,

111

but closer to becoming a god.

The conference room's sheer curtains filtered the afternoon's sun and the few warm recessed lights created a soft yet functional level of illumination. Adler insisted upon a calm and comfortable work environment—what the Germans called gemütlichkeit.

Hidden from view, embedded within the walls and glass, was sophisticated counter-surveillance equipment, surrounded by copper mesh. This was no ordinary conference room, and the man seated at the far end of the table was no ordinary guest.

Sergei Petrokosov was of average height and build, someone you'd describe as neither good looking nor unpleasant. A face easily forgotten. As a former KGB field agent, this had been an advantage. Witnesses never remembered him. The rest of Sergei's life, however, was anything but ordinary. He served the KGB with distinction, proving himself capable at intelligence gathering and interrogation. And when required, quite deadly.

After the fall of the Soviet Union, he traded the covert for the comfortable. His hairline began to recede, his belly advanced, and he took a cushy, high-level position in the intelligence agency of one of the Soviet Union's former republics. A well-deserved reward after years of sacrifice. Sometimes, he'd confess to old friends that he missed the thrill of his former life—having traded his pistols in for the prosaic. Then he'd laugh it off as nostalgia.

Sergei was here by order of his government. They were cooperating with Morpheus in exchange for favored status, should they have a need for the firm's unique services.

Seated at the widemouthed bay end of the table's resin river, Sergei's smile appeared forced. He'd told his superiors that he disliked Daemon, and called him an arrogant prick.

Still, Sergei was a good soldier and orders were orders.

Adler smiled, finding the situation quite amusing. Where other corporations relied on private investigators or mercenary security firms for information, he commanded national intelligence agencies, entire governments. Four other countries had already offered their services.

Adler leaned casually to one side of his chair, displaying all the humility of an eighteenth-century shogun. Who could blame him? Once an academic pariah, now he was being wooed and courted by the most powerful men in the world.

He allowed himself this one hubristic moment, but Morpheus was still young and the need for good intelligence was critical. That's why Sergei Petrokosov was here.

Sergei sighed and slid a Manila envelope onto the table. It sailed, virtually friction free, across the mirror-polished resin and into the hands of Adler Daemon with momentum to spare.

"Inside," Sergei began, "you'll find the dossiers and photographs identifying the organization behind the man that approached your agent. We've seized the machine they used to identify your agent, the—" He paused to refer to his notes. "—the MEG, along with the hard drives, files, and any other backups used to support their efforts. You're probably aware that there was an incident during our operation. The German, Reinhold Haas, returned unexpectedly. It became necessary to eliminate him. Unintended and unfortunate, but it does ensure they'll be unable to duplicate his work anytime soon."

He looked up at Adler. "I believe you indicated that a modest level of violence was acceptable?"

"Do they have a name?" Adler asked, conveniently ignoring the reference to murder.

"Not that I'm aware of."

"Doesn't matter," he said, waving off the comment as he thumbed through the short stack of dossiers. He gave each one a lengthy look, furrowing his brow. An unorganized, ragtag bunch—not the threat he'd been warned about.

"I'm curious," Adler asked, "have you found any evidence that they've learned to manipulate the dream environment? Something to indicate they're approaching—" Adler froze mid-sentence, staring at a photograph.

Sergei noticed Adler's reaction, watching quietly, as if returning to his interrogative past. At the same time, Adler was battling to control his emotions. Mindful of his facial expressions and body language—anything that might feed Sergei's predatory instincts.

Adler's fingers trembled as he held the photograph in his right hand. It was Olivia Abbott.

He felt completely lost—almost paralyzed.

How had Olivia become part of this group?

Adler always suspected that someone from his old research project had betrayed him to the university. Until this moment, he never considered that someone could be Olivia. The thought was unbearable.

Olivia was twenty-five when they first met at the Université de Montréal. He was looking for research assistants for what would become the Human Consciousness and Cognition Project. From the start, Adler wanted her—not only for the project—but for himself. Nothing else mattered, not the impropriety, not the age difference. He was used to getting what he wanted, and readily dismissed their twenty-year age difference as insignificant.

Olivia was beautiful, brilliant, and to his slightly masochistic pleasure, irreverent and challenging toward him. It was part of the allure. A man like Adler could never be with a woman too willing to please. They grew close—colleagues at first, then as lovers. Adler approached consciousness from a quantum mechanical perspective, while Olivia focused on the brain's biochemical functions. They were a strong team: one peering into the brain, the other looking out.

Adler Daemon was at his best during this period. He may have found some happiness in his academic achievements, but he found his joy with Olivia. For the first time in his life, he'd felt content.

Soon after, the project began to skid off track. Even in hindsight, it was difficult to explain. The breakup felt destined, almost organic. Adler maintained that if the goal was to expand consciousness, then the first step would be to escape the trappings of the current consciousness—to shatter the existing mindset—and that meant drugs, specifically psychotropic drugs. His ethical perspective had skewed. People talked, but he ignored them.

"Who would dare to dispute such incredible results?" he had asked.

As it turned out—the university dared. Where he saw brilliance and hope, they saw recklessness and liability. The Board of Regents rejected his ends justify the means approach, and terminated the project.

It was a wake-up call for Olivia. She distanced herself publicly, blaming the long hours and a misguided admiration for Adler's brilliance. An abrupt end to a wild ride. Somehow, she escaped unscathed.

Adler had tried to advance the cause of mankind, and in return, he'd been maligned, misunderstood, and now, betrayed. The university's Board of Regents were fools. Were they stupid enough to presume that any significant progress in astronomy, anatomy, physics, or psychology had been made without involving great personal or social cost?

When the project dissolved, Adler almost sank into despair. But a few former project members suggested secretly continuing the work. He regained his composure—replaced the emptiness with the white heat of anger and revenge. Dr. Daemon departed Montreal on the road to what would become Morpheus. He never saw Olivia again.

Still holding her picture in his hand, his initial anger had softened to a profound and unexpected hurt, like someone cut a deep valley into his chest with a dull blade. It eclipsed everything else.

"Are you sure this woman is part of the group?" Adler said, turning the picture toward Sergei.

"Quite sure," Sergei said. "Do you know her?"

"No," Adler lied.

Sergei nodded, watching closely. A habitual interrogator, he seized every opportunity to gain an edge. Adler refused to give him satisfaction. If Sergei was disappointed by this, he did a masterful job of hiding it.

"She still lives in Montreal," the Russian added, "but I'm told she's spending more time in New York with Sean Hastings."

Chapter Sixteen

New York City

The polished steel doors of the elevator parted on the fifth floor, and Sean stepped into the elegant foyer of Farber Investments. The receptionist, an attractive Gen X brunette, was busy on the phone. If asked, she would claim that this was only a temporary job. But after several months of unanswered applications and several rejections, her voice betrayed an underlying doubt. So here she was, working at Farber Investments, and seated behind an enormous reception desk that was only dwarfed by the size of her student loan.

She raised a perfectly manicured finger and signaled for Sean to wait. She hung up the phone, and without directly looking at him, said, "Mr. Reynolds wants to see you in his office—nine o'clock."

Sean nodded and continued to his desk. Fifteen minutes to go.

He dropped his briefcase and coat, then strolled toward the break room. Reynolds's office was upstairs, on the sixth floor, along with a slew of other vice presidents. Twenty-one in all, at last count. Reynolds had recently received a promotion and his new title was Vice-President of Securities and Trading, or Trading and Securities. Honestly, Sean didn't know or care. Farber's corporate titles were liquid. Either way, Reynolds was Sean's boss, albeit a level or two removed.

At nine sharp, he was shown into the spacious and handsome office. From the matching furniture to the generic wall art, it was obvious that a professional design company had decorated it throughout. The complete lack of personality struck Sean as a fitting match for its current occupant.

"Sean, thanks for coming in," said Reynolds.

He was around five years older than Sean, but their career trajectories could not have been more different. Reynolds had hammered out his promotions through grueling ninety-plus-hour workweeks, highly aggressive sales, and more drunken nights with clients, brokers, and call girls than any unsuspecting liver should ever endure. Sean knew the type. That's what it took. It also explained why Sean's desk was one floor below.

"We're letting you go," Reynolds said, wasting no time.

It was short, blunt—and shocking.

Sean blinked, half waiting for the punchline.

Reynolds's voice came across flat and uncaring, as if his mind had already moved on to his next meeting.

"I don't understand," Sean said, astonished at how calm his voice sounded. He suspected that his body hadn't had time to generate an appropriate reaction.

"A report of insider trading was leveled against the firm," Reynolds said. "Trades you recommended, the same ones we executed. For Christ's sake, do you have any idea how bad it looks to have the SEC on the property?"

Reynolds circled his huge desk, looking stern. Evidently, over the years, he'd found the time to perfect a look of righteous indignation. It was useful on occasions like this.

"If you've got a credible explanation for how these trades came to your attention —and can prove your workflow—now's the time to speak up."

In all probability, Reynolds couldn't have cared less whether Sean had an explanation or not, but he must have thought his concerned query would look good on the final HR report.

Sean stared at Reynolds in disbelief.

"You're asking me to prove a negative. Show evidence that I didn't receive something."

"Well?"

Sean's emotions finally caught up: anger, frustration, guilt.

"I've never engaged in insider trading," he insisted, his voice steady but troubled. "I resent the accusation."

Reynolds appeared disinterested. "A security guard is waiting outside to escort you from the building. You can come back after hours to pick up your personal belongings."

Sean stood there, silent.

"It's our corporate policy," Reynolds said with a soulless shrug.

"Don't want anyone going postal around here," he added, most likely for his own amusement.

***

By midafternoon, Sean had walked himself senseless. Regret, self-pity, and anger churned through his mind. After hours of meandering through half of Manhattan, Sean was tired—and alone. He'd been unable to reach Keenan, and presumed that Karen would start hounding him about alimony. Finally, he phoned Olivia.

She was walking along the Chemin de la Côte-Sainte-Catherine, near the Université de Montréal, when her mobile phone rang.

"Bonjour," she said, pinning the phone between her shoulder and ear while she fished through her purse.

"Olivia? It's Sean."

Her tone was light and warm, soothing his fractured spirit like a balm. Finding a nearby park bench, she sat down. Sean told her about his dismissal. He led with the heartless executive, the SEC investigation, and the accusation of impropriety. He ended with the company's lame concern that he might shoot his coworkers. As he hoped, Olivia's response was appreciably sympathetic, but it was the care and warmth in her voice that he found the most comforting.

When he finished, she paused. "Sean, may I ask you something? Your boss said someone filed a report. Who knew about this?"

Sean's mind was busy connecting the dots.

"After all," she continued, "this information came from dreams, and the dreamers are unaware. There are no witnesses, no paper trail. Unless you told someone—it's all very suspect, no?"

Sean stopped walking. The crowd flowed around him.

"I—I never even thought of that," he murmured.

By now his mind was in full gear. "The SEC goes after larger schemes that have dragged on for years. This doesn't fit the mold. It's too small—too recent. This must have come from Morpheus."

"How did they even know about you?"

"Not sure—probably from the Sydney dream, or the ski dream in Switzerland."

"But you never identified yourself."

"No, it must have been the agent—" Sean stopped midsentence. His hands began to shake, the color draining from his face.

"Shit," he said, vigorously shaking his head. "No, no, no, it can't be."

"Sean?" Olivia asked, the alarm in her voice apparent.

With a deep breath he said, "I think I led Morpheus to us—to our lab. I think Reinhold Haas is dead because of me."

On the line, only silence.

"Olivia, what am I going to do? Who could be next?"

***

Karen's motionless body lay perfectly still, tangled in the twist of a comforter. At some point, her left leg broke free in search of cooler air, but most of her lithe body was still tightly wrapped in the strange paralysis of deep sleep. Well after midnight, a sound began to pierce the layers of slumber. At first, it blended into her own dream, but like a distant train approaching, it grew louder and louder— until it demanded her attention. A young cry tore through the haze, striking at Karen's maternal cord like a sledge hammer.

Abbie!

Adrenaline raced through Karen. She ran barefoot through the darkness toward her daughter's room. Abbie was in the midst of a nightmare, thrashing about and kicking the sheets.

Abbie was safe—Karen could finally breathe.

She sat on the edge of the bed, gently stroking her cheek, and softly calling her name. Soothed by the warmth of her mother's voice and the feel of a familiar touch, Abbie woke from her nightmare. Confused and scared, her young mind tried to process what had happened. Karen whispered to her softly, "You were having a nightmare. It's over, you're safe."

The little girl gently sobbed, unable to shake the fear or escape the chill in her bones. They hugged for a while.

"Do you wanna talk about it?"

She shook her head, her lower lip quivering. She buried her head in her mother's bosom, while Karen softly rubbed her daughter's back. The light friction slowly caressing away the chill. Soon the sobbing began to subside, but like a contained brushfire, with an occasional flare-up. In the glow of the faint blue-purple light of Abbie's Frozen nightlight, the two sat quietly.

Then Abbie said, "It was about Dad."

Karen's heart skipped a beat. "Your dad? What happened?"

"I was at the dog park, playing with the puppies. A man asked if I like doggies and—" Abbie's voice trailed off.

Karen wrested a brave smile and hugged Abbie even tighter. She wanted to scream, but forced herself to stay calm to avoid Abbie shutting down. Her stomach knotted with fear. Was this just a nightmare, or something darker and more troubling? Had she missed the signs?

By now, Abbie was fully awake. Though her mother seemed upset, she continued remembering the dream.

"Then he picked up a little white puppy and threw it over the fence. It got runned over." Abbie checked her mother's reaction before going on. "He said more puppies would die if Dad didn't stop what he was doing."

Karen looked utterly lost, unable to make any sense of Abbie's dream. It was awful, but did it stem from abuse or trauma?

She whispered softly, "It's okay. Remember, it was only a dream, and dreams can't hurt you."

***

By morning, whatever semblance of calm Karen managed to cobble together the night before was gone. She told Sean she was taking Abbie to a child therapist.

"Why? What for?" Sean protested.

Karen told him about the nightmare, exactly as Abbie described it. She insisted it was a reflection of some suppressed trauma, or the divorce, or…

Sean was half-listening to what Karen said. His mind seized on that one particular line.

Tell your dad to stop what he is doing.

Sean suggested that it was something she saw on television, but underneath it all, he was haunted by the phrase. He kept repeating it in his head, and each time it sounded more sinister.

Tell your dad to stop what he is doing.

Karen kept talking, seemingly unconcerned whether Sean was listening or not.

His palms began to sweat. This hadn't been a random dream. In fact, this wasn't Abbie's dream at all.

It was a message, a clear warning. His jaw tightened and his face flushed with anger.

She's only nine years old.

He thought of going to the authorities, but what could he say? It sounded absurd. Besides, his potential legal woes with the SEC were enough of a concern—he had little interest in inviting another law-enforcement agency into his life.

He called Morgan instead.

After expressing his sympathy and regret, Morgan said, "Sean, I'm afraid we're entering a new and dangerous phase with Morpheus."

"So what? We just quit?"

"No," he said reassuringly, "but we can't go on the same way. The game has changed. We've allowed ourselves to think of Morpheus as a collection of scientists and semi-drugged graduate students, but to continue to do so would be unwise. Think about their clients: corporations, organized crime, governments, intelligence agencies. People with vast sums of money and reach. Morpheus has gained considerable power and influence—now, we're standing in their way. That makes Morpheus truly dangerous."

Sean swallowed hard. "Dangerous? Do you mean, getting in our dreams dangerous—or, back-alley, violent dangerous?"

Morgan paused.

The silence was answer enough.

Chapter Seventeen

A business professor of Sean's once said, in a rare sage-like moment, that you can have anything you want, as long as you're willing to give up the belief that you can't have it. As an ambitious business student, Sean took it as a rallying cry for budding capitalists, a never-surrender credo about persistence and grit. Now, in light of what Ulgen Khan had said about rejecting self-imposed limitations, he realized he'd never truly understood its meaning. It was about unlocking potential.

Sean sat sideways on his daybed, legs bent, his back braced against the wooden frame. Peering through the water-spotted windows at the crowd of pedestrians below, he thought of the eccentric bunch that was occupying his mind: shamans, physicists, fringe publishers, and rogue professors. And, of course, there was Abbie. Every thought seemed to circle back to concern for her safety.

Even if Morpheus never physically harmed her, how much damage might they inflict through manipulating her dreams? These were not ordinary dreams and he shuddered at the thought of their long-term effects. He was desperate to protect her, but how? And from what? His group still hadn't found a way to stop the incursions.

He wondered how this had become his life—this tangle of spirit and science that he barely understood. Somehow, whether it was the result of divine intervention or flawed impulses, this was now his path.

He gazed out at the city, mindlessly twisting the ring he still wore on his left hand. He thought of the Morpheus agent on the ski slope. Where had all that information come from? If Winston Waxman was right, then Sean had fallen into the deep end of human consciousness. It was time to sink or swim. He needed a plan, not only to protect Abbie and Olivia, but to bring an end to Morpheus.

***

The next afternoon, a light drizzle seemed to change the city's rhythm. Olivia had just flown in from Montréal, and agreed to meet Sean in the lobby bar of a Tribeca hotel—a softly lit, upscale, fusion of cocktails and ambition.

"I'm so sorry about Abbie. Is she okay?" asked Olivia.

Sean nodded. "She's fine. I spent yesterday with her, but she doesn't understand what all the fuss is about."

"So," she said, tilting her head, "now what?"

The question hung in the air—vague and open-ended. Was she asking about the loss of his job, or his encounter with universal consciousness?

Waiting for his reply, Olivia reclined into the cream-colored sofa; legs crossed, stylish and regal. It was just past five in the afternoon and the lounge was busy. Olivia smirked. A subtle sign that she was fully aware of the wolfish attention she attracted from the happy hour suits—several cocktails into it and still far from their wives, lives, and homes.

Sean was no less mesmerized by her open-back crimson dress, white stiletto heels, and red nails. She transferred the cosmopolitan from hand to hand—the bright candy-red liquid perfectly complementing the color of her nails. Lately, he'd found himself daydreaming about her often, and hoping for a sign that she felt the same.

"Is there a choice?" Sean finally asked, assuming she asked about Morpheus. "Using Amplius while in theta waves will open up new opportunities—maybe even to get inside Adler Daemon's consciousness."

He paused while a loud and obnoxious party passed. Then turned to Olivia. "I tell myself that Daemon is just another man, but you know him. Should I worry?"

Olivia uncrossed her legs, leaned forward, and placed her drink on the glass coffee table.

"The Adler I knew was curious and altruistic—sometimes kind. I think that man is gone."

Olivia took Sean's right hand, sandwiched it between her palms, and looked into his eyes.

"This new Adler is completely unknown to me. Someone capable of anything.

Whatever you choose to do, don't underestimate him. He is smart, calculating, and dangerous."

***

The next day, Olivia stood in Sean's hallway and smoothed her skirt. She let out a nervous giggle before knocking. Sean opened the door, still in his work suit, his tie loose around his neck.

"Hi. Come in."

Olivia knew the invitation was a ruse, but she had her reasons for accepting. The first visit to a man's home was a milestone, a window into his soul. Neat or cluttered? Professional designer or self-decorated? More like Architectural Digest or Maxim?

Olivia took a seat on the overstuffed couch while Sean poured the wine in the kitchen. She used the time to discreetly look about the room. A little surprising: masculine tones, but softened through the use of natural woods, accents, and delicate fabrics. She nodded. Perhaps even a little impressed.

"Here you go." Sean said returning with two glasses. They toasted and she turned to him.

"So, what's so important?"

"I managed to connect with Daemon in universal consciousness."

Olivia looked stunned. "Are you sure? How?"

Sean spoke slowly. "I focused on his image, on what little I knew about the man. But it wasn't clear, just glimpses, like a train going in and out of tunnels. Still, I must have done something right because I learned how they control the autonomic system in dream incursions."

Sean took another sip of wine before clearing his throat.

"Our method—it's intuitive. It's done by feel. I can't explain how it works, but it works. In contrast, Morpheus is entirely technical. Their agents act like conduits—a piece of a greater man-machine interface."

"Conduits? I'm not following," she said, her interest piqued.

"They train their agents by using the drug to rewire their neural pathways. Keeping the brain in a constant state of flux. Eventually, they're connected to a machine that runs the dream incursion program."

"So they need the machine to do incursions?"

Sean nodded.

Olivia looked half-amused. "You make it sound like they're trained monkeys."

"No, far from it. Their backgrounds are in military, science, or psychology—they know what they're doing."

"What about the autonomic system?"

"Something they stumbled upon, I think," Sean said. "While trying to manipulate dreamers, Morpheus found that using hypnotic suggestions during incursions could override a person's autonomic system. Whether accidental or not, they learned that hypnosis can kill."

***

Karen was unhappy. Unhappy in a way that bordered on seething anger. A familiar tone, one that Sean still recalled from their marriage. Thankfully, he was not the target of today's fury. It was the child psychologist that Karen's friend recommended after Abbie's strange nightmare. After a battery of psychological tests, the doctor ruled out the usual suspects—ADHD, autism, traumatic stress, etc.—and pronounced Abbie a normal, healthy child.

"She's a quack," Karen shouted into the phone. Sean winced, pulling the cellphone farther from his ear. He listened quietly—without offering much of a response. A return to his old marital reflex.

She'd accused him of indifference, but that had never been the case. He had loved Karen, but struggled to communicate his feelings. Over time, he surrendered to the force of her will, like a shoreline erodes to the tide. In the silence, Karen grew resentful. Neither liked what was happening, but still, they couldn't untie the knot they'd created. The marriage ended in quiet exhaustion.

Sean felt older now, calmer. He better understood who he was, and what he wanted. Most of his life had been spent pleasing others, pursuing goals and family expectations that never resonated with him. Working with Olivia and the group felt different. Letting go, as Ulgen had phrased it, had given him his life back.

When he returned to the call, Karen hadn't let up. He was half-listening, as his thoughts returned to Abbie.

Tell your dad to stop what he is doing.

The threat kept replaying in his head. How could he tell Karen about the dream incursions, or about Morpheus? Or that he was the indirect cause of their daughter's nightmare, or that it might happen again?

Obviously, any mention of Reinhold's murder was best avoided altogether.

He reasoned that distance might be the safest solution—a move to Florida should keep them safe.

Karen paused, and Sean asked, "I'm sorry?"

"I said we should look for another therapist."

"Right," Sean grunted, but his attention was elsewhere. His mind spun through the logic of using the move as protection, but flinched at a stark realization.

If they can get to Abbie in a dream, then they could physically harm her—anywhere, anytime.

He shook his head as the truth settled in. As long as Morpheus existed, Abbie would never be safe.

"Karen," he said softly, "let's give her a little time. You may be right, but let's see how it goes this week. If it's still a problem, I'll back you."

Karen paused, perhaps caught off guard by his tone, but then agreed.

Sean bit his lower lip. He had come to three conclusions:

Morpheus could reach inside a dream—and no place was safe.

Reinhold's death had changed their circumstances.

And, their point of no return was already in the past.

Chapter Eighteen

Paris, France

Adler Daemon followed the brunette hostess to the table, avoiding unnecessary eye contact with the other patrons. Dining at Le Chemin was usually a pleasure, but tonight he resented being here. Meeting with clients was below his station, but he yielded to the argument that only their top executive could explain the latest offering. Still, these things were personally distasteful—and unnecessarily risky.

Located a few blocks from Sacré-Cœur, the two-star Michelin restaurant had been a favorite of Adler's over the years. So much so that he took it as a personal affront when they missed being awarded their third star. In addition to the main dining room, customers could select one of the alcoves near the rear. These recessed tables afforded a remarkably high level of discretion. Very useful for occasions like tonight's meeting.

An agreeable blond girl in a short green dress soon appeared in front of him. He smiled back, but his brief optimism vanished when she turned to present an older Hispanic gentleman to the table. As she walked away—Adler sighed—another harsh reminder of his advancing years. He forced a generous smile, and the two men exchanged greetings.

Miguel Sopras admitted to carrying a few more pounds than he preferred, but blamed it on age, not diet. Still, he was physically strong, the result of a lifetime of military discipline. Tonight, he was out of uniform because this was not an official visit. He wasn't here as a high-ranking representative of his nation. Miguel had come to strike a deal for his country's future.

"Dr. Daemon, thank you for meeting me. I'm afraid my situation is desperate, and I hope you can help." Though his voice remained steady, his face betrayed his consternation. He'd spent a lifetime projecting a calm, forged sense of strength, but tonight he was on edge. Reputation or humiliation were trivial concerns compared to the fear of failure that gripped Miguel. Treason, and there is no doubt that's what they would call this, was no small matter.

"Call me Adler." His tone soft, a rare display of warmth. He swirled his Bordeaux and inhaled its aroma. "I suspect that you and I are more content to steer events from the shadows and leave the limelight for others. Nevertheless, here we are." Adler raised his glass in a toast. "By chance or destiny, may Lady Luck or God look upon us favorably."

When the seven-course meal arrived it was a delicate balance of color, texture, and shape—playful and amusing. Miguel Sopras appeared impressed by the presentation. As the evening wore on, they chatted and took measure of one another—agreeing to delay their business until after dinner.

Miguel set down his glass and began. "I have served in the military for thirty years, always in the interest of my country, no matter who held power. My late wife always shared my dream of open and democratic elections, a day when the people would be given their say."

Miguel paused, as if he could hear her once again. "That day is fast approaching, but there is a problem." Miguel looked down as he chose his next words.

"Of the three leading candidates, two are good men. The front-runner is not. He's corrupt, and backed by the country's largest drug cartel. If he's elected, my country will return to its dark past. We cannot allow him to take power, to corrupt our future."

Adler's fingers traced the rim of his glass. "May I ask how you came to learn of us?" It was an unnecessary question. Miguel had been fully vetted by Morpheus, and Adler had finished reading his dossier hours earlier. Still, he believed there was much to learn about a man through his tone and gestures.

"I've spent a good portion of my career in the intelligence branch. The world of spies is much smaller than people imagine. I learned of Mr. Bishop, and that led me to you." His words were confident and matter-of-fact.

"And now you want Mr. Serrano removed?" he asked, watching Miguel's face.

"Permanently," said Miguel, his voice firm and unflinching. "My country is far too fragile to survive this man's rule. We cannot risk his victory." Miguel scanned the restaurant and turned to Daemon. He leaned forward and whispered. "It's my understanding this could be done without attracting scrutiny."

A rare twinkle came to Adler's eyes. He disliked face-to-face meetings, but always enjoyed an opportunity to share a complicated scientific process with a willing audience.

"Are you familiar with anesthesia?" he asked without waiting for a reply. "Anesthetics suppress autonomic functions—heart rate and respiration being two of the primary ones. If misused, they can easily kill, but those deaths can be detected postmortem. We have another way. We enter the mind through a portal, a gateway from which no one is immune—the dream."

Miguel looked puzzled. Adler let his words hang in the air, barely concealing the full extent of his vanity.

"We've been experimenting with dream incursions, or dream traveling. At first, it was simply a profitable trifle, but this," he said, gesturing in a circular motion, "this is the real prize. After manipulating the constructs of the dream, we turned our attention to directly influencing the dreamer. Adjusting the dream scenario in order to control the dreamer's autonomic response."

Miguel's eyes narrowed, unsure where Daemon was headed.

"Imagine that you are drowning in a dream," Adler continued. "Your natural instinct is to gasp for air. Normally, you would wake up with your heart racing, and the sheets soaked in sweat—but you do wake up. Now, let's consider what happens when your autonomic system is suppressed. The body's natural response fails—no breath, no automatic reaction, no waking. The line between dream and reality has blurred. The dream has become real, at least in the sense that you are really asphyxiating—drowning in your own imaginary waters."

Miguel sat very still. He'd heard faint whispers and innuendos, but never imagined that such a capability really existed. He had seen plenty of death, but he'd never encountered anything like this. The two men sat in silence, occasionally tilting their heads back to drink from their brandy snifters.

Miguel looked troubled. Finally, he said what was on his mind. "This is unlike any killing that I have ever known. I'm here looking for an assassin, but somehow this feels wrong. No one is there to pull the trigger or plunge the dagger—this is killing—like a god."

"You just might be right about that, General." Adler said, amused and visibly pleased with himself. "Still, the emphasis should be on the 'killing.' Isn't that why you came here?"

Adler swirled the wine in his glass and shrugged. "Weapons have evolved from simple rocks to swords to the modern machine gun. Morpheus is simply the latest iteration in the evolution of killing."

He tapped his fingertips together, enjoying the logic. "One more thing, I believe you insisted that his death be discreet."

Miguel nodded. "This man can't become a martyr—the cartel would retaliate with violence. It must look like an accident."

"We can do much better than that, my friend," said Adler. "Accidents involving prominent individuals tend to attract suspicion. We deliver death by natural causes —completely indistinguishable from a natural death. Undetectable through an autopsy, entirely free of forensic evidence. No cries of foul play. No conspiracies. No demands for investigation. Even the most ardent skeptics will accept that Serrano died of natural causes—fate having taken him before his time."

Adler grinned at Sopras. "Only you and I will know the truth—that his death was your will, not God's."

***

New York City

Sean spent the afternoon in a dense fog of regret, introspection, and worry. Tucked into his favorite leather chair, he propped his feet on the second shelf of an overstuffed bookcase. The air around him was thick, almost suffocating. He exhaled—a long, tired breath that carried with it the weight of Reinhold's death. The image of his friend, lying lifeless on the floor, seemed as immediate as if it had just happened.

Only days ago, everything was so clear. Morgan had finished delivering his evangelistic tale of good versus evil and Sean had been inspired. It struck all the right chords. But now, as he thought of Reinhold, he wondered why no one had foreseen the tragedy. What else were they missing?

Morgan and Olivia's plan had revolved around using Reinhold's technology to stop Morpheus, some elaborate face-off of scientific wizardry. But now Reinhold was gone and they were floundering. It brought to mind the Mike Tyson line:

Everyone's got a plan—until they get hit.

As the last of the day's light faded away, Sean felt uninspired to get up and turn on a lamp. The dusk brought shadows that matched his mood. He replayed the recent encounters in his mind: the dream with the Morpheus agent, the conversation with Winston Waxman, the esoteric talk with the Fordham physicist. Different roads perhaps, but all leading to the same place: universal consciousness. Was that really the path to stopping Morpheus?

Sean decided to try again, to find the agent in the Swiss Alps and learn more about their intentions. He closed his eyes and slowed his breath until the weight of his body fell away. The physical world began to recede like the tide.

As his inward descent began, the same uneasiness came over him—the fear of losing control. Though he was calmer than before, his ego still fought over every scrap of self-control—a push and pull between the rational and the unexplainable. Letting go was a battle. After a few more deep breaths, the turbulence settled down; the worst of it behind him, like a spacecraft safely re-entering the atmosphere.

Now, fully immersed, he arrived at the bottom like a deep sea diver touching the ocean floor. But something wasn't right.

Where was the dream? Where was the Swiss agent?

It felt different and it made him feel off-balance. His anxiety swelled and he was again reminded that he was not in control of this process.

The weightlessness transformed into shapelessness. He sensed himself dissolving, losing the edges that defined the contours of his body. He'd become liquid, moving and flowing, splashing through crevices like a raging flash flood.

In his apartment, his physical body threw off a faint shiver.

But in his mind, he was alive with unimaginable beauty and wonder—an explorer in uncharted territory, like Magellan or Drake.

Then came the light. A blinding brightness that wrapped him in warmth and serenity. It felt ancient, like a peace that predated humanity. It overwhelmed him, yet he couldn't bear the thought of losing it.

And then just like that, it was gone. Sean emerged from the meditation in an abrupt fashion, as if being dropped off at the curb.

What a strange experience.

Still, some of the wonder lingered. Sean's body gave off an involuntary shiver—the aftershock from an intense experience.

He reached for his glass but stopped, staring at the floor. Images flashed before his eyes—the same kind of delayed information dump that he'd experienced from the Swiss dream. He jumped up and grabbed a scrap of paper, and jotted down everything. When he was done, the page was covered with sketches, symbols, and words. Much of it was illegible, a hurried scrawl that filled every empty space either horizontally or vertically. Sean bit his lower lip and turned the scratch paper from side to side, trying to decipher the words he'd written.

He scanned the paper and squinted. Nothing was matching the pattern from his first encounter. Was this what Ulgen Khan had meant—information cascading through him, as if it had been trapped in some neural-synaptic traffic jam?

No, he thought, there had to be more. What he'd experienced was extraordinary, but was it universal consciousness? The imposing term implied something greater.

Sean exhaled sharply—he'd been warned that feeling disoriented was part of the process. He glanced at the paper, and laughed. No shortage of disorientation here.

He studied the sheet and started to pick out fragments: names, places, dates. In the left margin, underlined several times, was a name. He stared at it.

Who in the world is Miguel Sopras?

Chapter Nineteen

In a quiet neighborhood of a South American capital, General Miguel Sopras sat in his living room and fidgeted. For each of the past few days, he'd carefully checked the newspapers for one story in particular—the unfortunate passing of presidential candidate Gualtiero Serrano. It hadn't happened. Not yet.

A few miles away, Serrano wiped his mouth with a white cloth napkin and let out a burp. Ten pounds overweight by his own estimation—and forty pounds by his doctor's—he practically inhaled his dinner of feijoada, rice, and collard greens. The Brazilian national dish was his favorite comfort food, but tonight, it sat heavy in his gut. He pushed his chair back to give himself some breathing room, lifted a glass, and proposed a toast.

"Un futuro próspero."

Seated around the table were several deeply compromised politicians from the current administration, his campaign manager, and the local drug cartel boss with his top lieutenant.

Serrano was an arrogant man with a natural gift for politics. Ambitious, self-centered, and shamelessly opportunistic, he had nonetheless convinced the country that he was merely a humble servant. A man of the people. In fiery speeches, he dismissed the corruption, cartel influence, and the country's failing economy as mere fantasies. Lies perpetrated by the opposition and the dark forces that loomed across the border.

"Let them say what they want," he joked to friends, "so long as we're victorious."

Serrano was a master of deceit—and favored to win next week's election. His opponents were a pro-business civil servant, and a university professor campaigning to restore many of the country's long-abandoned social programs. Both were decent men. Neither stood a chance.

Late that night, after his guests had left, Serrano sat alone at the long table. His cigar had burned down to a stub, and he cursed. It refused to stay lit, and he ground it into a pulp of tobacco and ash, twisting its end into submission. His nose scrunched, eyes narrowed, and he snarled at nothing in particular. Even Serrano might have struggled to explain the source of his rage. The election was going as planned, his finances secure. It might have been simple pre-election jitters—or the result of too much wine. He exhaled sharply, smacked his lips, and stood to stagger toward the bedroom. Perhaps a good sleep would silence whatever gnawed at Gualtiero Serrano.

Across town, General Miguel Sopras listened to his favorite Chopin concerto. Assured that Dr. Daemon was a trustworthy man, he nevertheless grew impatient. These methods weren't as simple as a hollow-point bullet—patience was the price of being undetected. That, and the substantial sum he'd wired to Daemon's Swiss account.

The piano entered the adagio movement, and Miguel closed his eyes to let the slow, soft notes gently flow over him.

The election was one week away.

***

New York City

Sean's mind was made up, his moral compass firmly set.

He thought of Morgan's warning that interfering with the assassination might have consequences, but easily brushed it off. The people willing to pay this price to Morpheus—these shadow governments, corporations, ideologues—all had powerful motivations. Altruism was not one of them.

Sean had learned the target was Gualtiero Serrano, a South American politician. But now what? How could he block a method that hijacks the nervous system inside a dream?

Too many variables. Too many unknowns. Sean had no idea where to begin—his moral compass failing to point to a solution. One idea after another fell short. He reasoned that even if he blocked an attempt, Morpheus would keep trying until Serrano was dead.

Sean rummaged through his desk drawer looking for scratch paper, and found an appointment reminder. He flipped it over, but when his pen touched paper, he stopped and read the note.

It was a reminder for his immunization shot.

He pinched his lower lip with his forefinger and thumb, and then smiled.

Could it really be that simple?

If Morpheus used hypnotic suggestions to suppress autonomic controls—could he fight their suggestion with a suggestion of his own—a virtual vaccine?

The idea had a certain symmetry to it, an elegance. Sean would implant a subconscious trigger in Serrano's mind, to act as a virtual immunization. When Morpheus inserted the hypnotic suggestion, Serrano's body would see it as a threat —and restore all autonomic functions to normal.

Not long ago, Sean would have dismissed such an idea as metaphysical rubbish. Now, the lines between science and mysticism had become razor thin. The possible and the impossible were no longer opposites, just variations of a common truth.

The big question was how to send the message to Serrano's subconscious. He'd never attempted a transfer through universal consciousness.

Sean closed his eyes and entered the meditation. Once he located Serrano, he found himself shaping and reshaping the message until it sounded right. Was it enough? Sean had no idea, but felt he'd done all he could.

Without the benefit of feedback, moving purely on instinct, Sean resigned himself to the lack of certainty.

He'd simply have to wait to see if Serrano stayed alive.

***

A South American Capital

Gualtiero Serrano slept soundly. His window open, the night's gentle breeze brushing against his face. The air was cool. He pulled the black-and-gold comforter a little higher around his neck. The king-size bed had four thick posts of ornately carved wood, matching the bedroom's heavy Spanish motif. Outside, the branches of a tree swayed, their movement casting eerie, animal shadows against the plaster wall. The whole scene seemed to come to life, as if it had been plucked from a child's nightmare. But to Serrano, it was home—and he slept soundly.

His steady, ratcheting, cigar-scented snore came in low and steady, reverberating against the high ceiling. His eyes darted back and forth beneath tightly closed lids. Gualtiero was dreaming.

The dream opened: a sheer granite wall, and the morning sun glaring off the stone. He reached for a small handhold, his muscles flexing, his thermodynamic rock-climbing shoes gripping the granite.

Earlier that night, Serrano had watched a documentary about a solo climb of El Capitan. Now, he was the one on the mountain face.

Below him, four climbers followed, their ropes weaving back and forth, slapping against the rock. Serrano moved effortlessly, displaying a strength that, in real life, he could have only dreamt about.

What Gualtiero couldn't see was the fifth climber, a Morpheus agent. Invisible, stealthy, and watching every move with cold calculation—waiting for the right opportunity.

Now, Serrano was in a jam—stretching for a handhold slightly beyond his reach. The agent smiled, and shifted the landscape to move the crack a few inches further away. Gualtiero strained to get a hold. Unable to extend far enough, he cursed, and unhooked his safety line.

The trap was set.

Serrano would soon exhaust all other options—leaving him with only one move.

He lunged at the crevice, his fingers scraping at its edge, his foot sliding from the narrow ledge. Then he felt his hand slip. He was in trouble.

Serrano fell.

Morpheus's plan unfolded like a script.

The rush of wind was shocking—and deafening. Serrano's body hurled down the granite face, his eyes fixed on the tree line below. His muscles twitched, his arms flailed. His hands grasping for something, anything. This was it. This was the end.

Gualtiero was about to die.

Although, if he'd been more self-aware in that moment—and, in all fairness, he was distracted by the fall—he would have noticed that his heart was no longer beating. For it was his heart, and not the imaginary fall, that would result in Serrano's death.

The agent watched, and smiled with satisfaction.

Seconds before impact, Serrano screamed—bolting upright in his bed. His heart thundering—but still beating. His chest heaved and his lungs drew in as much air as possible. Rivulets of sweat ran down his chest, and the thick dark hairs on his back bristled.

Gualtiero had experienced nightmares before, but nothing as visceral as this one. He kicked the dampened sheets off the bed. He fumbled for the bedside lamp, switched it on, and went to splash cold water on his face. He stared into the mirror. Though the icy fear was still lodged in his bones, he was glad to be alive.

***

The Morpheus agent was stunned. Serrano had woken up. But that was the problem.

It was a fairly standard assignment: take Serrano's dream scenario, manipulate the environment, and engineer a scheme to force the victim to dream about their own death. Adler's agents had complete discretion in choosing which autonomic function to inhibit. This agent chose Serrano's heart—a logical choice given his weight and lifestyle.

But somehow Serrano had disappeared from the dream. Had he escaped death as well? After replaying the incident in his mind, the agent was unable to find a mistake in their process. What happened?

In the Morpheus lab, he unhooked from the equipment and cursed under his breath. They'd better figure this out—and fast.

***

In his Geneva office, Adler Daemon spent the afternoon engrossed in Homo Deus: A Brief History of Tomorrow.

The book discussed techno-humanism, the idea that, in order to survive an increasingly technological world, man needed to become superhuman—to become a god. Adler smiled, amused as he turned the pages of the hardback. What would the author think about Morpheus—and its lethal marriage of technology and consciousness?

Curling his right foot under his left leg, he relaxed into the soft green leather chair. From this corner spot in his office, Adler enjoyed a breathtaking view of Lake Geneva and the distant mountains. As the afternoon sun gently pressed against his upturned face, he closed his eyes to drink in its warmth—this was a perfect day.

It wasn't meant to last.

His secretary entered with a flustered agent close on her heels. The agent got straight to the point: the attempt on Gualtiero Serrano's life had failed. Everything had been checked and double-checked beforehand, every protocol followed, but something had gone wrong—Serrano might still be alive.

Daemon listened without expression, while the agent braced himself for Adler's usual rebuke: soft, quiet, and totally eviscerating. None of that came. The agent waited nervously, unwilling to speak, unsure what to do with his hands.

"Run the diagnostics again," Adler said firmly. "And get confirmation from our team in South America. If he's alive, we'll make a second attempt tonight."

"I won't let you down."

Adler glared at the agent, his eyes cold and cutting.

"No. You won't—Jakob will replace you."

***

On a dusty soccer field in South America, two men watched an enthusiastic, most certainly alive, Gualtiero Serrano give a rousing campaign speech. The taller man stepped away, took out a satellite phone, and delivered the bad news to Morpheus.

In Geneva, Adler hurled his wine glass against a wall. This wasn't just a failure, it was an embarrassment. Morpheus's reputation was impeccable, but now it was forced to make an unprecedented second attempt. Gualtiero Serrano had become Adler's personal Rasputin.

That night in the laboratory, the tension was abnormally high. A technician fitted a headset onto Jakob—their best agent—and administered the right dose of the drug. Each agent's dosage was calibrated to optimize their individual performance.

But an hour later, Jakob woke and removed his headset. Shaking his head, he said, "It didn't work."

Chapter Twenty

Geneva, Switzerland

Adler Daemon had a fondness for rituals, patterns that made sense of the world around him. The unpredictable nature of his current situation had disrupted that order. It was driving him mad. This wasn't fate. Something else was at play. Either Serrano possessed some natural, innate capacity to counter their hypnosis—an extremely remote possibility in his view—or the man was getting help.

Had someone blocked access to Serrano's autonomic system? Thwarting Morpheus's actions? The idea soon hardened into a strong conviction. Adler summoned Jakob and gave him specific instructions.

"Tonight, go ahead with the assassination," he said. "Watch Serrano closely. Look for any anomalies in his subconscious or nervous system. Test each of the autonomic functions. Watch his pupils, breathing, even basic reflexes like sneezing. Anything that indicates his system reacts as expected, but then rejects the suggestion. I suspect that someone has implanted a resistance into Serrano's subconscious."

With his orders in hand, Jakob prepared for the evening, everything planned down to the smallest detail. But by the end of the night, their third attempt had collapsed into failure.

Serrano reveled in life's indulgences: cigars, liquor, fatty foods, and a contempt for exercise. Nonetheless, he was in remarkably good shape for a man that survived three assassination attempts. With his every labored breath, he squeezed Morpheus a little tighter. The election loomed—only days away—and time was running out.

The life of Serrano—or his death—meant absolutely nothing to Adler Daemon. It wasn't personal. But Morpheus had taken this contract—and now they needed to deliver. Adler rubbed the pad of his thumb against his palm. A nervous tic.

In hindsight, he'd made a mistake. Several lucrative contracts were coming on the market and Serrano's death would have made a nice little addition to Morpheus's portfolio. The business decision had been sound.

Unfortunately, the bastard was still alive.

***

After the third failure, Jakob and the team worked throughout the night, combing through the waveforms and data logs. While Adler waited for their report, he weighed his options.

Morpheus needed a win, or at least, to avoid a loss. If they couldn't kill Serrano, perhaps they should just kill their client. Quietly closing the contract—and erasing the problem. Adler nodded, satisfied with his contingency plan.

This would end in the death of Gualtiero Serrano—or, General Miguel Sopras.

Adler looked up when Jakob returned.

"We ran the diagnostics several times, but found nothing," Jakob began. "We almost gave up, but then one of the technicians noticed a glitch in the printout of the waveforms. They dismissed it as electrical noise."

Adler's eyes began to sparkle and he leaned forward. "But not you?" he asked smiling. "You thought it was something more?"

Jakob now wore a broad grin. "We pulled on that one thread until we discovered that the noise in the readings lined up with our hypnotic suggestions to his autonomic system. Statistically, this couldn't be random. After every attempt, Serrano's hypothalamus responded by first recognizing, and then cancelling our signal."

"Like an immune response? Automatic?"

Jakob thought about it for a moment. "Yes, but not a natural one. This was deliberate. His body responded as we expected, but then a secondary response canceled our hypnotic suggestion. The rejection behaves similar to the body's natural defense against foreign stimuli." He paused before looking up. "Serrano is being protected."

Adler stood, leaned on his desk, and stared blankly out the window. His facial expression appeared calm, but Jakob seemed to sense the brewing storm.

In some other time, Adler might have enjoyed all of this—the intellectual challenge, another move in a strategic biological chess match. This was not one of those times. Tensions were high, and Morpheus stood to lose everything. Adler needed those two lucrative deals.

"Stay on it," he said. "Find a way to stop them."

Jakob excused himself. Adler sat behind his desk. "Scheiße!" he cursed.

He could think of only one group with the skills to pull this off. Adler frowned and shook his head. But how? Sergei Petrokosov delivered a crippling blow to their laboratory, stole their equipment, and killed their technician. So how had Sean Hastings come this far?

No longer just an annoyance, they were now a threat. And every option needed to be considered. It was time to set aside the metaphysical games—and resort to brute force. Sean Hastings and his people had to be stopped—by whatever means necessary.

***

Montréal, Canada

The message blinked across her laptop screen. "Postponed: Today's budget meeting."

Olivia Abbott sighed, appreciative. She detested the administrative side of academia, but couldn't deny that modern university systems had become big business. She decided to take full advantage of her newly freed afternoon—and for Olivia—that meant shopping. Deciding to steal a couple of hours away for herself, she drove to the Les Cours Mont-Royal, a downtown shopping mall with high-end boutiques.

On the drive, she thought of Reinhold. Since his death, Olivia had held up fairly well, but whenever she heard a German accent, the memories came flooding back. Was any of it worth the horrible cost?

Pulling into a stall, she took a deep breath and straightened up. At least for today, she'd lose herself in a forest of clothes and cosmetics, the guilty pleasures of an urban life.

She stopped in front of a window mannequin wearing a long copper-colored dress with thin silver stripes. She eyed the dress, and giggled—surprised by how quickly her mind had flashed to thoughts of Sean. Another moment passed, and she shrugged before returning to the flow of blissful consumerism.

The automatic lights of the parking structure came on early, programmed for the shorter autumn days. Holding her key fob in one hand, her shopping bags in the other, she remotely unlocked her car. Olivia dropped the bags into the trunk before wedging herself in the narrow gap between her door and the inconsiderate red van parked next to her. Reaching for her door handle, she heard the sharp clack of a latch.

The sound of metal rollers.

In an instant, Olivia realized her mistake.

Two men in dark clothing and masks stepped out. Olivia was trapped between them. She fumbled for the alarm on her key fob, but the man on her left blocked her fingers from moving. Then a thick black vinyl glove smothered any attempt at screaming for help. In less than three-seconds, Olivia was lifted off her feet and pulled into the van. The only sound in the parking structure was the faint screech of metal rollers.

Olivia fought the urge to panic. They placed a black hood over her head. Her hands were restrained. She sat on the floor of the van, as it backed out of the stall. As it exited the building, no one spoke.With her hands bound behind her back, she struggled to maintain her balance.

Her mind raced with dark thoughts and images. Was she going to be raped? Murdered? No, she thought, that doesn't make sense. This was well executed—a professional job. This was about something else.

The van made a sharp right turn. Olivia toppled over, her face pressed against the floor, inhaling the pungent smell of rubber liner. She pushed herself upright. Over the pounding beat of her own heart, she heard an inner voice say—this was not random. Struggling to sit, she cursed. She wished Sean was with her. Then it hit.

Sean.

Of course. This had to be about Morpheus. What were they trying to prove?

Was this Adler's attempt at intimidation? Her mind reeled with question after question. And her anger grew. She wanted to scream. But then, beneath the black hood, she remembered the fate of poor Reinhold. Her emotions relapsed to fear.

Maybe they are going to kill me.

***

New York City

Sean stepped out of the shower and reached for a towel. A text message arrived on his phone. He swiped the screen a few times until his thumb was dry enough to be recognized. Looking down, he ran his fingers through his wet hair and tilted his head. It was sent from Olivia's phone, but the message only contained a single web link.

He tapped the screen.

A small video clip loaded. It showed Olivia, bound to a metal chair, a bare light bulb casting shadows across her face. Sean's stomach dropped, though he couldn't be sure of what he was looking at.

Olivia glanced up and to her right, as if receiving instructions. She nodded and then turned to the camera.

"Sean, I'm okay." Her voice lacked its usual strength and confidence.

A distorted, synthetic male voice said, "Olivia is unharmed. You are the key to keeping her safe. Undo what you did to protect Gualtiero Serrano, and Olivia will be released. We are watching."

The screen went black. Sean's left hand had unconsciously covered his mouth.

A flood of emotions rushed over him—all negative. In the past, he would have hurled his phone across the room, but now he stopped himself. He had to think. Taking a quick screenshot of the URL, he grabbed his coat, he needed to find Morgan.

In the back of the taxi, he looked out through the rain-streaked window and considered their demand. Was that even possible? He rested his forehead against the window and pressed his lips together. If he was being honest, he had no idea of how he'd protected Serrano in the first place. So how was he supposed to reverse this?

How do you 'un-immunize' someone?

He huffed, doubting such a word, or practice, even existed in the medical field.

After arriving at Morgan's office, they clicked on the URL link. It was no longer active. Sean's shoulders slumped. Morgan patted him on the back. "We have other options. My people still might be able to trace the source."

Morgan's secretary entered, bringing tea as a refreshment. Sean would have preferred something stronger. They waited for the call from the technicians.

"This is all my fault," Sean said, breaking the awkward silence. "If I'd only listened…if I hadn't been so damned arrogant." He rubbed his hands against his face. "If Olivia gets hurt because of me…" His voice trailed off, and Sean returned to staring at his hands.

A half hour later, Morgan jumped to answer his office line. All Sean could hear was a string of his utterances, "Uh-huh…I see…I understand."

When Morgan hung up, he looked as though he'd absorbed some great revelation. "Have you ever heard of an onion router?" Sean shrugged. "It's a form of encryption with many layers. That's how it gets its name—like peeling an onion, layer by layer. The tool erases the message, so if there was anything helpful on the video, we're out of luck. Fortunately, we should still be able to locate the original IP address."

Sean gritted his teeth. "I keep thinking there's something I must have missed, it just happened so fast." He stopped and looked up at Morgan. "Wait…did you say you can trace their location?"

Morgan nodded. "We should be able to come up with something. Until then, we need to stall. Like it or not, you'll need to find a way to fix this Serrano thing."

***

That night, standing in his kitchen, Sean closed his eyes and cursed.

How could he undo what he'd done with Serrano? It felt impossible, like trying to unsee something.

No easy internet search or reference guide would help solve this problem. He rubbed the back of his neck. He needed to focus, to find a starting point. If only for the time being, Sean needed to shove aside his worries about Olivia.

He opened his phone and found her picture—the one they took at the Lebanese restaurant. He smiled fondly. They'd made the poor waiter take almost a dozen shots before Olivia was happy. He remembered that night, her smile, her passion.

And then he had a thought.

He had protected Serrano through visualization. Sean imagined the body's natural defense, then pictured it responding to Morpheus's hypnotic suggestion as a threat. He then implanted those triggers into Serrano.

Now, to save Olivia, he had to visualize the opposite—to make Serrano's system accept the attack. One that would ultimately kill the man. Sean found the idea repugnant. How could this align with Ulgen Khan's grand vision: a possibility greater than you've ever imagined?

He stared at the photo again—the warmth of her smile, the sparkle in her eyes. He felt his resolve harden. It was clear—he knew what he needed to do.

One hour later, Sean opened his eyes and blinked—nothing more could be done. Whatever Gualtiero Serrano's fate, it was out of Sean's hands. Now, he'd wait for Morpheus's call.

***

Geneva, Switzerland

Jakob sat across the lacquered conference table from Adler Daemon, his fingers drumming the tabletop. The election was now two days away, and they could not afford another misstep.

"We should have killed Sean Hastings and been done with it." An uncharacteristic outburst for the normally reserved Dane. His frustration was something that Adler shared.

"Killing Hastings would have left Serrano invincible," Adler said with a sigh. "And we'd be no closer to understanding how this happened." Jakob said nothing, his expression skeptical.

Adler ignored him and continued, "Even if we had taken Hastings hostage, there's no guarantee he'd cooperate. Olivia was the leverage we needed—the logical move."

Jakob appeared to accept the reasoning, but still looked at him in an accusing manner.

Adler became defensive. It'd struck a chord. "What's with that look?" He bristled. "I know—how could I do this to Olivia? Well, she picked her side. Besides, I've got it under control." Adler walked toward the window, casting a distant stare at the street below. Although his smile was confident, he carefully tucked his trembling hand from Jakob's view.

Earlier that day, Adler received a call from Sergei Petrokosov, the former KGB agent. He reported that Hastings had given in—and Serrano's subconscious firewall was gone. Serrano was alone and exposed.

Before ending the call, Sergei pointedly asked, "What should I do with the girl?"

His first instinct was to kill. Not out of any particular malice toward Olivia, but because the clandestine world had taught him to be wary of loose ends—they always came back to haunt him.

Adler snapped. "Olivia is not to be harmed—under any circumstances! Do I make myself clear?"

After a brief pause, Sergei said he understood.

The call ended and Adler held the phone in his hand, unable to shake the uneasiness. He frowned. Sergei was headstrong, the classic loose-cannon type. He'd made his instructions clear, but could he trust Sergei with Olivia's safety? Despite Adler's obsession with ritual and order, he could sense that it was slipping away.

***

A South American Capital

With a crisp snap, Serrano shut the elegant box containing the solid-gold Rolex watch, and slid it into his bedside table drawer. A recent gift from a generous cartel. He smiled. Though beautiful, it would be unwise to display something so ostentatious in public, especially while campaigning as a man of the people.

Recent polls were running strong in his favor and his supporters, of both the legitimate and criminal varieties, were pleased. In just two days, he would be president.

Turning off his bedside lamp, he rolled into his eight-hundred-thread-count sheets. He lay on his bed and rehearsed his first hundred days in office, his vile grin cloaked in the darkness. A crackdown here, a relaxation of regulations there— ample rewards for the loyal, harsh retribution for his enemies. The thought of wielding absolute power soon lulled Serrano to sleep. His breath shallowed. A gentle snore emanated from his reddened nose.

On the ragged edges of Gualtiero Serrano's dream, Jakob waited patiently. Like an artist with a blank canvas, he would soon transform Serrano's dream into a masterpiece of death. Though the first clues were subtle, Jakob sensed a shift in the dream's dynamics. He smiled. Nothing would stand in their way tonight.

In the shadowy world of dreams, Gualtiero Serrano was about to die.

Chapter Twenty-One

Chicago, Illinois

Hayward James reached down and tapped his spoon against a crystal glass. Heads began to turn, and the chatter died down.

"Gentlemen, and lady," he began, "we've waited an eternity for this moment, and now we're close to achieving our goal. Thank you for your dedication to our cause—and to this great nation of ours."

Iron-ore smelting had made Hayward James a wealthy man. The flag-pin on his lapel was his constant reminder of the nation that had made it all possible.

The seven people present, formed the inner circle of an organization called Americans for Global Equity. Though their meetings were highly secretive, the people here didn't live or work in the shadows. They were public figures: running big businesses, on the boards of major corporations, attending society events, and supporting vast endowments for the arts, music, and literature. Across the country, on museum plaques and hospital wings, their names were well known.

"So we've got our own Manchurian candidate," joked the lanky man from Nevada, slapping the table for emphasis. His rat-a-tat laugh clashed with his appearance.

Hayward said, "No, Jim, you have it all wrong. It's more like planting a seed—nurturing and protecting its growth. America will soon benefit from the bounty of our labor."

Hayward looked around the room, inwardly enjoying his televangelistic parody.

"Let's just cut through the metaphorical bullshit. How's this gonna work?"

William "Buck" Debrew's face was wrinkled from years in the wind and sun. He wore a Stetson hat, blue jeans, and an absurdly large belt buckle that hid beneath his ample belly. With massive land holdings in Texas, Montana, and Wyoming, he was the nation's largest independent cattle rancher—making him the undisputed authority on bullshit.

Hayward bristled, but nodded—anything to mollify Buck's in-your-face persona. He shuffled his notes, while reflecting on how it all began.

Years ago, at a dreary charity ball, he'd joined two men discussing politics. They said America had lost its way, caught in a tangled web of rights: civil rights, women's rights, gay rights, who-knows-what rights. What about their rights?

"We used to build great big beautiful things," one man lamented, "now we just apologize for them. The liberals have put this country on its heels, undermining and ignoring a nation that did far greater good than harm."

"No empire in history," said the other man, "has been kinder to friend or foe than the good old US of A. Certainly not the empires of Egypt, Persia, Greece, or Rome."

"You're right," Hayward chimed in. "Not even our closest friends, the Brits. Through some misguided sense of fairness, we've abdicated that role."

Hayward smiled fondly, then returned to his notes.

"John D. Rockefeller," he began, invoking the legendary capitalist, "once said that if you want to succeed, you should strike out on a new path. We've done that, refusing to sit and wait for a leader—instead, we've made one of our own."

"You're talking about Laney," someone said.

"Exactly," Hayward responded. "We selected Senator Richard Laney as our president of the United States. Universally popular, electable, a little malleable—the perfect candidate. After winning the presidency, Richard was to unveil his true agenda—which is to say—our agenda."

He paused, allowing his expression to drop slightly.

"Sadly, times have changed. Over the past decade, Richard's attributes: moderation, reasonableness, and rationality are no longer electable traits. He's an anachronistic candidate, a man molded for a time long passed."

The room fell silent. A flicker of doubt crossed Hayward's face as he gathered the courage to unveil the real purpose behind today's meeting.

"Now," he continued, "he's being crowded out by a charismatic forty-seven-year-old from San Francisco, named Gavin Peakes. Since Mr. Peakes is likely to win the general election, I've decided to have Richard accept the nomination as his vice-president."

Grumbles and dissatisfaction spread across the room. They shared an expression that elites get when they fail to get their way. A special blend of disappointment, incredulity, and disdain; perfected after attaining a certain level of net worth.

"How does any of this help?" asked the only woman present.

"Goddamn it Hayward!" Buck shouted. He was losing his patience—and he wasn't the only one.

"A couple of months back," Hayward said, his voice steady. "I was directed to a company called Morpheus Research. And I'm convinced we have our solution."

Over the next few minutes, Hayward spun such a fantastic tale that even Buck Debrew was left speechless. In describing Morpheus; Hayward highlighted their iron-clad discretion, solid record, and latest dark offering.

"So," said the lanky man. "Peakes wins—Morpheus kills Peakes—Laney becomes president?"

Hayward nodded. "It sets into motion the US chain-of-command protocols. An elegant work-around for an otherwise fickle and unpredictable electorate."

He scanned the faces at the table.

"Now," he said, setting his papers aside, "if there are no further questions, I'll need a unanimous vote to proceed."

***

New York City

Still wearing his suit, Sean lay on top of his comforter, and searched the ceiling for answers. He wasn't sure how long he'd been there.

Serrano is probably dead.

The thought sat heavy as a stone. With his hands folded on his stomach, Sean wrestled with his guilt. He felt responsible for Serrano's death, but anyone would have done the same to save the life of someone they loved. Resting an arm on his forehead, he tried to recall a quote—something about when good men fail to act.

It wasn't just Serrano's death that bothered him. It was the fact that he'd been naïve, stupidly naïve. It should have been obvious that this gift might come with impossible choices. Morgan had certainly tried to warn him. Saving Olivia was an easy decision, but would the next one be as clear? He blew out a long breath. Playing God had consequences.

A text message chimed on his phone and he looked at the sender. It was Keenan. For the past week, Sean had been avoiding him, though he wasn't sure why. Olivia's abduction seemed like a good reason, but he knew the truth ran deeper.

Sean was in over his head. And his decisions had only made things worse. Olivia's kidnapping, Abbie's nightmare, and Serrano's death were taking a toll. Guilt and turmoil gnawed at him relentlessly.

The phone rang again; but this time Morgan's name appeared on the caller ID.

"We got a hit," he said, when Sean answered. "An approximate location from the IP address."

Still mired in thought and regret, he wasn't sure what Morgan was talking about —but embraced his enthusiastic tone. "Great, now what?"

"We've narrowed it down to a town called Brossard—across the Saint Lawrence from Montreal."

"We need to get her back!" Sean blurted, his voice carrying all the hope, frustration, and fears he'd coiled inside.

"We will," Morgan said.

In spite of his reassuring tone, Sean sensed something else—conflict, evasiveness? He waited for more, but nothing came. Sean had long suspected that Morgan had his secrets, though he wasn't sure if they concerned the group, or if it was some unrelated deal. About to press him for details, he stopped when Morgan spoke again. "I have access to resources that can help."

"What do you mean?"

"Through my firm—I have an associate that works with private contractors."

"I guess I'm not following."

"Mercenaries, Sean. Ex-military, private contractors."

Sean's brow raised. Access to mercenaries? How the hell did this fit into Morgan's image of a respectable businessman.

"Think about it, Sean. Olivia was taken by professionals; everything they've done reaffirms that. We'll need to respond with skilled people of our own." Morgan waited for his response, but only silence followed. "I'll handle the details," he continued. "Just tell me when they contact you."

Sean let the phone slip from his ear. He walked toward the window, the carpet soft and reassuring under his feet. How had this small group gone from working on human consciousness to mobilizing a paramilitary unit? What the hell had he gotten himself into? He brushed the curtain aside, casting his gaze across the city: traffic snarls, street lights, a distant siren.

Morgan waited for a response.

"All right," Sean said, "Do whatever you have to do."

He scratched at the prickly feeling on his scalp. There was something about Morgan that simply refused to add up. Still, he needed his help.

"I'll call you when they contact me."

***

Later, in his high-rise office, Morgan swiveled his chair and scooted it closer to the desk. He took off his aviator-style glasses and gently set them on a legal pad. The hour was late, and the outer office was empty and quiet. The only sound came from the vibration of the city itself—taxi horns and ambulance sirens—muffled but still piercing the double-paned windows. He rubbed his burning eyes and his salt-and-pepper eyebrows. How much longer could he keep this up? Was there no end to what they asked of him?

Morgan thought about his call with Sean. How was he holding up? Any signs of cracking? He figured it had to be tough on the guy. He couldn't imagine what Sean was going through; the loss of his job, the threats to his daughter, Olivia—even his understanding of reality. He exhaled and returned his thoughts to the call. Had Sean responded normally? In light of the circumstances, perhaps.

Nevertheless, Morgan worried.

He slid open the second drawer of his desk. The top looked like a solid shelf, but in its center was a recessed keypad. His fingers swiftly entered the eight-digit code, and then lifted the lid.

Inside the drawer was an encrypted smartphone—and a tan-colored Sig Sauer military-grade handgun. He took out the phone. Holding it in front of his face, he mentally rehearsed what he was about to say.

The directory had only one entry.

"It's me," he said softly into the receiver. "No, not yet. But we may have a problem."

Chapter Twenty-Two

The very sound sent a chill through Olivia. It felt eternal. No matter how many times she told herself that this was only a psychological game, a ploy on Adler's part, when she heard the steel door slam, her chest tightened and a lone tear trickled down her cheek. Olivia felt hollowed, as if her identity had been stripped away, leaving her spirit bare and vulnerable. Emotions were the only things under her control. Everything else—her life, her future, perhaps even her death—was entirely at the whim of some faceless captors.

In the unfinished concrete room, Olivia shifted uncomfortably in the chair. She looked longingly at the simple cot in the corner, ignoring the onset of stiffness. The light bulb, still swinging after being bumped by one of the men, tossed shadows against the cement walls. She struggled to think clearly. Her ragged breath drew in the chalky smell of damp concrete. It was cold and the bare metal of the chair against her skin made it feel even colder. How long had she been here? When would they return?

She worried about the older kidnapper, the one with the thick Russian accent. There was something dangerous in his eyes. An uncomfortable stare—as if she wasn't a living, human being.

Her lip quivered.

***

Richard Laney's presidential dream had come to an end. It was official—and undeniable. At the national convention, as the balloons descended, the cheers went up, and the first bars of some co-opted pop song blared, Dick Laney put on a brave face. Tonight, standing next to his party's presidential nominee, he was second best, a man just outside the spotlight.

In the convention hall, the speakers blared:

"Meet Richard Laney, the next vice president of the United States of America."

Hundreds of miles away, in the exclusive Washington neighborhood of Georgetown, a much quieter event was taking place. Bentleys and Cadillacs were parked in precise rows beneath the glow of a street lamp. The mature elm trees swayed in the gentle breeze. Drivers in dark suits stood by, casually gabbing and smoking cigarettes.

Inside the restored nineteenth-century house, Vivaldi's The Four Seasons wafted through the marble-floored rooms. Holding chilled champagne flutes, the elegantly dressed men and women formed a circle.

"Tonight is truly a big night for us," the host said excitedly, "a toast, to our success…to the Americans for Global Equity!"

***

Sean heaved four grocery bags onto his kitchen island, and rubbed the reddened grooves the plastic had carved into his fingers. A normal part of New York living, today's walk to a neighborhood market was a chance to burn away some stress. As he prepared to stock the refrigerator, he set his phone down on the granite countertop. For the first time, he noticed the alert.

Damn it.

Sean took a deep breath, his heart pounding, and settled onto a kitchen stool. He tapped on the link, his leg bouncing in nervous rhythm.

The video opened to the image of Olivia's face. She looked all right—at least physically. The camera panned to the left, and revealed a figure wearing a black hooded cloak and an ornate golden half-mask. In spite of the seriousness of the situation, Sean couldn't suppress a slight smirk. The man looked like he'd just walked off the set of Eyes Wide Shut.

"Don't lose sleep over Serrano," the synthesized voice began. "You've done well. However, there is another condition—an exchange—you for Olivia. Agree, and she will be released unharmed. Reply for details."

The screen went black. Sean continued to stare at the phone, muttering a curse under his breath. Another condition—of course. Changing the terms came as no surprise. Olivia had been leverage, forcing Sean to strip away Serrano's protection. But now, as long as Sean was alive, he was a threat to Morpheus's business. Being their primary target, he had no illusions about what this demand would mean. The exchange would put him in mortal danger—but at least Olivia would be safe.

Sean pulled a container of juice from the plastic bag and poured a glass. Taking a large gulp, he was struck by two ideas.

First, why hadn't Morpheus just killed him—like they did to Serrano—by using a dream incursion? Why go through this pretense? After a few puzzled seconds, he swallowed hard, a cold realization set in. Maybe they had tried—and failed? He rhythmically tapped his lower lip, and shook his head. He still didn't understand how any of this worked. Was he simply wired differently? He visualized their frustration—and grinned.

Second, maybe he could turn this to his advantage? Adler must be feeling pretty confident by now. The situation seemed back under his control and he was free to dictate events going forward. Sean smiled. That arrogance might be his opening.

He mentally worked through all the ways the transfer might play out. Would they kill him outright, or hold him for interrogation? He considered Morgan's offer of mercenary support, and soon, a plan had formed in his mind.

He spent another half hour running through the knowns and unknowns. Though nothing was assured, for now he was satisfied.

He dialed Morgan's number. If this was going to work, he needed help.

***

Geneva, Switzerland

No one paid much attention to the single-story gray stone building located behind Morpheus Research. More than two hundred years ago it had stored wine and cheese for the local markets. Now, it sat empty, fronting a small alleyway that saw almost no automotive traffic. An unassuming building, easily blending into the background. People rarely gave it a second thought. That is, no one but Adler Daemon.

He wasn't interested in its historical significance, for it had none. Hardly UNESCO heritage material. What Adler saw—what he absolutely loved—was its close proximity to his office building.

He asked Armand to acquire the property through one of their shell corporations. The two buildings, separated by a mere six feet, were perfect for Adler's plan. After the purchase, a secret tunnel was constructed connecting the two. The gray stone building became Morpheus's off-site research facility—and underground escape route.

Adler paused at the tunnel door and pressed his thumb against the biometric scanner. The electronic latch buzzed open. Inside the renovated barrel room, Jakob was hunched over his computer, typing away between bites of a luncheon baguette. Startled, he forced down his last bite with a sip of orange Fanta.

"Adler," he said, still swallowing. "I didn't expect you."

"Yes, well…I wanted to discuss something with you," Adler said, his tone contemplative. "Besides, I needed to be sure the tunnel door functioned properly."

Adler began walking around the room, mindlessly touching things, pretending to examine various equipment. Jakob stopped to observe his curious behavior.

"How do you think they do it?" Adler finally asked. "Have you ever wondered?"

Jakob blinked for a moment, and then realized he was asking about Sean Hastings.

By now, Adler had reached the far side of the room. Shaped like a half barrel, with red bricks lining the walls and forming an arched ceiling, the open space created an acoustically clear sound. Adler's soft mumbling could easily be heard at the other end.

"They started with nothing," he continued. "Then Sergei took what little they had. What is it, some innate ability to breach the human subconscious?"

Jakob remained quiet, not wanting to interrupt Adler.

"How is it that this—hack stockbroker—has disrupted so much of our work? Is he blessed by the divine?"

Jakob chuckled softly. "Divine inspiration, Adler? An atheist referring to God's design?"

Jakob was their most talented agent, but without Morpheus's technology, he couldn't do a dream incursion. No one had been able to explain how Sean Hastings achieved similar results without any supporting equipment. Still, to deny the truth would be foolish.

Jakob sat up. "I think there's a much simpler explanation. Probably something they stumbled onto—or a side effect of combining Amplius with some other drug.

Strange drug interactions happen every day."

Adler stopped pacing, and smoothed his tie before lowering himself onto a small swivel stool. "You might be right. But if this is something we've missed, we must correct it. We can't allow flaws in our system." Adler began swiveling his stool back and forth like an unruly child. A curious Jakob stared at this disturbing glimpse into his employer's psyche.

"I've instructed Sergei to take Sean in exchange for Olivia's release," Adler finally said. "I have to know what Hastings knows." Then Adler grinned. "Either we'll find out…or he'll die."

Back in his office, the rumination continued. Despite having devoted his career to proving the existence of universal consciousness, he was blind to its presence. Adler had fixed on an idea of what consciousness looked like, its shape and substance.

Sean Hastings wasn't it.

Adler had come to think of universal consciousness as an abstract term, some far-off concept, a theory that might never be proven. Oblivious to the irony, Adler was incapable of recognizing its actual presence. It never crossed his mind that lowly Sean Hastings might be living proof of his most cherished academic theory.

Adler had become trapped in a paradigm of his own making. Forced to react defensively, to dismiss it as some form of trickery. A parlor trick perpetrated by a Wall Street charlatan.

Chapter Twenty-Three

New York City

As soon as Morgan picked up, Sean asked, "How'd it go?"

"Not quite like calling a plumber, but all things considered, finding a mercenary wasn't all that hard. And you?"

"Well, they've made another demand."

Morgan waited quietly, while Sean went through the details: the surrender, the exchange, Olivia's freedom. He jumped ahead of Morgan's objection by laying out the details of his plan, step by step. Yes, he acknowledged, the risks were high, but if it worked, the game would tilt in the group's favor.

"What makes you think they'll actually let Olivia go?"

"A gut feeling," Sean said, knowing how feeble that sounded. "It's something I picked up in universal consciousness. I'm sure they enjoyed forcing my hand with Serrano, but hurting Olivia had never been part of the plan. I sense that Adler still cares about her."

"Do you think he knows about the two of you?"

"I'm sorry?" Sean sputtered.

Morgan laughed. "For two exceptionally clever people, you and Olivia are really terrible at hiding your feelings. Honestly, none of us ever understood why you bothered."

Sean was grateful that his cell phone couldn't reveal the sheepish, schoolboy grin that had spread across his face. Hearing Morgan confirm it out loud, somehow made it feel more real.

"So," he said, returning to the task at hand. "What do you think? Will it work?"

"Maybe," Morgan muttered. "But first, I want to take a precaution—a new sub-dermal tracking device. It transmits to satellite using short, irregular bursts. They say it's virtually undetectable." Morgan paused for a beat. "Are you sure you're up for this? If you're right about Daemon's feelings for Olivia, then that's what's kept her alive. I wouldn't count on receiving the same courtesy."

"I know, but what other option is there? Adler thinks he's got us on the ropes—that we're about to surrender. We can use that to buy some time."

Sean cleared his throat. "It's curious. I can understand their need to resolve this, but this feels rushed—like there's a deadline they need to meet. Whatever it is they're planning, it must be something big. I'll get a better idea once I'm taken. Right now, I can only be certain of one thing—they want to keep me alive long enough to confirm that every one of their problems will die with me."

***

"Ouch! What the f…?" Sean rubbed the underside of his left arm, just above the elbow. He glowered at Morgan and shifted on the exam table, crinkling the liner paper underneath.

"Why do they always say this might hurt?"

Morgan responded with a simple shrug, finding the situation a little too amusing for Sean's preference.

"Dr. Toliver explained that the device needed to be inserted a little deeper to avoid detection by touch. More than you expected?" He smirked. Sean nodded in equal parts of annoyance and pain.

Dr. Toliver had built a lucrative practice in the field of dermatology: poking, prodding, piercing, freezing, and burning his way through the intolerable imperfections of his well-heeled Upper East side clientele. Morgan had a long history with Toliver and trusted his discretion.

Sean nodded politely, still curious about how Morgan gained access to such high-tech surveillance equipment.

"Keep the gauze on the puncture for an hour or so, and you should be fine. Give me a call if any redness develops over the next couple of days…otherwise, you're good to go."

Toliver smoothed down the edges of the adhesive tape against Sean's arm, and removed his latex gloves with a sharp snap.

***

The wheels of the regional jet touched down at the Montréal-Pierre Elliott Trudeau International Airport. It was just past four in the afternoon. Sean had been instructed to be at the Parc Jean-Drapeau at six sharp, and wait by the reflecting pool on the south end of the Biosphere Environment Museum.

Unsure about how to pack for a prearranged abduction, he traveled light—just a small leather bag with a handful of toiletries. After clearing Canadian border control, he made his way to the taxi stand. The rush hour snarl was already underway and Sean anxiously checked his watch. The knot in his stomach tightened. He voiced his concern to the driver, who responded in a blend of French and English wrapped in a thick Vietnamese accent. Sean waited with a vacant expression, not sure whether he'd been understood. Seconds later, the cab was darting between lanes and slipping through yellow lights. They crossed the Jacques Cartier Bridge, the Saint Lawrence River gleamed in the late afternoon sun. The taxi continued south on the Chemin Macdonald until reaching its destination.

Hair-raising ride notwithstanding, Sean felt relieved when he glanced at his watch. 5:35 p.m.

The Parc Jean-Drapeau stretched across two man-made islands—the Île Sainte Hélène and the Île Notre-Dame—both built for Expo 67. When he stepped from the taxi, Sean took a moment to picture what it must have been like during the Summer of Love. He wistfully smiled at the architecture, the oddly retro-futuristic vision so popular in that era.

He glanced around to get his bearings, and his eyes fell upon the six-story Alexander Calder sculpture called L'Homme. Standing in the distance, it looked like an alien ship against the Montreal skyline.

***

Meanwhile, not far from the park, Olivia fought to stay upright in the back of the moving van. Blindfolded, with her hands tied behind her back, she had no way of anticipating the turns or sudden stops. Cursing, she whipped her legs around, thrashing at whatever, or whoever was nearby. Then her right foot hit something solid. Olivia pushed herself upright and braced a leg against the hump of the wheel well.

***

Sean reached the rendezvous spot—a quadrilateral reflecting pool near the entrance of the Biosphere dome. He checked his watch. Fifteen minutes to go. He killed time by reading a tourist plaque—but the words didn't register.

Are they watching me?

The harder he tried to blend in, the more conspicuous he felt. Scratching at the tracker in his arm, he turned back to the plaque.

"The park is accessible by foot, car, rail, or by boat."

Plenty of ways in—and out. A reluctant smile formed. Morgan was right, these men were polished and precise.

***

The van pulled into the stall and stopped with a sudden jerk. Olivia lost her footing and tumbled forward. One of her captors helped her upright, removed the blindfold, and snipped the zip tie that bound her wrists. Then they sat, quiet and motionless in the back of the van. Olivia did the same. The captors offered no instructions, no reassurances—nothing about what was to come. She exhaled slowly. Though she'd been treated well, these men weren't a particularly chatty bunch.

***

Sean's phone buzzed, and he flinched.

"Walk to the north end of the Biosphere. At Stationnement P-12, you will see two identical red vans parked a few spaces apart. Get in the van on your right and Olivia will be released. Leave now."

It was time. A sudden wave of fear swept over him. His breath stuttered, and he could hear his pulse pounding away. For a brief moment, he was tempted by an urge to turn and run.

This was a bad idea.

Doubt crept in. Suddenly he was unsure about everything. Had he misread Daemon's feelings for Olivia? Would they discover the tracking device? Would they kill him right away? The rush of adrenaline wasn't helping his mind—and he raced through every worst case scenario. Would Abbie grow up fatherless?

Damn it. Stop.

They say there can be no courage without fear. He was here for Olivia, and because of Morpheus's callous disregard for life, and the murders of Reinhold and Serrano. Slowing his breath, he exaggerated a long, controlled exhale. If this was where fate steered him—then so be it.

As he followed the path around the globe-shaped museum, his shoulders pulled back and his chest rose. The early panic eased into a steady confidence. Fight over flight.

The van had backed into the stall. The sliding doors of the two vans now faced one another. As he approached, two masked men waited inside. They didn't bark orders, or jump out to grab him. No aggressive actions whatsoever. They simply sat there.

Confused, Sean identified himself, and with a resigned shrug, he climbed inside. One of the men secured his wrists with zip ties, the second prepared an ominous looking black hood.

***

Within seconds, the other van's door flew open. One of the kidnappers extended a hand to help Olivia down.

The late-afternoon sun shone directly in her eyes, leaving her squinting and disoriented. As soon as she stepped from the van, the door slammed shut behind her. Tires squealed as the van sped away, leaving Olivia in a cloud of dust. Standing alone, she reached up and shielded her eyes against the harsh light. As they adjusted, she started to make out the other red van nearby.

***

The first van peeled away, Sean's head snapped up. Olivia was right there, only forty feet away. Thank God. She's safe. He opened his mouth, ready to shout to her, but heard the metallic click of a pistol being cocked. He froze in place. Sean held his breath. She needed to see that he was here—before the black hood went on, before they could shut him away—possibly forever.

Then Olivia turned and her eyes met his. Before she could speak, his captors slammed the van's door. Sean dropped his head and fell into despair. Olivia was only forty feet away, yet the distance felt vast.

Will she understand? Does she know that I love her?

A thick, oppressive hood came down over his head. The van rushed away, and Sean knew there was no going back. His fists clenched. A trickle of sweat ran down his cheek. Beneath the dark hood, his world was fading away. His resolve shaken, his body jostled by the movement of the van.

Sean struggled to maintain both an emotional and physical balance.

***

The instant she recognized Sean, Olivia broke into a full sprint, screaming his name and waving her arms. But the van had already accelerated, leaving behind a spray of gravel in its wake. She took a few more steps before surrendering to the futility of the situation. Her pace began to slow, and then stopped as the van—and Sean—disappeared beyond the tree line. The parking lot was empty.

It took her less than a minute to work it out. Her trembling arms clutched at her torso. Whatever fleeting relief she'd felt at being freed, it had turned to anguish.

Sean had put himself in danger—and all to save her.

Olivia needed to contact Morgan. She took a deep breath to steel her nerves. She spotted a teenager sitting on the rim of the reflecting pool, earbuds in, sandwich in hand. Olivia approached and stopped in front of him. He looked up to see her warm smile.

"Hi," she said softly, "could I borrow your phone?"

The teen blinked: confused, wide-eyed, a little in awe. Then, with a coquettish giggle, she added, "I think I lost mine."

He nearly dropped his sandwich as he fumbled to hand over his phone.

He would have let her call China.

Chapter Twenty-Four

Adler Daemon typed in the secure IP address and waited for the connection. The early sun had angled across his kitchen table, catching the steam from his coffee. Adler appeared relaxed this morning. At home, comfortably dressed in a Real Madrid T-shirt and a pair of light-blue pajama pants, he bit into a fresh chocolate croissant. A copy of the Le Matin newspaper lay folded next to his coffee cup.

The laptop's progress bar finished, and the screen came to life. In a dimly lit room, the image of Sean Hastings, handcuffed to a metal chair, appeared in view. A smile of satisfaction crossed Adler's face.

Sergei had suggested using the high-definition feed to allow Daemon to watch the interrogation in real time. Adler agreed, not only for the voyeuristic thrill, but because he doubted Sergei's capacity to comprehend and relay any technical information Sean might provide.

Inside the cramped concrete room, the restraints bit into his wrists as he tried to stretch. The clank of metal against metal. How much time had passed since they left the park? Maintaining his bearings would be a challenge.

An older man with a thick Russian accent, or one of his subordinates, had been taking turns asking the same questions again and again. "Which government agencies are helping you? What technology do you use to dream travel?"

They were throwaway questions—Morpheus already knew the answers. But as the hours passed, it dawned on Sean that these were only meant to wear him down —a prelude to the actual interrogation. The thought was demoralizing.

A few minutes later, a burly man in his early thirties came in, carrying an army cot under his arm as though it were a paperback. His cheek was scarred, his forearms absurdly thick and tattooed with various insignias and words written in Cyrillic. He removed Sean's handcuffs, pointed to the cot, and muttered something incomprehensible. Then he left.

Sean rubbed his aching hands. He moved to sit on the edge of the cot, careful not to lie down. Though he was exhausted, he couldn't risk falling asleep. He had to get his blood flowing. This could be his only chance to see what Dr. Daemon was planning.

In spite of the less than ideal surroundings, he would need to focus to enter universal consciousness. He took a long, deliberate breath, but concentration eluded him. Even the slightest sound made him jump. Every muffled noise, every creak of the air vent caused his eyes to snap open.

When will they return?

Exhausted and dangerously close to collapsing, he closed his eyes again and repeated the mantra. After a minute, it seemed like things were working—a soft, placid wave began flowing over him. A welcome sensation.

Then—nothing. Sean toppled over, overcome by sleep.

When he woke, he was being hoisted like a sack of flour. The big man picked him up with ease, and plunked him back into the metal chair. Sean blinked, wondering how long he'd been out. Would there be another chance?

Seconds later, the door opened. Sergei had returned.

Shit!

Sean looked at their faces and his chest tightened. Something had changed. The mood shifted. It felt like the temperature in the room had dropped ten degrees. In Sergei's expressionless face, Sean saw a new resolve, an eagerness to end this tiresome game.

Sergei asked, "How did you keep Serrano from harm?"

It was straight to the point—although Sean thought the term "harm" was a gross understatement. Seeing no reason to be evasive—they wouldn't believe him anyway—Sean went with the truth.

"I connected with him in a form of consciousness. Then I warned his subconscious about the attack."

Sergei Petrokosov stared at him dispassionately. He had spent a lifetime interrogating all manner of spies, double agents, and organized crime bosses—people with deep secrets, bent on deception and subterfuge. To Sergei's mind, these were his people: fighting to withhold names and dates, locations and plans, real tangible information. Now, his expression seemed to ask—was that even an answer?

"Who else can do this?"

"I suppose we all can," Sean said. "I mean—it's part of the human experience. Something we've forgotten, along with our true identity."

Sergei's sigh was heavy with frustration. The Russian's instincts may have told him that Sean wasn't trying to be funny or evasive, but then what was this? Were these the correct answers, a string of lies, or the rantings of a lunatic?

Sergei's phone rang. Adler's name was displayed on the caller ID. He stepped away and took the call in the next room. When he returned, his expression had darkened.

"Who else," he repeated sternly, "besides you?"

"I told you—"

Sean screamed out in pain.

The man with the tattoos had twisted Sean's right arm back at an unnatural angle. His vision blurred. He bit his cheek. Sure that his shoulder had dislocated, he started to yell out, but stopped, not daring to say another word. His eyes watered. The metallic taste of blood lingered on his tongue.

Sergei leaned in until his face was mere inches from Sean's.

"Again," he said softly. "Who can do this also?"

Sean fought his panic, sensing the other man was still standing behind him— eager for Sergei's next command.

Decades ago, Sergei studied physiology. When he joined the KGB, he applied his anatomical knowledge as an effective interrogation tool. Most of his classmates went the usual route of using drugs, electricity, or even crude beatings, but Sergei chose to perfect his method of moving limbs in a way that caused excruciatingly painful soft tissue damage.

Like physical therapy—only in reverse.

"Wait…wait…don't!" Sean pleaded. His voice raspy, his breath labored. Sergei offered a thin, insincere smile. Sean's initial shock passed and settled into a steady, throbbing agony. For the first time since the park, he doubted his plan. He took several deep breaths.

Sergei's patience had worn thin. After another signal, Sean's arm was bent backward at the elbow, hyperextending the joint—threatening to tear. He grimaced, bracing for the dreadful sound of snapping bones and popping cartilage. But there was only silence, except for Sean's muffled scream. They'd stopped short of doing actual damage. Sean's soft whimper brought a perverse smile to Sergei's face.

"Synovial, condyloid, ball and socket…I could go on. Did you know the human body has three hundred joints? I think you did not know that."

Sean's face was coated in sweat, his nose dripping snot. He took Sergei's question as rhetorical, and slowly nodded his defeat.

"I…I don't know of anyone else that can do this. At least no one in our group."

Sergei looked at Sean and exhaled in disappointment. He glanced at the burly man, as if to say, "These amateurs break far too easy." Nevertheless, Sergei must have been glad that this would soon come to an end. From the beginning, he'd been perfectly clear—he disliked these people—they were all nuts.

He leaned toward Sean. "How did you protect Serrano? Can you do it again?"

"It happened by accident," he said, his lip quivering. "I was deep in meditation, but then slipped into this strange place—I think it was universal consciousness."

Sergei's phone rang and he gritted his teeth—Adler again. After cursing in Russian, he stepped into the other room. The other man followed. As Sergei exited, he looked over his shoulder and sarcastically said, "Wait here."

Alone in the room, Sean's heart hammered against his chest. Each heartbeat radiating pain throughout his shoulders and arms. Any second now, the door would open and it would start again. Sean waited—the anticipation nearly as bad as the pain.

But minutes passed—and no one came. He forced himself upright. This was his last chance.

Sean began to meditate—using breathwork to block the pain. Gradually, his awareness opened up until he sensed every element in the room: muffled sounds from outside, vibrations from the vent fan, the temperature of the air on his skin. His awareness widened, the pain subsided. Sean focused on finding Adler Daemon.

Colors began bleeding into view, building from all sides. Fractals, geometric shapes, kaleidoscopic images. These were now familiar to Sean. A sinking sensation going deeper and deeper until the warmth enveloped him—a feeling of great bliss. A vibrational energy ran up his spine. He felt incredibly alive.

He had entered another dimension, one that defied terrestrial references like time or space. Sean found Adler Daemon. It lasted a split second—or it might have been an hour—in truth, he had no idea.

He snapped back into his body as the foggy haze began to lift. Shuddering at what he'd learned.

Serrano's death was nothing more than a demonstration, a sample of their work. But killing Serrano was only the beginning.

Morpheus was going to assassinate the president-elect of the United States. Sean exhaled sharply, never imagining something so brazen.

Now, the potential consequences of Morpheus's ambition dawned on him. Left unchecked, they could impact geopolitical events for years to come. Tipping the global scales in favor of every despot, autocrat, and nefarious character with an ability to pay. How many fairly elected leaders would inexplicably die of "natural causes" in the years to come? Sean's shackled hands clenched until the metal began to cut into his skin.

What happened to Adler Daemon, the idealist who once hoped to raise the level of human consciousness? That man seemed gone forever. Reduced to the worst elements of human behavior. Sean needed to expose him for the vile predatory creature he'd become. With renewed determination, he scanned the concrete room.

First, I need to get free.

The door opened and the two men returned. Not surprisingly, Sergei looked even more agitated. He barked orders in Russian, before turning around. Sean saw the pistol tucked into his belt. Sergei pulled a chair directly in front of Sean. The other man moved behind him.

"We start again, Hastings."

Sean swallowed hard. He fought the wave of nausea that rose from his stomach. He trembled at the thought of his limbs being torqued to their limits, but Sergei's gun hinted at a more lethal outcome. The time for questions would soon be over.

Then, two canisters rolled in. The soft clinking sound of metal on concrete. Sean looked up, confused.

What are those doing here?

Then the steel door flew wide open and slammed against the wall. Sergei spun around and reached for his weapon. Sean tried to duck, but came up hard against the restraints. The burly man leapt forward to block the doorway, but fell backwards with two gunshots to his chest. Sergei shouted in Russian.

Three men burst in wearing full body armor and gas masks. Sergei tried to use Sean as a shield—grabbing at his neck and raising the gun to his head. The soldier in the middle came in low—firing off three short bursts. One shot to the head. Two to the chest.

Sean felt Sergei's tight grip weaken and then release. The Russian's pistol fell to the floor and clanked against the concrete. Sergei was dead before the last two bullets hit his chest. His body slid down the concrete wall, and slumped motionless on the floor. A bright streak of blood smeared across the wall. Sean's eyes were wide.

Dazed, he watched the men check the bodies. A voice was shouting through the haze. "Sir, are you all right?" Choking and coughing from the gas, he nodded to indicate that he was okay. Two soldiers lifted him by the arms. He winced at the pain from his battered shoulder, but he was grateful to escape the gas.

Once safely in the next room, he walked around a couple of bodies that lay on the floor. Sergei's perimeter guards, he assumed. "How'd you guys find me?" His voice was scratchy and irritated from the gas.

"You can thank Mr. Maxwell for that. We got your location from the tracking device in your arm, but the real credit goes to one of Mr. Maxwell's people. They tracked the IP address to this location and hacked an intercept of the video signal. Once it was up and running, we were pretty amazed to watch things in real time."

***

Geneva, Switzerland

Sergei was dead. Sean was free. And Adler had watched it all with a lukewarm cup of coffee and a half-eaten pastry by his side. He could have been angry, or discouraged by the setback, but it wasn't in his nature to sulk. Wasted energy.

When the soldiers cut the feed, his screen went black. Adler continued to stare at the empty monitor, stitching together the fragments of what he'd just learned.

First, Morgan Maxwell was better funded and better connected than he had suspected. And the use of a paramilitary unit showed his willingness to use those resources. Adler would never underestimate him again.

Second, Sean wasn't using technology at all. He was some kind of savant—some metaphysical freak. However he was doing this, none of it was of practical use to Morpheus. It also meant that Adler could safely reason the threat would end with Sean's death.

Fortunately, nothing in the video indicated that their plan for the US presidential assassination had been compromised. Adler assumed he could safely proceed. But then he paused. Sean remained a threat, and Adler decided to make adjustments to his plan to counter the uncertainty.

Sergei's death, however, was a real problem. Before long, his identity would be traced back to his country's intelligence agency and then, possibly, to Morpheus. Adler would have his staff terminate any links and erase all connections.

Which left Sean Hastings—a problem in need of a permanent solution. Adler gently shook his head. This time, it would be different—nothing elaborate—just a simple knife or bullet would do.

Uncomplicated. Assured. Lethal.

He rubbed his upper lip as he went back over things. Satisfied with the soundness of his plan, he stood and looked down at his unfinished croissant. Adler frowned. The morning's events had killed his appetite.

***

The day after being rescued, Sean returned to his apartment. Reclining on his sofa, he took a moment to look around. The curtains, chairs, even the fruit bowl on the counter, exactly as he'd left it. Nothing had changed.

But was the same true of Sean?

His ordeal wasn't easily brushed aside. The images ran through his mind: the paramilitary unit, the brutal death of Sergei's crew, the torture, the smoke and gunshots—all more dreamlike than real.

He rubbed his palms firmly against his eyelids as he turned his thoughts to the assassination of the president-elect. Why were there so many gaps? Had he missed something? Or was Morpheus's plan simply unfinished?

He felt a flutter in his stomach. There was only one way to be certain—and it fueled his decision to return to universal consciousness. To learn the truth, he needed to find Adler Daemon.

Sean settled in to meditate, and slowly drifted into theta. The first sensations were now familiar: the descent, the vibration, a flush feeling. He knew what to expect next: the colors, the shapes, and then the revelation.

But a few minutes later—Sean was back, sitting in his apartment. His body threw off a slight shiver. He blinked and leaned forward.

What the hell just happened? It wasn't what he expected. Where were the details of the plan: time, place, date?

Sean stood and went to the bathroom. Splashing cold water on his face, he stared into the mirror. Would he ever fully understand any of this?

On his way back to the living room, he stopped mid-step. A pressure was building behind his eyes—then came a rush of information—like the type he experienced in the Swiss dream. He stood perfectly still; stunned, fascinated. Instead of learning about the assassination plot, he got insight into Dr. Adler Daemon.

How could one determine the worth of a man? Was it his best moments? His worst? Or was there some formula to calculate the statistical average? Sean reached for his Scotch glass, slowly shaking his head.

Adler Daemon was far more complicated than he expected. In many ways, Sean wanted—even needed—Adler to be pure evil. But that wasn't the man he found.

Sean saw Adler's idealistic side, the brilliant mind that once believed in the potential of consciousness. A mind convinced that we'd become lost in a sea of societal manipulation and religious doctrine.

Tapping the rim of his glass, Sean felt conflicted. How could he share common ground with a man that wished to kill him.

He saw Adler's desire to be embraced as the father of a new age of enlightenment. He sensed Adler's doubts, felt his anger, and his betrayal at being rejected by academia. And how that deep resentment led to the formation of Morpheus.

Two things surprised Sean.

First, he learned Adler secretly despised what Morpheus had become, loathing the perversion of his vision into a weapon. The power and money—the organizations and governments—had boxed him in on all sides.

Second, Adler had once been romantically involved with Olivia. Sean's grip on his glass tightened. Was that a betrayal? No, he supposed not. It was in the past, but that didn't sooth the pain he felt deep in his chest. She should have told him. Why hadn't she?

Sean had long sensed that Adler was protective of Olivia—now he understood the reason. His feelings for her still ran strong.

Sean lifted his whisky glass and took a sip. His heart felt heavy. Sometimes, the truth had a dark side.

Chapter Twenty-Five

Geneva, Switzerland

The morning's first rays crept across the bed, and a drowsy Adler Daemon rolled away from the light. The sheets were kicked aside and hung halfway off the edge. Very unusual for Adler, for even in his sleep, the man was meticulous. But this morning felt different. Adler was uneasy. And it wasn't from a nightmare—something else, something he simply couldn't identify.

Over breakfast, he mentally replayed the events of Sean's capture. Recalling with tender fondness, the image of Hastings writhing in pain, with snot dripping from his nose. As satisfying and rewarding as that image was, he couldn't shake this troubled feeling. The sensation followed him to the lobby and, while patting his trouser pockets for the mailbox key, the answer hit him.

Universal consciousness.

Sean had used the term during Sergei's interrogation. Adler's face contorted as he weighed the possibility. No, he told himself, that couldn't be it, it had to be a trick—some combination of dream traveling, with a dash of clairvoyance.

The uneasy feeling stayed with him throughout the day. By early afternoon, Adler finally came to admit what he'd sensed since this morning: someone had entered his dream. The prospect of Sean Hastings wandering around in his head was jarring—and revolting. Adler hated feeling vulnerable. Had Sean learned anything valuable? Was the assassination plan compromised? What would it take to make Hastings disappear for good?

His initial fury settled into a calculated revenge. Above all, Adler was a pragmatist. He would take care of Hastings, but first, one issue demanded immediate attention. If the plan to assassinate Gavin Peakes was compromised, then the plan had to be changed.

He checked the time difference between Geneva and California. It was still early, but in a couple of hours he'd telephone Hayward James and propose a new assassination schedule to the Americans for Global Equity.

Hayward would no doubt throw a fit, but Adler had crafted a reasonable explanation for the change. He let out a slight laugh. By the time he finished with Hayward, that simpleton would be the one thanking him. But first, Adler needed to confirm something with his attorney, Armand C. Locke.

The light-blue glass door was partially open. Adler knocked on the narrow steel frame.

"I have a question."

Armand looked up from his computer screen, his brow furrowed—as though this was the worst possible time. In truth, it never seemed to be a good time, and Adler sometimes wondered if he viewed life itself as an inconvenience. Though to Armand's credit, he understood that it literally paid to accommodate his one and only client. He gestured toward an open chair, and forced a smile.

"How may I help?" The smile only further deepened the laugh lines of a man who rarely laughed.

"What happens in the United States, if someone is elected president but dies before taking the oath?"

"Well," Armand paused, recalling his constitutional law, "it's addressed in the Twelfth and Twentieth Amendments. It depends on when the death occurred—and how you define the term elected."

"Explain."

"You're aware that US presidential elections are indirect? The general populace votes, but the Electoral College actually elects the president. The general election takes place in November and the apparent winner is regarded as the new president-elect. However, the true election occurs in mid-December, when the electors cast their ballots. If the president-elect dies before those votes are cast, then the vice-president-elect would likely receive the votes, although his party is free to select another nominee."

Armand paused. Adler waited.

"Once the Electoral College votes are cast, it becomes official in January when

Congress counts the votes. The candidate with two hundred and seventy electoral votes is declared the winner."

"And if this winner dies before then?"

"Then the Twelfth Amendment stipulates that all votes be counted…even if they're for a dead candidate."

Armand paused, his expression curious. He continued.

"So, the casting of the Electoral College votes is the deciding moment. Once cast, we can safely say that the Twelfth and Twentieth Amendments both stipulate that the vice-president-elect will become the next president."

Adler considered all this, while mindlessly playing with a crystal globe on the desk. Armand gritted his teeth. He appeared eager for Adler to either respond, go away, or just stop playing with his damn globe.

"Thank you, you've been most helpful."

"Of course. Anything else?"

Adler shook his head. He stood and straightened his jacket. The two men gave each other a quick nod, and Adler left.

In an odd way, their relationship seemed to flourish in the cool air of suspicion —a peculiar dynamic.

***

Chicago, Illinois

"What in the blazin' hell happened?" asked an unbridled Buck Debrew.

Typically boorish, the wealthy cattle rancher's behavior frequently bristled the other members of the group, but to his credit, his question cut to what was on everyone's mind. How could their well-executed plan be in danger of failing?

"A transitioning chief of staff, and a bit of bad luck," Hayward James cautiously explained. They were intolerant of excuses, and rustles and murmurs of discontent flew around the table.

Adler had fabricated the story, out of concern that Sean had learned about the plot. Fearing he would block the assassination, Adler simply moved up the time line. No one would know of Sean's interference, or Morpheus's fallibility. In the new plan, Peakes would be murdered soon after the casting of the electoral college votes, prior to the inauguration.

"Let me explain," said Hayward, addressing the seven principal members of Americans for Global Equity. "As his chief of staff, Gavin Peakes has chosen a meddlesome woman. She's doing due diligence on all prospective cabinet and staff members, including the vice president. If she connects Richard Laney to our work…well, it's no secret that Peakes opposes our group."

"Who the fuck cares?" asked a man with a buzz cut. "He can't fire Laney. His hands are tied, right?"

"True," Hayward said, "but he could harm Richard's influence with the legislators. It would paint Laney as our puppet—and draw unwanted attention to the Americans for Global Equity. I'm sure we can agree that it's desirable to do our work out of the spotlight."

They murmured their agreement.

"Do we have a backup plan?" asked a tall man with an equine face. His company designed weapons guidance systems.

Hayward nodded and said, "A slight adjustment, really, but one worth discussing." He outlined the new, accelerated timeline.

"I'm not comfortable with this," said Margaret, the sole woman at the table. Hayward looked at her with worry. In her mid-sixties, her family's wealth could safely be called a dynasty.

"After he's dead, how can we guarantee that Laney will become president?"

Hayward breathed a sigh of relief. Murder wasn't going to be an issue, only the succession.

"Well," he said with a chuckle, "there's lots of legal disagreement about when a president is actually elected…"

The next few minutes were spent explaining the intricacies of constitutional law, and how it pertained to the transfer of power prior to an inauguration.

Hayward watched them process and comprehend the details of the plan. Soon they would vote. Over the years, they'd met challenge after challenge—and they would prevail again.

Richard Laney would never learn of this meeting—or about the plot to kill Peakes. None of that mattered. By early next year, Laney would be president.

***

Geneva, Switzerland

The demise of Sergei's team was a second page newspaper story in Le Journal de Montreal. The Canadian government had no appetite for a scandal, eager to avoid investigations into a covert Eastern Bloc intelligence agency setting up a torture site on Canadian soil. All done under their noses and without their knowledge. Rumors of a Canadian hostage only made things worse.

Sergei and company were described as members of a Russian drug cartel running a heroin pipeline into Canada. The official version said the group was the subject of a month-long investigation spearheaded by the Drug Enforcement Division of the Royal Canadian Mounted Police. During the raid, shots were fired, and the Russian narcotics dealers were killed. No mention of foreign government involvement.

Adler leaned back from his computer, and smiled.

Is it any wonder that I'm free to operate with such impunity?

He mused that the largest government agency in the world should be the CYA, the official organization of "Covering Your Ass." Adler chuckled softly. The loss of Sergei was regrettable, but only a minor setback. His backup plan was already in motion. At any moment, he expected a call from a lieutenant general in Myanmar. He tapped on the dossier sitting on his counter.

Lieutenant General Aung Win started his military career with the Tatmadaw, the official name of the armed forces of Myanmar. Despite his high rank, Aung Win remained uncelebrated in his home country. He worked from the shadows, in charge of covert military operations for the Sa Ya Pa, the intelligence branch of the military.

Adler's phone vibrated and danced across the granite countertop.

"General, good of you to call," he said warmly. "Yes, yes, we are pleased as well. I'm looking forward to our collaboration. I'm sure you're aware of our situation, so let me get to the point."

***

New York City

"We have to warn them," Olivia said emphatically.

"Not the best course of action," Morgan mumbled.

Olivia had insisted they tell the US Secret Service about the plot to assassinate President-Elect Peakes. It was their duty, their moral obligation.

"And what do you expect them to do?" Morgan asked, uncharacteristically terse. "Only one person in the world can prevent this." He jabbed his finger toward Sean.

Olivia acknowledged, but said, "Someone needs to put Morpheus on the radar of law enforcement. If a plot to kill a president-elect doesn't qualify, then what does?"

Sean noticed that whenever Olivia was angry, she tensed her jaw and put a hand on her hip. Sean watched from the couch, finding it oddly attractive.

"I know these people," Morgan said. "They'll see our warning as a thinly veiled threat. We'll end up being the ones on the watch list. Morpheus will check out—an innocent consulting firm, unfairly maligned by us."

Sean cleared his throat. "Don't you have some government contacts? People who could vouch for us? To say that we're not a bunch of nutcases?"

Morgan tugged at the knot of his tie, shaking his head. "No. They won't help on this one. Let's just focus on immunizing Peakes before the inauguration. Maybe we can find something else on Morpheus—something less mystical—like tax evasion?"

Sean and Olivia exchanged a look, clearly thinking the same thing.

Morgan may have been right about alerting the Secret Service, but tax evasion? Feeble.

Sean frowned, still getting odd vibes from Morgan. What was it? He watched Morgan's behavior—his little tells—playing with his tie, the careful choice of words, or slight evasiveness.

He's hedging. But why?

"You're probably right," Sean said abruptly.

He noticed Olivia's hand return to her hip.

"Let's stop this assassination first," Sean said, "then we can look for a more permanent solution."

He extended his hand to Olivia, and she reluctantly took it. As they walked toward the elevator, neither spoke, but Sean could feel her grip tighten.

Reaching the lobby, Olivia spun around. "What the hell was that?"

"I thought we should leave."

"Damn it, Sean—you didn't say a word. Why didn't you back me up? Morgan is dead wrong and you know it."

In a whispered tone, he asked, "Do you ever get the impression Morgan's not entirely on our side?"

Olivia stepped back, looking confused. She shook her head at Sean's insinuation. "No, Morgan's been with us from the start. I can't believe he'd work against us." Her voice sounded tight.

"Maybe not against us, but he must have another agenda. It's just a feeling. The little things he says, or the way he's says them, or these little tells he has, like fumbling with his tie."

Olivia gave him a curious look.

"What?" he said with a shrug. "I play poker sometimes. Don't you find it odd that he'll use his government contacts to keep the process going, but refuses to outright shutdown Morpheus? He's got to be working with someone else—maybe a government agency? I just can't shake the feeling that he's hiding something."

Olivia said nothing, but Sean could see that he'd struck a chord. He wondered if she'd been having similar thoughts.

They walked out of the building.

"Let's keep this between us," Sean muttered. "At least until we know more."

Chapter Twenty-Six

The call was long overdue, but after two weeks of soul searching, Sean finally reached out to Keenan.

He'd spent many late nights reflecting on recent changes, and trying to steady his doubts about what it meant for the future. All of which fueled his desire to find balance in his life. Sean started by reconnecting with the one friend who had always kept him grounded.

On Friday night, they met at Quintana Roo, a Mexican restaurant on Eighth Avenue. Keenan appeared genuinely glad to see him, and graciously omitted any mention of his many unanswered calls. In spite of Sean's initial apprehension, halfway through their first round of margaritas, the two friends were back into their old rhythm—talking about college days, old girl friends, past embarrassments. Their laughter peeled away the layers of stress he'd been carrying. In many ways, Keenan had become Sean's touchstone.

On the waitress's recommendation, they ordered tikin xic, a Yucatán dish consisting of a whole fish with achiote marinade and sour orange juice, wrapped in banana leaves. The conversation drifted into the night. Sean felt his shoulders relax, the tension in his jaw ease, and he remembered how good it felt to laugh. Still, even in this relaxed atmosphere, he was careful to avoid any mention of Morpheus, dream traveling, or universal consciousness.

Standing outside after dinner, Sean shivered in the chilled night air, as it cut through him and moved down Eighth Avenue. He zipped up his jacket. After saying good night, they separated. Keenan headed one block up to catch his train, while Sean turned south to cut through an alley.

A little farther down the block, a man leaned against a streetlamp and blew out a billow of smoke. Nothing about the five-foot-five, black-haired man in the leather jacket appeared threatening. None of the passersby gave him a second glance—certainly not Sean or Keenan.

His name meant "lion" in Burmese, but Thiha served as a lieutenant in the Sa Ya Pa. He watched the two friends part, stomped a cigarette out under his boot, and tugged at his jacket, concealing the knife under his belt.

Sean turned into the alley.

Thiha entered a few paces back. Reaching around, his fingers found the handle of his Ka-Bar combat knife. Sean had slowed to check his messages. The steel blade glimmered in the orange light of the lamps above the alley's service doors. Thiha spun the handle in his grip, then turned the long blade of the knife to face inward. He raised his right arm in preparation.

The sheer force of the hit knocked the wind out of Thiha. His feet left the ground. The air left his lungs. He slammed onto the uneven cobblestones with a thud. A large man was on him in an instant, driving punch after punch into his head and chest. But the Sa Ya Pa are well-practiced in the martial arts, and within seconds, Thiha broke Keenan's hold. He jumped to his feet.

Sean had been knocked down during the tackle. He looked up and saw a sidekick slam into Keenan's side. Keenan tried to grab Thiha's leg. But he missed and took a fist to the temple for the mistake.

"Get the knife!" Keenan shouted.

Sean scrambled, eyes darting, disoriented. Where the hell was it? Could it have skidded under that garbage bin? Thiha looked like he was searching for the weapon, but as he turned back, Keenan hit him with a brutal front kick to the chest.

By now, Sean had gathered his courage. He lunged at Thiha, but missed. The attacker moved with blinding speed. Keenan landed a few punches. None of them clean. Sean then noticed Thiha's right eye had begun to swell.

This was his chance.

Sean moved to flank Thiha who shot him a cursory glance, but kept his focus on the more powerful Keenan. Sean tried to lunge at him, but he was too slow. The lieutenant stepped forward and spun into a roundhouse kick. Keenan and Sean jumped back. Their split-second of hesitation was all he needed to bolt and make his escape. By the time they reacted, Thiha was halfway down the block. He was gone.

Keenan reached around and held his left side, moaning as he slowly lowered himself onto the ground.

"You okay?" he panted. "Hell of a mugging…"

That was no mugging.

Sean sat next to him, and tried to steady his breath. Thoughts of Abbie, Olivia, and Reinhold raced through his mind. "Morpheus," he whispered to himself as though the name was venom. They would stop at nothing.

He looked down, watching his hands tremble. Sean's heart was beating so hard that it seemed as though it was trying to break free from his chest. Overcome with emotion, he squeaked out a shaky, "Thank you."

Keenan lifted his head from his hands. "I looked back and saw him following you. Something felt off. Then I saw his knife…I just went full out."

Fear. Guilt. Regret. Sean felt the weight of the emotions like an anchor. He darted a glance at Keenan before returning to stare at the cobblestones. The moment kept replaying in his mind. When would this end? Would this end? His secret had almost resulted in the death of his best friend.

"Not your typical mugger," Keenan muttered, surprisingly calm. "Did you know him?"

"No," Sean said softly, now clear on what he needed to do. He stood, extended his hand to Keenan, and blew out a long breath. "I've got a lot to tell you and I don't know where to start. I owe you a drink…well…probably more than that."

An hour later, the whole story was out: the sleep clinic, universal consciousness, Russian operatives, the dream assassinations. Keenan listened quietly, without interruption. A nervous Sean fidgeted with a salt shaker, wondering whether his friend thought he'd gone mad. When he finished, they sat in silence, staring at one another.

"Why didn't you tell me any of this?" Keenan finally asked.

After a heavy sigh, Sean said, "At first, I was ashamed to admit my stock trading success was based on dreams. That seems pretty trivial at this point, almost funny, still it crossed a line for me. Then, everything got out of hand. Before I knew it, I didn't know where to begin."

"So," Keenan said, gesturing outside, "who was that guy?"

"Mercenary? Agent? Anyone's guess."

Keenan laughed, surprising Sean by his odd reaction.

"Sorry. It's just that, not too long ago, you complained about how boring your life had become—a stereotypical stockbroker, I think you called yourself."

"So you don't think I'm crazy?"

"Maybe a little," he said with a wry grin. "But I believe you. Though it might take some time to wrap my head around this consciousness stuff." He reached down and pressed a hand to his ribs. "One thing's for sure, that guy wasn't imaginary—he was real." He winced at the pain from his side. "Maybe a little too real. So, what now?"

With a vulnerable shrug, Sean turned his palms skyward.

Keenan shook a finger at Sean. "You're going to need some protection—professional protection. Some of my former Ranger buddies run a private security firm here in the city. Let me give them a call."

Sean lowered his head. There was no point in denying the reality of the situation. "Thanks."

Keenan seemed happy that there was no argument on the issue. "So, no more secrets?"

Sean nodded.

"Good. Now, tell me more about this Olivia. Just friends?"

***

The next morning, Sean downplayed the incident. Someone "got rough" with him, and Keenan intervened. He sat back in one of Morgan's office chairs and nodded to himself, as if that pretty much covered everything. He left out a few details: the trained assassin, the combat knife, or the fact that Keenan had nearly died.

Morgan and Olivia exchanged skeptical glances, indicating they weren't buying Sean's version. When pressed for details about the attacker, Sean said, "I think he was Asian."

Morgan held a tight expression. He must have assumed that, after losing the services of Sergei, Adler had called in a favor from the other side of the globe.

Sean cast a furtive glance toward Olivia. Wondering whether she still believed that Adler would never harm her. Sean was under no such delusion. In his mind, Adler Daemon was capable of anything.

As Sean left the building with Olivia, he questioned whether to tell her about Keenan's offer of protection. Would it frighten her? Or reassure her? His thoughts then drifted to Abbie. Had her nightmare been a one time thing, or would there be more? How had he let things come to this? And what, if anything, could he do about it? He pressed his thumb hard into his palm.

Sean had become increasingly concerned about the people he cared for, Olivia included.

"Where are you staying?" he asked.

"At my usual hotel…why?"

"Is there another place you can stay?"

Olivia gave him a coy look—uncertain whether the question was out of worry, or hinting at something more.

"I have a friend in Murray Hill," she replied. "I suppose I can stay with her for a while."

Sean nodded. He was constantly on edge, bracing for Morpheus's next strike. This time, with luck, Keenan's friends would be ready for them.

***

Geneva, Switzerland

Adler was happy to sneak off for a midafternoon's indulgence. Geneva's Richter Cafe was renowned for its Pflaumenküchen, a plum cake with an astringent bite. Adler intended on making the most of the warm weather before the gloom of winter descended upon the city. Casting an eye on a large bowl of fresh whipped cream, he hesitated, glancing at his waistline. Then, he recalled Oscar Wilde's famous quote about surrendering to temptation, and plopped a generous dollop on the top of his cake.

Jakob entered the cafe, scanning the room before approaching Adler's table.

"Sorry for the interruption. Something's happened."

Adler was annoyed, but hid his displeasure under a graceful smile. He had been looking forward to a quiet afternoon, but now he put down his fork and gestured for Jakob to sit.

"Would you like something to eat?"

"Just coffee, please."

The waitress placed an extra cup on the table. While she poured from the porcelain pot, Jakob relayed the bad news.

"Sean Hastings is still alive. The Burmese operative failed in his mission."

Adler scoffed, before taking a bite of cake. He closed his eyes, savoring the contrasting flavors of sweet and tart.

"So what—we try again."

"That might not be so easy. Hastings had help. Now, he's being protected by a private security firm."

Adler brushed away Jakob's concern with a wave of his hand, as if he couldn't care less.

Jakob drew in a breath—Adler's peculiar indifference was well known at Morpheus, and his refusal to see Sean as a legitimate threat only deepened the confusion.

Adler's thoughts turned to Sean, *who is this inconsequential fool, really?* It was his ego talking—and he knew it.

"There's more," Jakob said quietly. "Morgan Maxwell is aware of the contract on the president-elect. He's making inquiries into who's behind the order." Jakob sighed. "Our efforts to dissuade this group have only strengthened their resolve."

Daemon frowned, pushing his plate of Pflaumenküchen away.

"Now it makes sense. I received a call from our American partners—they've become concerned. I thought it was merely jitters, but maybe not. In either case, this is an unwelcome bit of news." Adler dabbed his mouth with a white cloth napkin, his eyes narrowed.

Jakob waited.

"This little group of theirs has three leaders and a few minor characters. Take out the top three, and everything will fall apart. Wouldn't you agree?"

Jakob inhaled sharply. He immediately understood Adler's implication.

Olivia.

"You want Olivia dead?" he asked, stunned. Jakob stared at his boss.

"What I want is irrelevant. It's what has to be. These three are a threat to our organization." Adler's eyes looked past Jakob and into the distance. "She has made her choice—now she must bear the consequences."

Jakob could see the determination in Adler's eyes. Everyone at Morpheus had seen that look before. There would be no changing his mind.

"Have Armand ready a transfer to General Aung's account. I'll call him later with the details."

Still shocked by Adler's decision, Jakob rose from his seat. Though he hesitated for a moment, it was clear that he wouldn't stand in his way. Adler sat quietly before lifting his head. For a moment, Jakob hoped that he'd reconsidered.

Then Adler waved him away with a brusque and dismissive gesture.

***

New York City

Noble's flight touched down at JFK airport under a light drizzle. Looking up at the overcast sky, he chortled. It was as if he'd never left Scotland. He smirked and then headed toward Madison Avenue to meet with Morgan and Olivia.

Noble walked into the lounge: old brass fixtures, checkerboard tile, darkly stained wood yellowed under years of varnish. Nothing contemporary. Utterly perfect.

He greeted Olivia with a kiss on both cheeks, but immediately flinched. Something about the exchange felt off.

Olivia tilted her head. "Is everything all right?"

"Aye. Forgive me—must be a touch of jet lag."

Morgan briefed him on the chaos of the past week, but Noble's mind had already returned to the odd sensation from his contact with Olivia. It felt foreboding, and he'd sensed it the instant they touched. Still sorting through his thoughts, he heard Morgan mention something about staying alert.

"I said, keep an eye out for suspicious Asian men."

Noble chuckled with a raised brow. "Suspicious? Shouldn't be a problem, I'm staying with a friend in Chinatown."

Morgan shrugged with a weak smile.

They reconfirmed their plans to meet with Sean later that night. As they stood, Noble looked outside. The drizzle had turned into a downpour.

"I think I'll stay out of the rain—wait for my ride-share inside."

When they left, Noble stretched, a little tight and uncomfortable from the long flight. Then he noticed Olivia's scarf was still draped across the chair.

Picking it up, the same uneasy feeling descended upon him. No clear images. No flashes. Just a feeling of dread. Noble frowned.

His visions were usually more like photographs—something he could stitch together into a narrative. This was different.

Noble glanced up at the sound of the rain driving hard against the windows.

Looking at the street through rain-streaked windows, he wondered why he felt so uncertain—and worried.

***

Later that day, while getting ready to meet with the group, Noble picked up the scarf again. The same uneasiness returned—only sharper now. He sat on the edge of the bed.

What the hell is this?

Determined to get to the bottom of it, he gripped the scarf tightly and held it close. With eyes shut, he concentrated, pushing for meaning. It began as a mere trickle, but soon the images rushed in like a flood.

Olivia. A doorman. A flower shop. A traffic walk symbol. A dark-gray sedan.

Noble's eyes went wide and his heart jumped. He grabbed his cell phone to call, but Olivia didn't answer. Then he frantically called Morgan.

"Where's Olivia?"

"Murray Hill, I think. I can text you the address." Morgan sounded flustered and confused, but Noble hung up before he could ask any questions.

In the taxi, Noble tried Olivia's cell again. Straight to voicemail. He cursed, startling the driver.

As they approached the address, Noble wondered why the vision had taken him so long to see. Maybe it's a false reading? Although quite unusual—it gave him hope that this time, of all times, his premonition was wrong.

At the curbside, Noble stepped out and faced the entrance of the building. In his peripheral, he spotted Olivia. She was fifty yards ahead and walking away. He shouted her name, but an accelerating delivery truck drowned him out. He started to sprint toward her.

As he ran, he compared the street scenes with the images from his vision. They aligned perfectly. The doorman. The flower shop. The intersection.

No, this was no false reading. Despair washed over him. He pushed himself to run faster.

The walk light illuminated, and Olivia stepped off the curb. Noble screamed her name again, just as the echoed sound of screeching tires bounced off the glass and concrete buildings. He saw the gray sedan—same one from his vision—barreling through the red light—accelerating toward Olivia.

Hearing the noise, she turned—and froze. Noble flew across the curb. Olivia was staring directly at the speeding car when Noble's hands hit her squarely in the back. It knocked her off her feet. She screamed and tumbled into the lane divider.

Noble's momentum carried him forward, just not enough to clear the speeding sedan. The car's left front bumper clipped him right below the knee. His body was spinning like a doll in mid-air. His head slammed into the rear door. The force of the blow knocked him clear and he landed with a thud.

The gray sedan continued ripping through the red light, screeching as it turned the corner.

It was gone.

A horrified crowd swarmed around Noble, trying to render aid. A few feet away, a stunned and disoriented Olivia struggled to her feet. With only a few scrapes, she'd been lucky. When she regained her senses, she pushed her way through the crowd. "Noble! Noble!" Her limbs shook from the adrenaline. Bending down by his side, she winced at the sight of his twisted body. Then his shoulder moved and he groaned. He was alive, but writhing in pain. She closed her eyes and took a deep breath.

Noble's left leg was a mess—a pale-white fragment of his tibia protruding from the ripped leg of his trousers. He was bleeding. The compound fracture had bent Noble's lower leg at an altogether unnatural and unholy angle.

For a moment it looked like he recognized Olivia, but before she could say anything, his eyes rolled backward and he slipped into shock. She grasped his hand: shaking, crying, angry. It seemed that there were so many emotions racing through her body that she couldn't begin to keep up.

The distant sound of a siren was soon upon them and the crowd parted for the paramedics. Olivia asked to ride with Noble. Initially, the paramedic refused, but after seeing her cuts and abrasions, he helped her inside.

The police soon arrived on the scene and began taking statements. Although there were plenty of eyewitnesses, the descriptions they provided were a little shaky. The hit-and-run car was a gray, or white, or black sedan with two doors, maybe four. Almost certainly a late model Lincoln, or possibly a Mercedes.

The cops taking the statements smiled and exchanged glances. Just another day in the city.

Chapter Twenty-Seven

Returning from the hospital, Morgan tossed his keys into an ebony bowl by the door, the one he'd picked up during a trip to Johannesburg back in 1984. It had been his first exposure to the injustices of apartheid and it left a lasting impression. A harsh reminder that fairness all too often became lost among the world's other priorities.

Pouring himself a couple of fingers of Scotch, he eased into the couch and pushed a few buttons on his remote. The room filled with the sound of classic jazz. With eyes closed, he took a slow, deep breath.

Noble was now in stable condition and resting under an intravenous cocktail of painkillers. The orthopedic surgeons had performed their magic and were anticipating a full recovery. With Noble sleeping soundly, Morgan decided to call it a night.

The first few notes of Miles Davis's muted horn enveloped the room. Morgan felt his muscles relax, his anxiety drain away.

Then his phone rang.

Concerned, he sat up, wondering if Noble's condition had worsened. But when he picked up his cell phone, it wasn't ringing. A pained looked crossed Morgan's face. With a sigh, he reached beneath the coffee table, and unlatched the bracket that held his encrypted phone.

"Yes?"

"Code in, please," said the cold voice. Morgan recited the numbers. The dispassionate voice told him to stand by for the director.

"It looks like you're on to something," the director began. "We've picked up chatter about an assassination. It seems you might be right, it's domestic, not foreign."

"As I said, my source is reliable."

Morgan clutched at a throw pillow. He always kept his responses to the agency as short as possible. Less room for error.

"Our vulnerability goes up with each passing day," the director insisted. "This threat must be neutralized. We need to know if this technology can be safely confiscated and of some practical use to us." After a long pause, he cleared his throat. "Don't make me remind you of how you got yourself into this mess. Just do your job. This will be over soon."

Morgan inhaled slowly. "I think we're fairly close to the answer."

He was hedging with half-truths. He wasn't ready to share Sean's theory. Not yet.

"Well hurry. Time is running out. Get your guys on this."

The line went dead.

Morgan tossed the phone onto the table and turned to stare into the fireplace. He closed his eyes once more, and let the gravity of the day settle upon him.

Yeah. Hell of a day.

***

"Are we safe talking over the phone?" Hayward James's voice faltered, a man attempting to sound calm in an unnerving situation.

"The line is secure," replied Adler Daemon, his impatience creeping into his tone. "There's nothing to worry about."

"Really? Because it seems like there's a lot of things worth worrying about. Like these rumors I'm hearing about a group that could fuck this whole thing up."

Hayward was on point—and Adler knew it. The threat to Morpheus was real. Sean Hastings and his band of misfits had worn Adler's patience thin.

"Don't worry, it's under control."

"I don't need to be placated," he snarled. "I need results, not patience." Hayward was under pressure because he was the one who'd brought Morpheus to the attention of the Americans for Global Equity.

"We have a plan," Adler said softly, "but I'll need to ask a small favor first. I understand that you have connections—people who could leak a credible conspiracy to the FBI?"

Silence followed. Hayward seemed reluctant to share the true extent of his influence. Though, eventually, he let out the low grunt of acknowledgment.

Adler then laid out his plan: plant fake evidence on Morgan's servers, stage a cyber-breach, and trap Morgan between his clients and the FBI. He would find himself battling multiple fronts.

"And Hayward," he added. "There's an ancillary benefit to this plan. Whatever suspicions may arise after the death of the president-elect, they'll implicate Morgan Maxwell and his people. The Americans for Global Equity will be clean—and above suspicion."

Hayward must have known he was being manipulated by Adler, but it was too late to back out. "All right fine," he grumbled.

Daemon's smile could almost be heard over the phone.

***

When Morgan arrived at his office, the staff was in disarray.

Perhaps it had been naive, but Morgan had hoped for just one day to breathe—to push aside the chaos of the group and the shadow games of the NSA—to return to normal.

Their computer system had been hacked and the IT people were scrambling. They acknowledged that some of their data had been compromised, but no one could give him a straight answer on what that actually meant. Morgan retreated to his office and waited for the crisis to pass.

Gripping the armrest of his chair, he swiveled back and forth. He thought about who might be behind the hack. What were they looking for? When will the pieces ever begin to fit the puzzle?

At 11:17 a.m., his phone chimed. A text message appeared:

AN INVITATION TO A SEMINAR: RETIREMENT INVESTMENTS!!!

Written in all caps and followed by three exclamation marks. Morgan shook his head and sighed. What madness. The text header was his signal to make immediate contact—the exclamation points denoting urgency. Well, at least that's what he'd been told. Until now, he'd never seen it used. He picked up the encrypted cell and, after a moment, a voice came on the line.

"Take your phone, weapon, and hard copies of confidential documents and exit the building through the rear service entrance. A black Camry will be waiting. The FBI will raid your offices in eight minutes."

The line went dead.

Morgan exhaled a long, annoyed sigh. He hated being played. But then being cuffed and dragged out by the FBI wasn't very appealing either. He tossed the essentials into a messenger bag and grabbed his jacket. On the way out, he made a few half-plausible excuses to his staff.

Once in the elevator, he wondered what had prompted the FBI to raid his offices. He'd been disciplined about keeping the group's activities separate from the center's operations. And the CCP had always operated legally and aboveboard, even if some of their clients tended to be less so.

His jaw clenched. Morgan assumed that Morpheus was behind the raid, but to what end? And how in the hell did the NSA know the FBI raid was coming? More puzzle, he thought, even fewer pieces. He shifted from side to side, unable to connect the dots.

The elevator door opened on the service level, one floor below the lobby. Morgan slipped out and scanned the corridor. Cautiously making his way toward the back service entrance, he checked the corner before swiftly descending the concrete steps. As he moved toward the street, weaving in-between the service trucks and garbage bins, he was struck by a strange thought:

Who sends a Camry for an extraction?

***

After a quick calculation, Sean learned it was a little past four in the morning in Geneva. The timing was right. Adler Daemon should be fast asleep.

Over the past few days, Sean had become troubled by Morpheus's behavior. It seemed desperate, aggressive. He'd come to view Adler as cold, calculated, and ruthless—but his latest actions seemed more reactionary than rational.

At least Olivia's kidnapping had made sense, it was leverage to force him into undoing Serrano's protection. But what about these recent actions? The attempt on his life, on Olivia, severely wounding Noble, and the raid on Morgan's offices.

Why?

As far as Sean knew, Adler was unaware that they knew about the plot to assassinate Peakes. But it was the only thing that could explain the sudden aggression. He tapped his lip with his fingers. There was really only one way to know for sure—a return to universal consciousness.

He dimmed the lights and settled into his favorite chair. Closing his eyes, he slowed his breath and let his thoughts dissolve into the layers of theta. Sean began to relax. He focused on Adler Daemon, allowing his intention to guide him.

In the hallway outside of his apartment, a small man knelt down and picked at the lock of his front door. He made it look easy; a little pressure here, a slight jiggle there, and the tumblers fell away.

Sean heard nothing.

Dressed from head-to-toe in black, only the men's eyes were visible beneath the masks. They'd been forewarned about Sean's protection detail, and avoided the downstairs guard by gaining access through the building's electrical room.

A second man entered the apartment, following on the heels of the first. They used hand signals to canvas the unit and make sure that Sean was alone. Confident that no one else was there, the second man slowly reached into his side pack. He pulled out a garrote, a length of wire with wooden handles used for strangulation.

Aung Win's men used a modified version they acquired from the French Foreign Legion in Indochina. La loupe was a garrote, but it added a second coil of wire; the effect being that even if the victim managed to grab and pull free of one coil, the other would tighten even further.

Sean sat motionless, his eyes closed, his focus elsewhere.

A wicked smile formed on the man holding the garrote—this would be easy. Sean's chair faced away from the men, so it amounted to a repetition of their most basic training exercise:

Level one: sneak up and kill a mannequin.

The two men moved quietly through the apartment, stepping as soft as a feline. With the garrote pulled taut in his hands, the second man moved toward Sean.

The silence was broken by an explosion of sound.

The front door flew open, slamming hard against the stop. The masked men spun around in shock. It was too dark to see, but then, a sliver of light from the hallway glinted off steel. A split second later—a bright muzzle flash.

The first man collapsed instantly. The second man whirled around to lunge at Sean. Two rapid shots from the silenced pistol broke his stride. He took one last step before his lifeless body crashed into the back of Sean's chair.

Snapping out of his meditation, Sean leapt to his feet. Breathless and disoriented, dropping into a defensive crouch. He braced for the unknown, with no idea of how close he'd come to being killed.

Somewhere, out of the darkness, came a deep and reassuring voice.

"Sean, you're safe. It's okay. I'm Keenan's friend, Clyde."

He calmly went back and closed the front door. Clyde reached into his pocket and pulled out a cell phone. "No, it's just the two. Right…yeah…I'll text you the address."

Several minutes passed before Sean could think clearly.

Few meditations end with two dead members of the Myanmar secret police lying on the living room floor.

Visibly shaken, Sean made a beeline to the liquor cart. "I could use a drink. How about you?"

Clyde glanced around and shrugged. "Sure, why not?" His voice was remarkably calm, as though this was just another day.

"I was covering the ground floor, but somehow I missed these two. Fortunately, my partner's in the building across the street watching with a telescope and an electronic monitor. When he saw them enter your apartment, he alerted me and… well…here I am."

He made the whole thing sound rather routine.

Sean nodded with a weak smile. He swallowed hard and forced himself to take a closer look at the bodies. For the first time, he noticed the garrote clutched in the hand of one of the men. A cold shiver ran up his spine.

Clyde followed his gaze and smirked. "Probably best if we don't involve the authorities."

***

Geneva, Switzerland

The next morning, Adler woke up groggy. Very unusual. He'd always prided himself on his sleep discipline; in bed at a certain hour and rising at the same time each day. There was comfort in structure. He acknowledged his tendency toward obsessive-compulsive behavior, but he reasoned that these sleep habits were by far his healthiest.

He pressed down on the handle of the French press, and inhaled the aroma.

While impatiently waiting for that first kick of caffeine, he thought about his recent restlessness. Two reasons immediately came to mind, and perhaps a few more that weren't as clear.

For one, Lieutenant General Aung Win should have called. By now, Sean Hastings should be merely a footnote in Morpheus's story—another problem checked off the list. But the call hadn't come.

Second, Hastings's talk of universal consciousness was gnawing at Adler. What if it was true? A big "if" in his opinion—but it would mean that they could no longer be sure of what Sean knew. Though it seemed unlikely, Adler hated unknowns. Until Hastings was confirmed dead, nothing could be left to chance.

Just one more day, Adler muttered to himself.

Success was so very near, but time was running against them. Tomorrow, the Electoral College votes would be cast—and with that vote—all the variables associated with the executive chain of command would be gone. The timing was tight—a little too tight.

Sipping his coffee, he felt the caffeine amplify his apprehension. To quiet his anxiety, Adler poured over the details of the plan until he was satisfied that everything was in order. It settled his distraught emotions, and Adler was able to turn his focus to the days ahead.

He felt invigorated, anticipating the company's first major assassination. Adjusting his Hermès tie in the mirror, he allowed himself a vile grin. When President-elect Peakes went to sleep tomorrow night—it would be for the very last time.

Naturally, the world would mourn the loss. Rumors would fly. The media would speculate.

But within the hidden corridors of power and influence, the name of Morpheus would be recognized as the deadliest political force on the planet.

There was simply no rival.

Chapter Twenty-Eight

New York City

Olivia softly murmured, curling her right foot under her leg, and gently placing a hand on Sean's thigh. Her head rested softly on his shoulder. He had just finished recounting last night's bizarre attack—the two Burmese assassins, the gunfire, and a larger-than-life hero named Clyde.

This time, Sean didn't hold anything back. If Olivia held any fears about what might have been, she concealed them behind clear eyes and steady breath.

His story came across like some movie trailer from an action thriller, but the danger was very real. Too hard to dismiss. Reinhold had paid the ultimate price, but for now, the rest of the group had been lucky. When would their luck run out?

Olivia pointed to a spot on the living room floor. "So, they were right there?"

Sean nodded. "I don't think this was Clyde's first go at this sort of thing. He made one call, and then three men showed up with large wheeled cases and a host of cleaning equipment. Within an hour, the whole place looked untouched—no trace of the bodies, blood, or anything else." Sean scratched his forehead.

"It was so quiet afterwards," he said shaking his head, "that I started to wonder whether I had imagined the whole thing."

Olivia shifted closer, wrapping her arms around him, and resting her head on his chest. A delicate smile formed as she pressed against his warmth. She lifted her chin and kissed him on the lips—softly at first, then nibbling at his lower lip before gently flicking her tongue against his. Sean turned and cupped the back of her head and drew her into a deeper kiss, reveling in the taste of her lips. He pulled her onto his lap and felt the firmness of her breasts against his chest. His hope—his dream was becoming real. Their hands wandered, cautiously at first, but then more aggressively—freely exploring each other's bodies. Sean closed his eyes, quite content to remain lost in the moment. Then—Olivia suddenly pulled back and gave him an odd look.

"What's wrong?" he asked.

"Are Clyde's men still watching the apartment?"

Sean stopped. "I suppose so," he said grinning.

Olivia's smile was playful and mischievous. "I appreciate what they've done, but we should probably move this into the bedroom. I assume you have curtains?"

Sean let out a slight laugh. He stood and took Olivia's hand.

***

They woke entangled in the bedsheets—and nothing else. Two souls immersed in the warmth and fuzziness of an afternoon nap. Sean's eyes traced the length of her leg, and a sleepy smile crept across his face. The late-afternoon sun scattered its shimmery light across the bed. In the room's golden glow, he drank in every curve of her body and admired the gentle shadows they cast. He was at peace.

Waking with a soft murmur, Olivia turned her head. She smiled, then rolled her body over to drape her right leg across his thigh. "What time is it?" she asked, almost in a whisper.

"A little after four, I think," he said, straining to read the bedside clock that always seemed to point away from him. Relaxed and cocooned in her warmth— Sean seemed content to stay there forever. But Olivia had already shifted out of her tranquil haze, and swung her legs out of bed. He sighed, watching as the moment vanished. He stood to make coffee. Standing next to the bed, she stretched and tossed her hair from side to side. When the light from the window caught her hair just right, Sean was again reminded of the young professor's words:

Caramel balayage hair.

Sitting on high stools at the kitchen table, they discussed recent events. Olivia was quick to reiterate her position about notifying the Secret Service, but before she could finish, she noticed Sean's changing expression.

"These people are powerful," he said. "Morgan's right, the Secret Service can't stop this kind of assassination."

Olivia listened while fidgeting with a rogue strand of hair. She aggressively tapped her nails against her coffee cup and he could hear her breathe. After a long and tense silence, Olivia reluctantly nodded.

"Okay, fine," she said, "but you need to immunize—or whatever you call it—the president-elect right away. I can't shake the feeling that waiting will be a mistake." She left little room for debate.

"I suppose, but Morgan thinks that if we move too soon, we'll tip off Morpheus."

Olivia looked at him as if he'd lost his mind. "Are you a complete idiot?"

Sean blinked and sputtered.

"We've had three Asian assassins try to kill us, a maniac hit-and-run driver, and don't forget our sadistic Russian friends. I think Morpheus is pretty fucking tipped off."

He winced at her tone—but she was right. He wanted to back-pedal, to return to the warmth and intimacy of earlier. He stared deeply into her eyes and asked, "Are you sure?"

Olivia's face immediately flushed with anger—but when she caught the ever-growing smirk on Sean's face, she stopped herself. After a playful snarl, she stuck her tongue out at him.

Sean laughed. "Okay…I give up. You're right. Too much is at risk if we get the timing wrong." He reached out, held her hand, and in a soft voice said, "I'll take care of this tonight. If this thing works, at least we won't have to worry about President-Elect Peakes being taken out by Morpheus."

***

Later that night, having settled into his favorite chair, Sean prepared for the immunization of Gavin Peakes. He closed his lids and eased into the meditation—only to snap his eyes open again after a few seconds.

Is someone there? What's that noise?

He listened. Nothing.

Just the quiet hum of an air conditioning unit and the low rumble of city traffic. He sought to calm himself, to try again, but soon found he was squinting through a half-open eye—like some anxiety-ridden cyclops.

Every time Sean shut his eyes, last night's brutal scene came flooding back: the steel wires of the garrote, the masked assassins, the blood-stained carpet. Reflexively, his left hand reached up to touch his throat. He took a deep breath.

All right, he thought, maybe it's the chair. Same chair, same position—same disturbing memory loop. Sean lifted it and pushed it firmly against the solid wall—something he vaguely recalled seeing in a gangster movie. Was it silly? Absolutely, but somehow it felt comforting.

Now feeling calmer and able to relax, he sat back down. His breath slowed. His right hand slipped from his lap, as Sean dropped into the hazy darkness of Gavin's dream. A scene unfolded.

Pristine examples of automotive engineering, polished and shining in the sun, were displayed on a grassy field. He'd once read that Gavin Peakes was a collector of rare and vintage cars. Sean wandered around, admiring the autos, waiting for that one exquisite moment, that mysterious instant when he would slip into universal consciousness. How long would it take? Minutes? Hours? Seconds?

When it finally arrived, it was unlike any of his other experiences. It began with a distant light, like an oncoming train cresting over the horizon. It grew brighter and brighter, until it burst into a broad palette of colors, twisting and flaring from the center.

Sean focused all his attention on Gavin's subconscious—strengthening his defenses, giving him the tools he needed to survive an attack by Morpheus.

And then the vision simply fractured and vanished. Gone—as swiftly as it had come.

***

"Olivia told me you went ahead with the immunization of Peakes," Morgan said the next day. He made it sound unseemly, like an ethical breach.

When Sean had answered Morgan's call this morning, he'd hoped for something —well, something better than this. Caught between his principles and the chaotic demands the world was thrusting upon him, he was trying to do the right thing. In this twisted world, nothing was that clear. He didn't respond.

Morgan pressed further, "I thought we had agreed to wait."

"No," Sean finally said, sounding annoyed, "what we agreed to was not to alert the Secret Service. You know that Olivia's absolutely right—Morpheus already knows all about us. Protecting Peakes won't change that. I had to do something to safeguard the president-elect."

Morgan softened his tone, before retreating. "Yes, of course, you're right. Better safe than sorry. Although—" He stopped abruptly.

Sean waited for a moment. "Morgan?"

After some hesitation, Morgan finished. "I was going to say that the threat to Peakes might not last much longer."

Sean felt his stomach tighten. "What the hell does that mean?"

"Nothing. I've just heard…some things."

"Morgan, what do you know? I swear, if you're holding back—"

"I'm not. Really. It's just a few whispers for now. I'll let you know if anything comes of it."

Chapter Twenty-Nine

Morgan had known the call was coming. He'd been dreading it for several days. The NSA contact wasted no time, and went straight for the throat. He accused Morgan of holding back, of purposely sabotaging the process. Despite the multilevel encryption, the message came through loud and clear—especially the loud part.

After berating Morgan for a couple of minutes, the NSA contact paused to take a breath. His frustration all too clear.

"Well…all right. At least tell me that he's safe."

"Yes," replied Morgan, referring to the security of the president-elect.

He'd done his job; briefing the NSA on Sean's actions, the inner-workings of Morpheus's operation, and his best assessment on the viability of transferring and weaponizing Morpheus's technology. It was everything they demanded of him— but it never seemed enough.

"So then it's a go?" the voice asked.

Morgan chewed on a fingernail, before quietly grunting his acknowledgment. He rolled his tense shoulders.

This strained, involuntary servitude with the NSA stretched back many years— to a time when the Center for Change Potential was a fledgling consulting company. A South African client had hired them to consult for a new software firm operating in the emerging cryptocurrency market. Morgan had made a few calls, and arranged introductions with some bankers and European officials. Nothing out of the ordinary. All rather straightforward.

Only it wasn't.

In reality, the South African company was a front for money laundering. The funds were being used to buy weapons for regimes in war-ravaged regions in West Africa. By the time Morgan uncovered the scheme, it was already too late. Within days, the NSA contacted him with a simple proposition: allow the Center for Change Potential to serve as an occasional cover, or watch the case get handed over to the Department of Justice for prosecution.

Civil and polite.

Still, it reminded Morgan of watching Marlon Brando make a similar offer in The Godfather. Whether he liked it or not, this was his lot.

Morgan lowered his eyes to the floor. With any luck, this miserable chapter of his life was nearing its end. Though the NSA hadn't bothered to share their plans about Morpheus, it wasn't hard to guess their intention. He drew in a deep breath.

The thought of the NSA in possession of Morpheus's technology was sobering —if not terrifying.

****

Geneva, Switzerland

The twelve men sat shoulder to shoulder inside the unmarked van. Silent and motionless. Black helmets and masks, black combat fatigues, black boots, and black fingerless gloves. They were identical in every way—but one. Four of the men were missing an embroidered shoulder patch that read, "Polizei."

It had taken several high-level negotiations to persuade the Swiss government of the necessity for a joint operation. But in the end, the Americans prevailed. They'd maintained that two of Morpheus's principle players—its CEO and legal counsel— were American citizens suspected of stealing highly classified documents. The US government insisted that this was a matter of national security, and they needed to be on-site to discreetly recover the assets.

The four Americans were introduced to the Swiss authorities as members of Homeland Security, operating under the direction of the Department of Justice. In truth, all four were NSA operatives.

Morpheus Research was accused of corporate espionage, money laundering, and the support of terrorist regimes. Naturally, no reference was made to dream traveling—or the assassinations.

The Swiss commander signaled for the team to get ready, habitually checking his

SIG automatic weapon. Then the team began to move. First, they sealed off the exits, and then rapidly cleared floor after floor of the four-story building.

Secretaries and accountants, blissfully unaware of Morpheus's secretive side, screamed and scattered. The men, dressed from head to toe in black, seemed to burst through every doorway at once. With guns drawn, they shouted in French and German.

Show your hands. Don't move.

The intelligence had indicated the weapons and operative agents were located on the top floor. The Swiss police concentrated their efforts there.

While the chaotic scene unfolded upstairs, the four Americans quietly slipped away to the lower level.

Taking advantage of the few minutes created by the diversion, the NSA team gathered all the hard drives and proprietary hardware Morpheus used to dream travel and manipulate the autonomic system. The equipment was carefully loaded into four specially constructed backpacks. Before leaving, they used the remaining time to scrub the non-critical hard drives. All traces of Morpheus's activities and contacts were erased.

When the Swiss police reached the fourth floor, they stopped abruptly. Something was wrong. Perplexed looks were exchanged.

There was nothing here.

Executive offices, some clerical staff. Nothing more. One of the Swiss officers slowly lowered his mask and weapon, and looked to his team leader.

"Merde!" cursed their commander under his breath. They had been played—and he knew it. There were no weapons here—no terrorists—the intel was all wrong. And more likely than not, it had been deliberate.

If there was any criminal activity taking place here, it wasn't the kind that justified an assault team. The frustrated Swiss team began to stand down, going through the motions of gathering and grouping the various terrified employees of Morpheus Research.

Alone on the floor and leaning against the wall, Armand C. Locke exhibited an impressive level of arrogance. It was no small feat. After being dragged out of his office at gunpoint, he was told to sit on the floor with the rest of the employees. Armand looked to his left and then his right, and realized that he barely recognized any of the staff. He shrugged. That was fine with him.

A moment later, a member of the SWAT team towered over him.

"Well, if it isn't Mr. Locke. So nice to see you."

The accent was unmistakably American, and it took Armand about three seconds to connect the dots. Of course. Now it all made sense—the Americans were behind the raid. He smiled. What bullshit story had they given the Swiss to get them to go along with this charade?

Armand knew that, as far as Switzerland was concerned, Morpheus Research was a model corporate citizen—profitable, legitimate, at least outwardly, and, above everything else, highly discreet. Armand shook his head and muttered.

This has fucking America written all over it.

He watched in amusement as a heated exchange erupted between the Swiss commander and the apparent leader of the American team. As best he could judge, the Swiss commander was getting the better of the American. Armand smiled. It was one of the benefits of being trilingual—it tripled your expletives.

Eventually, the Swiss commander calmed down and pointed at Armand before storming out. Moments later, he was arrested by the Swiss police to await extradition to the United States. He was charged with corporate espionage, money laundering, and terroristic threatening. When he was informed of the charges, Armand laughed out loud.

Terroristic threatening? Seriously?

The last person he threatened was some fool of a waiter who brought him the wrong appetizer.

As he was led away by Swiss police, Armand searched the crowd for the one face he expected to see—Adler Daemon. He'd assumed that they'd been separated as part of an interrogation strategy, but now, he got the distinct impression that Adler may have escaped.

He recalled seeing him before the raid, so he knew he'd been in the building. So where was he? His eyes continued to scan the faces, even as he was led to the police car. In the back seat, Armand turned to look out the rear window—and there was his answer.

The gray stone building. Of course.

He'd completely forgotten that Adler had him purchase it through one of their shell corporations. Armand shook his head and smirked. Eventually, the authorities would discover the hidden passageway, or learn of the purchase, but by then— Adler would be long gone. Son of a bitch.

Adler had known the tunnel and building would be essential one day, but still, to make it work, he needed advanced warning. The raid simply happened too fast. As the police car pulled away, Armand bit his lip and continued to stare out the rear window.

Who tipped him off?

Two hours earlier.

Adler was quietly sitting at his desk, when his phone buzzed. No name appeared on the caller ID, only the number. They'd agreed that Ian Bishop's name could never appear in Adler's phone directory.

"Hello?"

"Listen carefully. A special weapons team is outside your building. They'll enter in three minutes. Leave now. If you can make it to Chambéry by morning, go to our usual café. Our friends are standing by. They'll handle the rest. My apologies for the short notice—I only learned moments ago."

Adler Daemon did not hesitate.

He flew down the fire escape from his fourth-floor office. Reaching the ground floor, he slipped into a small storage closet and moved the boxes that concealed the hidden entrance to the tunnel. A couple of the boxes tumbled and Adler scrambled to re-stack them. Barely inside, and still shutting the door, he heard the assault team as they breached the main entrance.

Scurrying through the dimly lit tunnel, Adler removed the battery from his phone. Once safely inside the barrel room, he took a few calming breaths to collect himself—and then kicked over a table in anger.

What the hell happened? Everything had been going according to plan. Despite his vast resources, Adler was left clueless and huddled alone in the dark with his thoughts.

Instead of being on top of the world, he would spend the next seven humiliating hours hiding in a corner of a two-hundred-year-old Swiss cheese and wine warehouse.

Later that night, with nothing but the clothes on his back, he carefully slipped out of the warehouse and made his way to France. To Chambéry. It would only be the beginning of Adler's journey.

A few days later, the secret door to the tunnel was discovered by the authorities. Adler was long gone.

Chapter Thirty

New York City

After only a few steps inside, Sean already felt the tension ease. The place was warm and familiar: open laptops, coffee cups with brown sleeves, hoodie sweatshirts brushing shoulders with three-piece suits. He threaded his way through the midday Starbucks crowd, and found Keenan at a small round table in the corner.

"Hey."

"Hey, yourself," Keenan said, sliding a fresh cup of coffee toward him.

Sean wrapped his hands around the cup and let out a slow breath. "I know I've been a little off this week—actually—more like a royal ass." He forced a slight smile and ran his thumb across the lid of his cup. "How do you ever repay someone for saving your life? Hell, for saving it twice."

"No one's keeping score," said Keenan graciously. "It'll take more than that to drive a wedge between us." He sipped his coffee, his eyes never leaving Sean's face, studying his friend's expression. Ever the psychologist, he asked, "So, how are you holding up?"

The response landed somewhere between a laugh and a sigh. Sean walked Keenan through a few of the events since the attack in his apartment.

"Gavin Peakes? Really?" asked Keenan in disbelief. "He hasn't even taken office —and someone already wants him dead?"

Sean cast his eyes to the floor and lifted his hands. "I think it's more about stopping his agenda—or pushing a new agenda."

Keenan winced. "Politicians. They're only interest is in special interests, I guess."

Sean's smiled, soft and ruminative. Every attempt at expressing his gratitude seemed to fall short. Keenan had stood by him, showing a willingness to accept this as something other than a psychotic break. If not for the man sitting opposite him, he would have died in that alley—and of course, Clyde would not have been there to save his life for a second time.

But Sean had come here for more than just expressing his thanks.

"Olivia insisted that I immunize Peakes."

"Did it work?"

Sean let out a slight laugh. "I'm never sure—there isn't any feedback. But I think so."

They sat quietly for a moment, and then Sean continued, "The good news is that they raided the offices of Morpheus in Geneva. They're finished. But now, I'm looking for some advice."

Keenan gestured for him to go on.

"After the raid, I've assumed that the threat to Peakes is now over. No one seems to know the whereabouts of Adler Daemon, and all of Morpheus's equipment and records were confiscated—"

"Confiscated by whom?" Keenan interrupted.

"Not sure," Sean said with a shrug. "I know the Americans arrested the attorney and extradited him. So…I'm guessing the US government?"

Keenan nodded knowingly. "It's not too difficult to imagine what their interest might be in this sort of thing. So what advice were you looking for?"

"Gavin Peakes has no idea that someone tried to kill him. I can change that. I could enter his dream and lay it all out—the role of Morpheus, his vice president's involvement, the Americans for Global Equity. So, I guess I'm asking: is there any point to that? I mean, Morpheus is gone."

Keenan gave it some thought. "We had a rule in my unit," he said. "Never turn your back on the enemy. Even if they're disarmed and on the ground, they're still very hostile. The people who hired Morpheus still want Peakes dead—and they're not going to give up. I think he deserves to know about the threat."

Sean nodded, and was already thinking about how that might be accomplished, when Keenan brought up another point.

"Morpheus may be gone, but the technology is still around. It's only changed hands."

Sean looked up and grimaced. "For better or worse, I suppose."

Meeting his gaze, Keenan said, "Something we won't know until it's too late."

***

Washington, D.C.

"Good morning," said Gavin Peakes, as he settled into the heavily padded chair at the head of the conference table. The beige-on-beige meeting room was on loan from the government, a temporary facility provided for the president-elect's transition team. It lacked any adornments—no plants or artwork—just old carpeting and water-stained ceiling tiles.

On Gavin's immediate right sat his newly appointed chief of staff. For the first time, the job often called the most powerful man in Washington, would be held by a woman. Raina Pope was barely five foot three, but she commanded an outsized respect from her colleagues on the hill.

Gavin let his eyes move around the table. He saw many familiar faces from the campaign, most hoping for a more permanent home in the West Wing. He flashed his signature smile to each, but saved a deliberate nod for the man seated at his four o'clock.

Phil Torbin was the deputy director of the NSA, and slated to be his new director of national intelligence. The two had been friends since college. Gavin smiled, still astonished by the path that had led them both here. He could never have imagined that one day, he would become president, or that his old roommate, would ascend to lead the nation's intelligence agencies.

After the morning's transition briefing, Gavin crossed the room and shook hands with Phil. He pulled him close and lowered his voice. "I need to talk with you later. In private."

Phil blinked, raising a brow.

"Today at two thirty. My hotel suite?" Gavin looked around the room. In a whisper, he said, "I've come across some troubling information and I need it verified. If I told you how I came to learn of this information..." He paused, long enough to arouse Phil's interest. "Let's just say I'd rather tell you when there's no one around to see your reaction."

Phil blinked again.

With a quick raise of his brow, Gavin smiled and gave him a cursory pat on the shoulder. Then he was back into the handshakes and discussions—fully absorbed in transition activities.

Phil stood motionless and watched as Gavin disappeared into the crowd.

***

A member of Gavin's Secret Service detail ushered Phil Torbin into the sitting room just before two-thirty. The hotel was one of Washington's famous historic venues, and its colonial decor reflected the nation's heritage. The salon featured a walnut coffee table flanked on either side by settees upholstered in a pale-yellow floral print. Phil's expression revealed that the decor was not his preferred style. It surely wasn't Gavin's either, but the presidency came with certain expectations— and respect for tradition was high on the list.

"Phil," a voice called from behind him. "Sorry to keep you waiting." The two old friends exchanged pleasantries. Gavin gave the agents a subtle nod, and they exited, closing the door with a soft click. Once they were alone, he sat across from Phil.

"I'll get straight to it," Gavin said, matter-of-factly. "I've learned that Richard Laney is part of a group planning to have me assassinated."

Phil Torbin froze. He could not have looked more shocked. With eyes wide and mouth agape, it seemed that he was still minutes away from being able to utter even the slightest guttural response. He quickly poured a glass of water from a pitcher and drained it in several large gulps. Gavin watched, somewhat amused, as his friend scrambled to regain his composure.

"We need to notify your Secret Service—"

Gavin was already raising his hand, shaking his head. "It's not that simple." He leaned back against the cushions. "In fact, the whole thing is pretty damn weird— so hear me out." He took a deep breath and cleared his throat.

"A few nights ago, on the night of the Electoral College ballot, I had a dream. A nightmare, really. I don't remember all the details, but the feeling still remains with me. I had this dreadful, almost visceral sensation that I was dying. I'd been in some kind of car accident, choking on this acrid smoke. It was so thick that I swear I could taste it. I remember thinking, this is it, this is the end."

He gave Phil a half-hearted shrug. "Then I woke up. Completely fine."

Phil looked confused, but said nothing, seeming to sense that Gavin wasn't done.

"A nightmare. No big deal, right? But then, last night, I received a message. Not an email, or a text. Nothing conventional. A message that was placed directly into my mind while I slept. Something—or someone—implanted these thoughts in my head."

After twenty-five years of working in national intelligence, Phil Torbin had heard a lot of bizarre stories. This was certainly one of them. However, the one thing his years of service had bestowed upon him was a keen sense of judgment; in other words, he had a nose for bullshit. Gavin wasn't exhibiting any of the usual markers.

No paranoia. No desperation. No pretense.

"What kind of thoughts? Why don't you start by telling me what you think you know?"

"There's an organization," Gavin said, before closing his eyes for a moment. "They call themselves Americans for Global Equity. They're wealthy, and far right. For years, they've planned to install their hand-picked candidate in the White House. That candidate was supposed to be Richard Laney. When his campaign cratered, they adjusted and worked to make him my running mate."

Phil leaned in, sitting on the edge of the settee.

"The plan was to kill me and have Dick assume the presidency. At that point, he'd be the tool for their agenda for the next four years."

Phil winced. "No offense, Gavin, but that's one hell of an accusation. Laney is liked and well-respected in Washington…"

Peakes nodded slowly, his head down. "I know that. To be honest, I don't think Dick was ever fully read into the assassination plot. But he's connected—I'm sure of that."

Phil's forefinger gently rubbed the stubble on his upper lip.

"So, when's this assassination attempt supposed to happen?"

"It already has," Gavin replied.

"What?"

"The nightmare—that's how I was supposed to die. Asphyxiating within the dream. They wanted me to believe that I was choking to death on the smoke." He leaned forward onto his elbows. "Here's the weird part…"

Phil's eyebrows arched.

"I think whoever put these thoughts in my head is also the one who protected me."

A long moment of silence settled between the two men, each carefully considering how their next words would sound out loud.

Finally, Gavin spoke. "What'd ya think, Phil? Am I losing my mind?"

Phil Torbin didn't answer right away, but avoided waiting too long, to suggest hesitation or doubt. He shook his head. "You're one of the sharpest people I know. I don't think you've gone mad. But I am very concerned about who did this to you —and how."

"That's why I asked to meet in private. As discreetly as possible, I need you to look into Dick Laney, the Americans for Global Equity, and whatever you can find on this dream thing. Only report to me—and don't document any of this."

"Of course. I'll get on it right away." Phil started to stand. "Anything else?"

Gavin seemed distant, deep in thought. Then he looked up.

"Have you ever heard of a company called Morpheus Research?"

Phil Torbin stiffened, almost paralyzed by the question. The current deputy director of the NSA swallowed hard and began a slow descent back onto the settee, as if he was losing an internal tug-of-war. The fingers of his left hand covered his mouth, as if guarding against the escape of rogue words.

Facing his old friend—and the next president of the United States—Phil took a deep breath.

"Actually," he said softly, "I have."

***

The next day, Gavin Peakes waited alone in his hotel suite, sipping a tall glass of sparkling water. Phil Torbin had already briefed him—on the assassination plot, the Americans for Global Equity, and the current status of Morpheus Research. There was nothing left to do, but wait.

At any moment, Dick Laney would walk through the door.

Gavin still wasn't sure how to handle the situation. He just couldn't believe that Dick could be part of an assassination plot. The two men weren't friends by any means, they were running mates. It was a partnership borne out of convenience and political expediency, not friendship. Nevertheless, he'd known Dick on and off for years, and doubted the man was capable of being a conspirator.

Gavin was still vacillating between two various styles of confrontation—fists and fury, or calm and collected—when Dick walked in the room.

Gavin stood and shook Laney's hand. All smiles and firm grips. So far, calm and collected was prevailing.

"Dick, I've got to ask you something," Gavin began. "There's no point in tiptoeing around."

Laney sat, holding a curious, if somewhat uneasy expression.

"What's your involvement with Americans for Global Equity?"

Gavin watched his reaction carefully. Dick's eyes went wide and he sputtered a bit. "Ah…well…" He looked away, but when he turned back to Gavin, he must have sensed that something was wrong—seriously wrong. He hesitated for another few seconds before sighing.

"They've been supportive of my political career."

If he'd hoped that was enough, Gavin's expression clearly indicated that it was not.

"Okay, fine. They've been my principal backers. From the start. In fact, they encouraged me to run for office." Dick's eyes narrowed and he grew defensive. "What's this about anyway?"

"We have credible evidence that Americans for Global Equity is behind a plot to have me assassinated—and elevate you to the presidency."

If Dick's first instinct was to laugh out loud, he held back as soon as he saw the gravity in Gavin's expression. Laney turned ashen and he sat speechless.

"Dick," Gavin said sharply. "Look at me. What can you tell me about Morpheus?"

"I…I don't know anything about that," he stammered. Sweat began to form on his brow. "I swear it's the truth. I don't know anyone named Morpheus."

Gavin's tone was biting. "But you knew that they wanted you in the White House."

"Everybody wants their guy in the White House," he shot back, annoyed. His arms spread wide. "That doesn't mean they're willing to kill to make it happen."

Gavin stood and began pacing. He wanted to believe Laney, he really did, but something wasn't making sense.

"But why you?" he asked, stopping to look at Dick. "You're a moderate, and they're far right. What's the connection?"

Laney was twisting his body to follow Gavin's rapid movements. When their eyes finally met, he exhaled a heavy breath.

"I'm not as moderate as I let on. It was always understood that if I reached a higher office, I'd promote a conservative agenda and improve the environment for American businesses."

Gavin's expression radiated his anger. How had his team missed this? He looked at Laney with open antipathy.

"Oh, come on, Gavin," he responded, bristling. "It's politics. Who hasn't put on one face for the public while keeping the other private?"

Gavin ignored the remark. "How did they make contact with Morpheus?"

Laney shook his head again. "Gavin, I've never met anyone named Morpheus. That's a name I'd remember."

The silence that followed stretched out, increasing the tension.

Laney broke the silence. In an exasperated tone, he asked, "What do you want me to do? Resign?"

Gavin's nostrils flared, he seemed on the verge of screaming, Yes, goddamn it!

"No," he said instead. "Not yet. You're going to tell Phil Torbin everything you know about Americans for Global Equity. After that, we'll see where we go from there."

Dick stayed seated, pensively rubbing his lower lip with his thumb. Weighing his options. Before he could say another word, Gavin said, "You should go."

Laney stood and looked at Gavin. Was he searching for some reassurance or support? Forgiveness? Whatever he hoped for—he found none of it in Gavin's grim face.

Chapter Thirty-One

New York City

Blunt, uncivil, snippy, discourteous—Morgan ran out of adjectives to describe the tone of the call he received from the United States Attorney's office for the Southern District of New York. There were no apologies, not even a mea-fucking-culpa. Only a flat statement: the FBI raid was in error, and no charges would be filed. When Morgan hung up, he was seething, the heat of anger prickling his skin.

His contacts at the NSA claimed they couldn't identify who ordered the FBI raid —though Morgan suspected they were simply unwilling to share this information with him. Being a pawn in someone's interagency chess match was an unenviable position.

A black town car pulled up to the curb of Morgan's building. He climbed inside and the car began inching its way through Midtown traffic. Morgan stared out the window, his reflection staring back. He focused his attention on the problems he faced.

First, he needed to distance himself from the agency's choke-hold. Second, he wanted—or rather, needed—to make things right with Olivia, Sean, and Noble. To apologize for his deception.

But his final thought was more opportunity than problem. Quite uplifting. Despite the many threats, and the death of Reinhold, the group had accomplished something truly extraordinary. He stroked his chin and smiled. Whatever lay ahead, Morgan wanted to be part of it. The NSA had stolen the technology from

Morpheus, but in his mind, it was crude and mechanical. In contrast, Sean had achieved something quite different. A vision of the future. A remarkable, elegant, and mind-blowing advancement of humankind.

When the town car stopped in front of the Center for Change Potential, Morgan stepped onto the sidewalk. His decision had been made—he knew what needed to be done.

It was time for a little mea culpa of his own.

***

Sean was alone in his apartment, when he reached over and picked up his phone.

"Hello? Karen?"

In the wake of everything that had happened, Sean sensed an opportunity, a chance to rewrite the script of his life. "How's Abbie?" he asked. "No new nightmares, I hope?" His tone was still laced with trepidation, though Sean was confident that the threat to Abbie had gone.

"She's fine," Karen responded. "She's doing well."

"Good." He let his words hang for a moment. "Listen, I'm making a few changes in my life—and I'm not really sure how they're going to play out. I just want you to know that, no matter what, I'll always be there for Abbie. Even after the move."

Karen muttered something that Sean couldn't quite make out. A few seconds passed.

"About the move…I think we're going to stay in New York after all."

Sean sat up. "Really?"

"I know it sounds strange, but I got this job offer—completely out of the blue. A well-respected company said I came highly recommended. It pays quite well—and of course Abbie likes it here, so…I guess we're staying."

"That's great news," he said, as a smile crept into his voice. "I'm really happy for you. And for me too."

They spoke for a while: about Abbie, her school, about life. It was the most agreeable conversation they'd had in a long time. A faint smile crossed his face as his thoughts drifted back to the talk with his friend Dr. Kate Keelson, and the discussion with the physics professor, Dr. Yong. He was reminded of a Marcus Aurelius quote —about how our life is what our thoughts make it. Things were changing. Was he beginning to create his own reality?

After they hung up, Sean thought back on the conversation and Karen's words.

Highly recommended?

A minute passed before the realization set in.

Morgan. Of course.

***

Washington, D.C.

The NSA had ambitious plans for the technology, but Phil Torbin told himself that they'd never be like Morpheus. The technology would be used sparingly—and judiciously—and only for the greater good. Morpheus had acted like street thugs, whoring themselves out to the highest bidder. No, the NSA would be different. They would never take a life—unless—it was morally justified.

After decades in clandestine operations, Phil Torbin was damn good at rationalizations.

Satisfied that his project was on track, he moved through the unadorned corridors of the federal building. Fluorescent lights buzzing, casting harsh shadows against the walls. He turned his attention to the Americans for Global Equity. Wealthy, influential, completely above reproach—or so they believed.

In Phil's view, they had crossed the line. This wasn't the way the game was played. Unacceptable. They acted with malice and cowardice. It was time for someone to knock the hubris from these people.

Phil Torbin was determined to be that someone.

***

Arlington, Virginia

In an understated Virginia law office, two men sat wearing giddy expressions.

"So, we're in agreement," Jerry Lovewell said. "From now on, it's just Lovewell and Jones. I have to admit, I like the way that sounds."

Lovewell was a portly man in his mid fifties, with intensely blue eyes that seemed both kind and unsettling at the same time. He sat back, using his right hand to hoist one leg over the other.

"If you ask me," Jones began, "it's long overdue. I think we're in agreement. In Locke-step, as it were." He laughed heartedly at his own pun. Both men were in jolly spirits today.

The law firm of Armand C. Locke, Lovewell, and Jones had just learned of Armand's arrest. Beneath the merriment, however, was pure relief. With Armand in manacles, they could finally be free. The two partners hastened to a couple of decisions.

First, they would not represent Armand in court, using the convenient rationale that this was well outside their scope of expertise. Second, they would exercise their proxy vote to remove his name from the firm. Easy choices.

After a moment, in a more serious tone, Lovewell remarked that Armand had "sullied" the firm's name. Phil Jones looked at his partner with a curious expression —but then the two men doubled over in laughter.

When they finally got a hold of themselves, Jones said, "We should do something, though." After discussion, they decided, as either a courtesy or an afterthought, to arrange for outside counsel for Armand's defense.

***

New York City

Most of the CCP staff had gone home, and Morgan sat alone, reflecting on the day's events. A few whispers, some murmurs, but overall it had gone better than he expected. He leaned back in his plush office chair and released a slow breath.

Two down, one to go.

Earlier, Morgan had gathered his office staff to explain about the events leading up to the FBI raid. One of their clients had been falsely accused of supporting a terrorist organization. When he was tipped off to the raid, literally minutes beforehand, he was forced to make a difficult choice: protect their client's confidential information, or hand it over to the FBI. He'd chosen the client.

Emphasizing that the FBI raid was aimed solely at collecting the documents, Morgan assured them that none of the CCP staff were ever at risk of being apprehended or detained. Now, with their client absolved of any charges, it was clear that the Center for Change Potential had done nothing wrong.

For now, it seemed enough to mollify his office staff.

Next, he'd phoned his contact at the NSA. In his most implacable tone, he declared that his debt to the NSA was paid in full. He maintained that the technology stolen from Morpheus was far more valuable than anything that he could still offer. Adding that if word of the program ever leaked, it would compromise its usefulness.

The contact was furious, ranting and accusing him of blackmailing the agency. Morgan flatly denied that it was a threat—only judicious. The call ended the way most did—hostile and abrupt. He'd have to wait to see how it played out.

Morgan closed his eyes, grateful for a brief moment of peace. Tomorrow night, he'd face his final obligation—the last stop on his personal redemption tour.

Dinner with Sean and Olivia at his home.

***

Arlington, Virginia

Armand entered the windowless government room wearing an orange federal jumpsuit that could never be mistaken for bespoke. His attorney, a younger man with a stellar reputation for defending clients in complicated, Patriot Act offenses was already seated.

With a curious expression, the attorney watched Armand's interaction with the guard, the confidence of his movement, and the sly acknowledgement he gave to him as he sat down. The handcuffs clanked against the metal tabletop. Silently, he studied his client for a moment. Armand seemed annoyed, but not worried. Not even a little.

"Well," the attorney began, "let's start with the good news. They've dropped the charge of terroristic threatening. I'm not sure why they chose to—"

"It is as expected." Armand interjected. He made no effort to elaborate.

He knew there were factions within the US government desperate to weaponize Morpheus's method of controlling the autonomic system. They simply couldn't risk any of that surfacing in open court. Armand's eyes dropped to the handcuffs on his wrists. He smiled at the irony. It seemed the government's hands were tied as well.

The attorney paused, then cleared his throat as he collected his thoughts. "That still leaves some notably serious charges. Corporate espionage. Money laundering."

An expressionless Armand looked at his attorney. "Yes," he said evenly. "They do sound most serious."

"I'm not sure you fully appreciate your situation," he said emphatically. "Aren't you worried?"

"Fuck 'em."

The attorney blinked and drew a heavy sigh. Within seconds, a regret registered in the attorney's eyes. Armand cleared his throat. The attorney looked up. With the fingers of his shackled hands, Armand pushed a few sheets of yellow legal paper toward him. Bewildered, the attorney picked up the sheets and began skimming through the hand-scribbled notes.

"The first page," Armand began, "is a list of the various statutes and case precedents relating to international and Swiss law. As the details of the money laundering charges come into focus, you'll see these references effectively cripple their case. For the record, any money moved by Morpheus Research was always in compliance with the applicable international and Swiss laws. As a company registered in Switzerland, we were under no obligation to abide by US statutes while operating outside of the United States."

Armand paused, then with a slight smile added, "Any money held by Morpheus, or handled on behalf of our clients, was fully compliant with Swiss banking regulations."

"How did you—" the attorney stammered.

"I think you'll find that the US attorney general will agree with me on this," Armand continued. "Considering his eldest son is the CFO of one of our client companies, and his wife is on the board of directors of another."

The attorney looked nonplussed—and perhaps a little frightened. His eyes narrowed as he rapidly thumbed through the papers.

Armand smirked. He enjoyed keeping his lawyer off-balance.

"Of course, we have files that can prove all of this. They're stored on an encrypted server that's—well, somewhere secure. You won't need everything, but I'll make sure you have what you need."

The attorney didn't respond. After a lot of frowning, lip biting, and page flipping, he looked at Armand.

"And you think this will lead to the dismissal of the money laundering charges?"

Armand gave him a textbook French shrug. Bien Sûr. Apparently, a little bit of

Europe had rubbed off on Armand after all.

"Even if this holds," the attorney countered, "you're still facing charges of corporate espionage." He seemed increasingly unsure whether he was defending or challenging his client.

"Unprovable," Armand replied flatly. "Knowing something is not, in itself, illegal. You'll find that they are unable to connect us to any wrongdoing using traditional definitions of spying. We've never recruited a disgruntled employee, bribed an insider, stolen any documents, hacked computer systems, or infiltrated these organizations. It's impossible to link us to these companies through any means, internal or external. We just happened to know—and that's not a crime."

"But," said the attorney, looking for weakness in the argument. "They'll argue that you gained this information through some other illegal means."

Armand brushed the statement away with a dismissive gesture. The handcuffs rattled. "That's like accusing someone of murder without witnesses, evidence, or a weapon." He paused and grinned, immensely amused at how close to home that statement was to reality.

"On the final page, you'll find a partial list of the corporations and government agencies that have enlisted our services. Most are one-time clients, nothing groundbreaking. Still, enough to embarrass some very influential people. No, instead of conjuring up some fantastic prosecutorial story, they'll see the wisdom in letting this one go. Besides, they have no real interest in me. It was all pretense for their actions in Geneva—an elaborate story for the benefit of the Swiss."

The color seemed to have drained from the attorney's face. Armand smiled, sat back, and refused to expound any further. In his gut, the lawyer must have known that he was being manipulated—but the quicker he put this behind him, the sooner he could return to life without Mr. Locke. He forced a deep breath and shook his head.

Even at a cursory glance, the legal notes Armand provided were compelling. He covered his mouth, and looked like he was formulating a valid counterargument. But in the end, he just shook his head and looked up at Armand.

"So that's it," he said, almost in a whisper. "You just intend to walk free?"

"Yes."

***

Three weeks later, Armand C. Locke did just that.

He walked out of the gated exit of a Federal Detention Center in Virginia, a free man. His orange jumpsuit replaced with the blue Savile Row suit that he instructed his still-flabbergasted attorney to bring along. The two rode together in the back of a hired town car. No one spoke. Their goodbyes were cold and brief—two men equally relieved that their unpleasant association had come to an end.

Armand climbed the steps to the lobby of his Falls Church apartment. He paused at the mailboxes. It was the usual clutter of unsolicited mailings, but one letter stood out. It'd been sent certified. Armand looked at the sender and let out a long measured sigh.

It was from the Virginia Bar Association.

Chapter Thirty-Two

New York City

After ushering his guests inside, Morgan set some cocktails on the coffee table. Probably hoping the warmth of the fireplace would help set the mood. He sat on one couch, while Sean and Olivia sat on the opposite.

"Any word on Adler's whereabouts?" Sean asked.

"Nothing. Gone. Vanished." Morgan replied in a deliberately staccato manner.

Olivia grinned. "He'll be back." She turned to watch the flames dance behind the glass. Sean frowned, tilting his head.

"His ego," she explained with a shrug, "it's the greatest driver in Adler's life—and his greatest downfall."

Sean turned to Morgan. "Have you heard that the American government was behind the raid?"

Morgan's jaw tightened. If he'd hoped to ease into the subject, that moment was quickly vanishing. With a faraway look, he forced a deep breath.

"Yes, I have. But let me start at the beginning."

He told them about the South African software firm, the money-laundering, and how it led to his obligation to the NSA.

"Damn it." Sean's anger rose quickly. "I've been telling Olivia that you were working against us—but she swore you'd never do that."

Morgan said nothing, minding his expression. Olivia touched Sean's arm. "Let him finish," she said, in a soft tone.

"My ties to the agency go back long before I met Olivia. When the NSA first took interest in Morpheus, I welcomed it. We were all trying to stop Adler

Daemon. Our goals and objectives were aligned. An effective partnership—or so I thought."

He paused, studying Sean and Olivia.

"Then they began asking whether the Morpheus technology could be transferred —and then it all became clear. They had no interest in stopping Morpheus. They only wanted the technology."

Sean leaned forward, ready to argue, but Olivia tightened her grip on his hand.

Morgan sighed. "I felt stuck, hopeless—and then you came along. You were the leverage we needed to turn this around. To finally stop Morpheus."

"Bullshit," Sean snapped. "I didn't end anything. The government did that." He was angry and discouraged.

"This whole thing—this stupid charade—was for nothing."

Morgan's expression turned compassionate. "You really don't see it? You really have no idea of what you've accomplished?" He chuckled softly, shaking his head.

"Sure, the government shut down Morpheus. But what they stole—what Morpheus actually had—is trivial compared to what you've been able to achieve. The NSA will never be able to comprehend the potential—or beauty—of an idea like universal consciousness. They have no interest—it's just another weapon. For someone who just wanted a decent night's sleep, your achievement is truly remarkable."

Sean had almost forgotten about the insomnia. He thought back on the causes of his sleeplessness: his constant worries, his stress, and his lack of purpose. Now, these were nothing more than vague and distant recollections from some other time.

Morgan cleared his throat. "From the moment I first learned about the Human Consciousness Project, I knew this was where I belonged. I can understand why you think this was all for nothing, but it's simply not true. This was your awakening. The chance to remake yourself. To discover your real purpose and potential."

Overwhelmed by his many conflicting thoughts and emotions, Sean desperately hung onto his anger. He wanted to feel maligned, betrayed by Morgan and the others. To free himself of this immense burden.

Sean stared into the fireplace. And suddenly, what he felt became so clear. He was scared. Afraid of what he'd become, afraid of losing himself. His ego still hoping to recreate the illusion of his limitations. Ulgen Khan's words came rushing back.

Keep your mind free, and you'll find your potential is more than you've ever imagined.

Why hadn't Ulgen explained that the process could be terrifying? Untethering one's self from the past—self-worth, self-doubt, self-loathing—throwing it all to the wind. Surrendering his old identity, and moving with blind trust into what lay ahead.

After a moment, Sean's expression calmed. He glanced up.

"So, what are you asking Morgan?"

"Simple," he replied without hesitation. "I want to restart the Human Consciousness and Cognition Project."

He studied their faces. Watching their expressions soften with cautious interest.

"It's simply a continuation."

Olivia glanced at Sean. "I think we're both—um—concerned about where your loyalties really lie."

"Fair enough—and for that, I'm truly sorry. But for this to work, we'll need each other. It's a paradox, but spirituality is going to need capitalism." Morgan took a quick sip of his cocktail.

"You won't get any university grants, not without the academic credentials of someone like Adler Daemon. This will require private funding: facilities, equipment, credible staffing." He looked at them both. "I can make that happen."

Olivia nudged Sean, playful but encouraging.

Morgan looked toward the dining table. "I didn't have time to cook, but I've arranged for catering. Shall we call a little truce and enjoy a meal together? For old times' sake."

When they stood, Morgan seemed in better spirits.

Perhaps, things could mend after all.

***

Turin, Italy

Jakob sat alone outside the cobalt-blue cafe, tucked under an ornate, arched walkway that lined the shops and restaurants of this small piazza. The morning sun softened the centuries-old walls, and left him with a sense of calm he hadn't felt in days. Jakob left Geneva shortly after the raid. Since then, he'd made several calls from public phones and sent emails from small internet cafes. Every attempt at reaching Adler had failed. He assumed the worst.

Fortunately, Adler was a detailed and methodical man, and had put a set of protocols in place. Two days after the raid, Jakob walked into a French regional bank in Lyon, and used a false ID to gain access to a safety-deposit box. Inside were encrypted backup files, the real names and contact information of Morpheus's agents, and a single phone number. The last item was critical. Adler had been quite clear. If things went wrong—horribly wrong—he should contact the man at this number.

A waitress, young and naturally beautiful, approached his table. Jakob looked up. "Buongiorno. Posso avere un cappuccino e una sfogliatelle, per favore?"

She nodded, stifled a slight giggle, and went back to the kitchen. Jakob grimaced. Italian was the weakest of his four languages. If he could stay alive, he would fix that.

Jakob had never met the man he was waiting for. Adler simply said, he will find you. No description. No instructions.

He was stirring his cappuccino when he felt the presence of someone. He looked up to see a white-haired man in his mid-sixties standing before him. His eyes were dark and sunken, and Jakob instinctively sat up.

"That looks rather good," he said pointing to the pastry. He gestured toward the empty chair. "May I?"

Jakob nodded. So this is the legend? The man behind the man behind the curtain?

"My name is Ian Bishop," he said evenly. "Jakob, we have much to discuss."

Wasting no time, Bishop spent the next twenty minutes laying out the future of Morpheus Research. Corporate espionage was finished. The firm would now deal exclusively in assassinations. Adler Daemon would be taking some time away. Jakob would head the new company, overseeing the technical rebuild, and reassembling their personnel.

Discretion, he explained, had never been Adler's strong suit. He'd foolishly allowed the company's public profile to attract too much attention—from too many governments. They would not repeat that mistake. From this point on, it would be so inconspicuous that, to most of the world, they wouldn't exist at all.

"And, Dr. Daemon?" asked Jakob out of caring, concern, or just idle curiosity.

"We have an understanding," Bishop said flatly. "For now."

Ian Bishop abruptly stood, indicating the end of the meeting. Reaching into his coat pocket, he handed a small card to Jakob.

"How's your Spanish?"

"Better than my Italian."

"Good. There's an address on that card. An apartment in Jerez de la Frontera in Andalusia, Spain. Be there by Friday. A man named Fenster will arrive that evening from Tangiers. He'll explain the rest."

Bishop straightened his jacket and said, "It was a pleasure to meet you, Jakob. Though, I doubt we'll meet again."

***

New York City

Winston Waxman was unaccustomed to visitors. Still, he politely welcomed his guests, and gestured to the two threadbare chairs facing his desk. The office, the hub of Noosphere magazine, looked exactly as Sean had imagined. Behind Waxman, a sagging bookshelf strained under the many volumes on spirituality, physics, UFOs, and astronomy. Volumes too tall for the shelf laid on their side, serving as makeshift bookends.

The wall to the right was plastered with mismatched frames: diplomas, awards, and photographs of Waxman alongside an impressive array of celebrities and politicians. To the left, a cork board burst with notes, newspaper clippings, and clusters of colored pushpins. Sean smirked. How many conspiracies solved? How many still ongoing?

"I must admit," Waxman began, "this is quite intriguing. I'm curious to learn how I might be of use to a financial magazine."

Morgan pivoted smoothly. "Perhaps we should start with a simpler question. Would you be interested in reviving the Human Consciousness and Cognition Project?"

Waxman blinked. His suspicion clearly evident. "Adler Daemon's old program?" His eyes narrowed. "I'm sorry, but I don't know either of you. What's your interest in this?"

Sean leaned in, resting his forearms on the desk. "What if I told you that universal consciousness is real."

He leaned back, letting his words register.

Waxman snorted. "I'd say—no kidding, Mr. Hastings. If you haven't noticed, this entire magazine is dedicated to the noosphere and universal consciousness." He made little effort to hide his irritation.

"I don't mean conceptually real," Sean explained. "I mean actually real. I've experienced it, more than once." Sean smiled, amused that those dedicated to studying universal consciousness were as skeptical as anyone else.

Waxman reclined in his chair, his hands naturally resting on top of his ample belly. He squinted, which only deepened the lines of his crow's feet. After a few seconds, a curious smile formed.

Morgan saw an opening and seized the moment. He began by describing the group, the evolution of Morpheus from corporate spy to assassins-for-hire, and the raid that ended it all. He spoke of Sean's remarkable path into spirituality, his experiences with universal consciousness, and the opportunity it presented. He closed by emphasizing that this was a rare chance to accomplish something extraordinary.

"A project of this importance should be a collaboration of like-minded individuals," Morgan said. He added that, as the editor of Noosphere magazine, Waxman was in a unique position to bring these people together.

"Well, Mr. Maxwell, that is indeed persuasive—" He grunted, struggling to lift his corpulent frame out of the reclined position. "I might know of a few people. In Adler's absence, who'd you have in mine to head the project?"

Morgan tilted his head. "Someone with strong academic credentials—and a solid reputation. We're open to finding mutually acceptable candidates." Morgan cleared his throat and then added, "There is only one condition: Adler Daemon can never be part of this project."

Waxman shrugged, unconcerned. "Sure, fair enough." He looked at the men and grinned. "Okay. Let's take the next step."

***

Amazonas, Brazil

Adler always laughed whenever he heard someone say, It's a small world, and it's getting smaller.

Nothing about that felt remotely true here. There was nothing small about this place—and that was precisely the point. If a man truly wished to disappear, this was a very good spot to be.

As he walked down the gravel pathway to his car, the soles of his leather boots kicked up little clouds of dust. The air was heavy and damp, and smelled of flora and decay. He was in Amazonas, a Brazilian state nearly four times the size of Spain. He slammed the door on his rusting Toyota Land Cruiser, and slowly drove down the winding dirt road that led back to his house.

When he'd first arrived, he was surprised by how little attention he drew from the local population. Mildly curious perhaps, but not intrusive. The small town was quiet. The genial people were inclined to mind their own business. A mash-up of English and German carried him through his first weeks, until he was able to converse in Portuguese. If asked, he claimed to be an anthropologist, studying the effects of modernity on indigenous tribes. But no one asked. No one seemed to care.

There was a pronounced wildness to these lands. In this northwestern corner of Brazil, the Solimões, Negro, and Madeira rivers converged to form one vast river—the Rio Amazonas. Take but a few steps from any road or village and the land was thick with vegetation—nearly impassible. The land was familiar to Adler. Years ago, as part of an academic research team, he'd come here to study tribal cultures.

The raid on Morpheus had been unfortunate—but it was also an opportunity. A chance to turn back the clock. In his enthusiasm for building Morpheus, he'd lost something along the way.

Adler continued to be preoccupied with thoughts of Sean Hastings. How could this unremarkable man have achieved such a breakthrough in human consciousness? If that weren't enough, he was troubled by another realization. While Sean was finding himself, Adler had become increasingly lost. The comparison angered him, the very idea grating his ego. This irritation gnawed at him, until it drove him halfway around the world—to study indigenous spirituality, to understand collective consciousness, to find wisdom beyond the technology.

An epiphany? Perhaps. A chance to redeem himself? A last attempt to set things right?

Or, maybe it was the sober realization that some very dangerous people were still looking for him.

Chapter Thirty-Three

New York City

"A TED Talk? You're serious?" Olivia's face immediately lit, excited by the prospect. "Did they say when?"

Sean shook his head and plopped onto the overstuffed couch in her office, his left leg dangling over an armrest.

"To be honest, I'm as surprised as anyone. Apparently our little project is starting to make noise outside of the usual circles." He quickly flashed a brow.

Olivia crossed the room and sat down next to him. "That's wonderful."

"No," Sean said, contorting his face into a half-grin, "it's beyond terrifying."

The new Human Consciousness and Cognition Project had settled into an old two-story office building in New York's East Village. It's redbrick facade, tiny Colonial windows, and white shutters seemed to be reaching back to a simpler time. The neighborhood was eclectic, a mishmash of boutiques and secondhand stores. On the left was a hip-hop recording studio, and on the right, a restaurant that specialized in Japanese-style hot dogs. Not a typical space for academic research which—somehow—made it feel perfect. A good fit in spirit and energy.

The reception and administrative staff occupied the first floor, while the upstairs belonged to the researchers, various labs, and testing rooms. As promised, Morgan delivered. Private donations were used to purchase the building and equipment.

Sean had once asked him, straight-out, if he'd been behind Karen's job offer. Morgan shrugged, denying any involvement, but Sean swore he detected a slight grin tugging at the corner of his mouth. They let their differences go over a large bottle of Sapporo and a Japanese Ume dog.

Morgan had been worried about attracting the caliber of people they needed for credibility. But the concern was unfounded. The interest from esteemed members of the psychology, scientific, and philosophical communities was astonishing. Some names familiar, others less so—but all with degrees and awards to spare. Olivia admitted that the original project had always struggled to gain traction within the scientific community. She wondered if this current interest reflected a significant shift in cultural and societal beliefs. A new willingness to study non-physical phenomenon, as Nikola Tesla put it.

Keenan would often stop by, looking for new approaches to treat his patients with PTSD. Dr. Carl Yong, the baseball-cap-wearing physics professor, handled all their quantum related matters. And, Winston Waxman added a regular column to Noosphere magazine, tracking the project's progress with enthusiasm—and some skepticism.

Morgan, still engaged with the Center for Change Potential, stopped by as often as his schedule allowed. Joking that this had become his second home. Thrilled with the response to the project, he proudly boasted of the momentum it generated. New money attracted renowned scientists, and they, in turn, attracted new money.

After a few months of physical therapy, Noble was fully recovered. On the Fridays when Sean had Abbie for the weekend, Noble could be found upstairs, cross-legged on the floor and playing games with her. She would laugh and giggle at his "silly" Scottish accent, while trying to figure out his magic tricks.

Olivia edged a little closer to Sean. "Do you ever wonder what happened to Adler?"

"No."

She arched a brow.

Sean smirked. "Well, maybe a little. Though I try not to think of him at all. Why do you ask?"

Olivia shrugged. "Sometimes I can picture him out there—somewhere—secretly creating a bigger, stronger, faster Morpheus."

Sean swung his legs down and gave Olivia a pained look.

"Looking back, I was naive. I thought this would end with the fall of Morpheus. But this technology is like some mythical creature—like the phoenix that refuses to die, renewing itself endlessly."

He patted her on the thigh before resting his hand there. "This will never be contained. The NSA won't give it up—or even admit it exists. And, we can never rule out a return from the dead by our dear Dr. Daemon."

He smiled softly at Olivia, then tapped his stomach. "It's getting late. Is there anything in the fridge, or should we grab a bite on the way home?"

Olivia put on her jacket. "Let's do takeout."

"Okay," said Sean. "Takeout it is."

As Olivia gathered her belongings, Sean stopped and smiled. His thoughts drifted, as they often did lately, to the impossible sequence of events that brought him here—to this moment, to this place. For the first time in his life, Sean was content with who he was.

He wasn't perfect—leaning more toward flawed—but he was aware. Grounded, with a sense of his true self, his ego, and of his place in the universe. Somehow, the universe felt bigger and Sean felt smaller—but in the best possible way.

He stood, and with a loving look, followed her out the door.

A few minutes later, the receptionist poked her head up the stairwell.

"Has anyone seen Sean?"

Morgan Maxwell was stacking papers, preparing to leave. "He just stepped out with Olivia. Why?"

"There's a phone call" she said. "From the White House. The man says it's urgent. His name is Phil Torbin."

9 798990 331808